D1526433

RABBI, RUN

A Novel

by

Elliot Strom

This is a work of fiction. Names, characters, places and incidents are products of the author's imagination. Any resemblence to actual events, locales, or specifiic persons (living or dead) is purely coincidental.

Cover Design: David Sandman

Text set: Adobe Garamond Pro, Calibri, Swiss fonts, Apex Lake

Manufactured in the United States of America

ISBN 978-1512073881

To Susan

my sweetheart, my love and
my partner in all things

f this was sleep, it was the deepest I'd ever seen.

Sharon's eyes were closed. She lay under the blanket with only her bare feet showing out the bottom, a nearly drained bottle of Grey Goose on her nightstand alongside an empty bottle of Percocet. Her wrists, neck and face were ice-cold, tinged slightly blue, her pulse weak and faint, her breathing intermittent and shallow.

I tried to wake her, shaking her at first gently then more forcefully, but nothing... no flutter of eyelids, no blurted-out fragments of words. Just stillness.

It was clear. She had done it, exactly as she said she would – gotten drunk, then swallowed every last one of her pills and lay down to die. I guess it was no surprise. She hated her life, she always said. She wanted out. And this time, she warned, this time she'd get it right.

I picked up the phone and hit 9, then 1, then another 1, missing that simple sequence not just once but twice. Finally, I got through. "It's my wife," I said. She's in bed and she's cold and she's almost not breathing. Please, come as quick as you can."

"Okay, sir, okay. Tell us your address. Where do you live?"

"422 Holden Lane."

"Holden Lane in Westover or in Fentonville?"

"I'm sorry. In Fentonville. Fentonville."

"Okay, sir, stay calm. We're sending an ambulance over right now. It'll be there in just a few minutes. Try to stay calm. Hang on for just a second and don't hang up."

The voice at the other end of the line shouted something to someone evidently in the room with him. "OK. I'm back. Now listen carefully: while they're on their way, I just want to ask you a few questions, okay? So we can be ready to help her as soon as we get there."

"Yeah, sure, of course."

"You said before she's almost not breathing. So, I need to ask you: Is she breathing at all?"

"I think so. I don't know. Maybe."

"Is her body still warm?"

"Not really."

"Do you have any idea how this happened?"

"No...well not exactly. I wasn't here. I was out and then I came home and I saw her in bed and realized right away something wasn't right. But there's a bottle of vodka and an empty pill bottle beside her bed so I figured..."

"Okay, sir. I understand. Someone will be there in a moment. Just wait by her side, keep her as warm as possible and we'll have someone there in just a minute. Okay? Just hold on."

"Okay. I'm standing beside her now. I've got her covered with blankets. Is there anything else I should be doing?"

"No, no, that's fine. Just hold her hand, okay? Someone will be there right away."

Not four minutes later, the doorbell rang. I saw the red lights flashing outside, reflected in the hall mirror. I opened the door to the emergency team, pointed them upstairs to the bedroom and Sharon's inert body, gestured with upturned palms "what-am-I-supposed-to-do?"

One of the team sat and asked me questions downstairs while the rest of them were upstairs with Sharon doing God-knows-what.

After several minutes of noises emanating from the bedroom, the paramedics hoisted the gurney up the stairs with professional efficiency. Then, using her blanket as a kind of hammock, swung Sharon's body from the bed to the gurney, carefully maneuvered it down the stairs to the front door and out to the ambulance idling in the driveway. Moving in a kind of trance now, I locked the front door behind me and followed behind the ambulance to St. Theresa's.

All the way there, falling further and further behind the speeding ambulance, I wondered if she really was dead this time and, if she was, what was coming next in the continuing soap opera of my life.

* * *

It's hard to remember now but the truth is: it used to be really good – Sharon and me. It feels weird, almost crazy to say it now. But it's true. It was good. The best thing in my life.

I remember the first time we met at that charity event. CityArtsRun, it was called, ten miles snaking through the streets of Center City on a Sunday morning, orange traffic cones and city police blocking roads all around. No prizes, no medals. Just the satisfaction of getting to the finish line as quickly and efficiently as possible.

Not so long ago, when I first decided I'd better start running or I'd turn into a big, fat blimp, it wouldn't have been quite so easy.   Back then, I couldn't go even 1K without having to stop again and again along the way, wheezing and panting and all bent over. By now, though, I felt like a real runner. Ten miles was no big deal. Anyway, that was what I was thinking as I got ready to start, stretching my legs, limbering up, waiting for the starter's pistol. But then I ran into Cindy What's-her-name and her very attractive friend and my attention quickly shifted in a different direction.

I hope it doesn't sound awful but I knew Cindy was interested in me, was hoping I'd ask her out. She'd made it kind of obvious, turning up at things at the shul - although she wasn't even a member -- and somehow finding her way to the front of the room where I couldn't miss her, especially in those low-cut tops and the push-up bras she was always wearing. Nice to look at, it's true, but I never got the feeling there was anyone home.

Her friend, though, intrigued me. I could see she was a bit shy, hanging back, pretending to check something on her phone while Cindy and I shot the breeze. I could see she was looking over at us and I, for my part, was looking over her way as well. I couldn't miss the athlete's slender body and the pretty smile and the obvious fact that she was flirting with me like we were in home room in high school. So, Cindy introduced us and we started talking. But then we heard the announcement that it was time to line up in front of City Hall; the run was about to begin. So I said goodbye and thought maybe I'd try to get her last name if I could figure out how to weasel it out of Cindy later on. I'm not really sure what happened but something did – something in the middle of the run. All I remember is that we found each other at some point along the way and we talked and we ended up at her place and, well, things went pretty fast and furious, and I thought maybe this might get interesting.

Anyway, it was weird dating her, trying to manage that while simultaneously trying to figure out how to be rabbi to this new congregation of mine -- how to connect with them, how to teach and counsel them, how to be open and friendly and strong and dependable and thoughtful and inspiring, all the impossible things they wanted me to be. It was a lot to manage without distractions. And then, into this crazy, crazy time in my life, comes this charming, shy, anxious, complicated, very sexy woman. How we got to the point of marriage -- and so quickly! -- I still don't understand, even now.

But anyway, we did. We had a wonderful wedding where everything went just as we planned. We made a life together. We figured out how to balance our own needs against the synagogue's, making sure my congregants got all they needed from me but with plenty of time for the two of us to try to make a marriage. She went willingly - well, mostly willingly -- to the Saturday night fundraisers and the parties full of Emmanuel regulars. She even went to services with me, this girl who had grown up so alienated from Jewish life! And she was happy. Or at least she seemed to be. And she made me happy. Almost all the time.

Looking back now, I'd have to say those were probably the best times of my life. With a beautiful bride and a new young congregation in the burbs, I felt like I had it all. Here I was, after all, finally a rabbi – as I'd wanted to be from the time I was a kid and they asked me to lead memorial services for my Bubbie. From that moment on, I remember thinking: this is what I was meant to do!

I guess I've felt that same thing – more or less – ever since. I felt it a few years later on staff at Jewish summer camp, singing and praying and talking – sometimes through most of the night. I felt it when I went to rabbinical school and got so charged up studying text and commentaries, history and theology. And I felt it – and still feel it – with the Hebrew prayers and the music here in this congregation, that feeling of serenity that comes over me sometimes in the middle of a beautiful melody. So I was happy. Because, you see, all I ever wanted to be was a rabbi.

I woke up every morning with the conviction I was doing something that made a difference. I had Sharon to come home to at the end of the day, to tell her my little adventures, to get her input and advice, to laugh with her, to make love to her. Before too long, there was Ari. And, of course, there were my congregants who, to my enormous relief, really seemed to like me. It all felt kind of charmed, I guess you could say. And I thought it would always be that way. But that's not the way this story goes. Probably wouldn't have been much of a story if it had.

Anyway...where to begin? I guess it could be almost anywhere, but if we're looking for the point just before everything started going bad, it was probably that class on "Finding God in the Prayer Book" I was teaching one Tuesday evening late in March.

For two hours, they had been sitting around the big conference table in the board room, my adult learners, faces turned eagerly toward me, awaiting some kind of epiphany. I didn't want to let them down.

So I picked up the prayer book, and proclaimed, imitating the bombast typical of the rabbis of my youth: "You should love the Lord your God with all your heart, all your soul and all your might." Then, more conversationally, more real: "Okay. Stop for just a minute. Listen, really listen to the words. And think about what they're saying."

"Stop and think about what it would mean to be that passionate about God. To love God with all your heart and all your soul and all your might. I wonder if any of us has ever loved anyone or anything that much. I doubt it and I think we all know why...it's just too scary. To be that intense, that passionate.

"Just think what we'd have to give up to live lives like that. Think how it would rock our world. Our jobs? Forget it. Marriage? Not important. Friends and family? Wouldn't matter. If we really loved God with all our hearts and souls and might - just like the prayer book says -- what would happen to paying the bills and changing the oil in the car and cleaning the dishes? We'd be too busy communing with the Almighty, like those cult members who can't be bothered changing their clothes or combing their hair or taking a bath because God is right there on their shoulder and there's no time to waste on piddling, everyday stuff.

"Obviously, we couldn't live like that, wouldn't want to live like that. It would mean giving up too much—our jobs, our friends, our community, our family, the stuff that makes our lives full and good and satisfying.

"Still, take a good look at the prayer book, people. It's asking a lot of us. It wants us to care – really care – about God, to be passionate about God, to make God a big part of our lives. And I wonder how many of us do that and what we're missing out on in our lives if we don't."

I stopped, looked down at my watch and back up for dramatic effect. Then, allowing myself to smile again, I said:

"My, my, where does the time go? Okay, seriously folks, there's a lot here to think about. So here's my suggestion: Do just that. Think about it. Think about it during services, when you pray. Think about it when you...take a shower or...rake the leaves. 'When you lie down and when you rise up,' like the text says. I know it's challenging stuff but don't be frightened off - and don't brush it off. Really think about it and I'll give you the chance next week to tell me how crazy I am. Alright, scram. Go home. I'm sure that's more than enough heresy for one night."

As I stood up from the table, collected my books and watched everyone head home, I knew something had just come clear for me, something pretty important. I had just given what I figured was the best impromptu sermon of my life and no idea where it had come from. Somehow it had just bubbled up from some deep and instinctive place in my soul -- which, after all, maybe it had.

Still, I knew what I was likely to do with this moment of insight. What I always did. Like a loaded gun kept locked in a cabinet, I'd store it away somewhere and try not to think about it too much. It was, after all, strong stuff - just as I'd said. To take it seriously would mean giving up everything - wife, family, career, friends. Which I wasn't about to do. I was too happy exactly where I was. Gathering everything up in my big, tan leather briefcase, setting the building alarm and locking the door, I headed out to my car, parked in the space marked "Reserved for Rabbi Chazen -- at all times." (Someone, years earlier, had written in black magic marker underneath those words: "THIS MEANS YOU." I decided to leave it there.) Settling in behind the wheel, I dropped my case on the passenger seat beside me, then turned the radio until I found something fast and loud on an oldies station.

Out of the parking lot, into the traffic, tapping my left foot to the pounding bass line of the song, I replayed the endless shuffle of a day that had begun with a breakfast meeting at eight and ended just now with this class over at ten PM. Does anyone have even the faintest idea how full my days are? Nope, none of them. Well nobody but Sharon.

Even at this hour of the night, the traffic was moving slowly, too slowly. What the hell was it with these people? I looked left, pulled into the passing lane and shot ahead of a line of too-timid drivers.

"Bunch of wussies," I said aloud. Then: "How long have I been talking to myself like this?" And then: "Too long."

As the light turned red, I slowed, then came to a stop. Looking to my right, I saw, in a white convertible, a young woman in a tailored grey suit, blonde hair gathered up in a red barrette. Then came the shock of recognition -- it was Sharon. She looked gorgeous. Of course, she was always gorgeous, but looking at her this way, she was, well, spectacular. She looked over in my direction, saw it was me and smiled. I smiled back. Then she winked at me and I understood - the 'game was on.' As the light turned from red to green, she streaked away.

Although she had a head start on me and was fearlessly zipping in and out of the twin lanes of the traffic, I wasn't about to let her get away. After all, this was how we played the game - I chased her until she caught me.

By the next red light, I had caught up to her and again was poised beside her. Pausing a moment, I lowered the passenger-side window and motioned for her - in universal drivers' sign language -- to lower hers as well.

"What do you want?" she asked, imperious.

"I think you know exactly what I want," I said, like some cheesy porno star.

I waited, locking her in my gaze. She seemed as if considering for a moment then nodded slightly.

"Follow me," I said as I motioned to her.

Driving now as quickly as my fairly elastic conscience would allow, I pulled in front of her, turned right, then left, then left again, constantly checking my rear-view mirror to see that she was still behind me. Finally, I pulled into the drive-way of our house. She parked behind me, our bumpers touching as if in heat, then looked over at me, measuring me. Entering the front door, I motioned to her as if to say "this way."

It was late. The house was dark. Standing right behind her, my hands on her shoulders, I directed her up the stairs to the bedroom, pressing against her from behind. I noticed there was actually a little light seeping out the bottom of the door to Ari's room; we'd have to be quiet this time. That was okay too. Made it seem more wicked somehow.

Standing beside the bed, I turned her around and planted a series of tiny bites on her ears, neck and shoulders. She offered no resistance, her breath coming in shorter and shorter gasps.

It was over in a hurry, pounding in mounting rhythm until we both came to climax, our cries muffled in the pillows. I lay there for a moment, pressed close to her, then rolled over on my back. We both lay silent for a moment.

Finally, she turned on the lamp beside the bed - the game now over -- propped her head up on one hand and said: "So...how did it go tonight?"

"Pretty well," I said, catching my breath. "Actually, really good. Lots of people. Lots of discussion. I felt good about it. How about you? Anything interesting at work today?"

"Is there ever?," she asked. "Nah," she said, "same old same old. But my dinner with Cindy was fun. We ordered a bottle of wine and sat there at the table for a long time after we'd finished and paid the bill, and we just talked and talked. The waiters were so ready to go home, they kept hovering over us, asking us again and again if there was anything else we needed. Finally, we took pity on them and left. Anyway, it was a really nice evening," she said, dreamily. "Then, when I saw you pull up beside me on the way home, I thought, maybe we could finish this day with a bang. I'm sorry, am I being too crude here?"

She was smiling. I was too. This was an amazing woman, this gorgeous blonde with the athlete's body, smart and interesting and...just a little wild. My Sharon.

I should have known it couldn't stay like that forever. And, if you go looking for reasons - which I've been doing more and more lately -- it's really not all that hard to figure them out -- equal parts work and my struggle for, I don't know, something bigger in life, something about God and the universe and I don't know what else. But it certainly did all come back down to earth with a thud. And I guess you could say this is that story, my story.

But there is another one here and it's Sharon's story. The one she was writing when...well, when our world was coming apart. I still have it, of course. I take it out and look at it sometimes, especially when I feel like I still don't get her, like I never really got her. I've got to warn you...she changed all the names. But you can figure it out. It's not that hard. It wasn't meant to be. Here...take a look.

* *

Chapter 1:

"Baby, We Were Born to Run"

I guess you could say we met cute.

At least that's how the lousy, third-rate paper I work for would have put it.

I looked up and there he was, stretching—preening, to be precise — light blue spandex shorts, tee shirt that almost matched, high-tech shoes that pro-claimed his "running cred," an outfit (like my own) that suggested: I'm here, I'm serious, but I'm also available.

I glanced over at Candy, my closest friend, the person who knew me best in the world and, without needing to say a word, she smiled and said: "Forget about it. He's the new rabbi at Temple Sinai, the one everyone loves. You don't stand a chance." I laughed out loud. If this was the rabbi, maybe I needed to re-think my whole approach to religion.

"Hey, I'm not out to marry the guy. Just looking for a good time. You know, like the song says, "Girls just want to have fun."

"Oy Cheryl," she said as she smiled and wagged a crooked finger at me. "I wonder what poor, sainted Momma Ruthie would have to say if she could hear you talk like that?"

"Oy indeed, Candy, oy indeed," I replied as I raised one eyebrow, turned away and began stretching, striding and jiggling in place, focused now on the task at hand.

As we massed on the street in front of City Hall, I made sure I was well-po-sitioned: not too close, but well within sight of "the rabbi." I could tell he'd already noticed me. He was trying extra-hard not to look but his eyes kept wandering in my direction, pulled by some invisible tractor beam.

Then the race began. Without a word, the three of us -- Candy, the hunky rabbi and me -- fell in together, finding a steady, shared pace. Already compatible, I thought, and smiled my best and brightest smile—not so easy at 6 am on a Sunday morning.

"So, sailor," I offered as we loped along, "new in town?"

To my relief, he laughed out loud. "I guess sort of—been here just over a year. I'm Dan Chafetz. And you're. . .?"

"Cheryl Kravitz. My friend here tells me you're the new rabbi at Temple Sinai."

"Guilty as charged."

Good answer, I thought. This could be fun.

And so it was. Running together, Dan and me, already a pair, perfectly in sync, with an increasingly invisible Candy fading from view. I guess we both felt the surge of energy between us as we kicked into higher gear, challenging, teasing each other. Edgy, I thought, but nice-edgy.

At exactly that moment, he let out a yelp.

"Shit! My calf!" Grabbing his leg, he hobbled off to the median, trying hard not to upend any of the other runners. I followed close behind.

"Can't believe this is happening again!" he bellowed.

I helped him walk off the cramp, then offered to stretch his muscle out.

He smiled, picking up the hint. "Well, well," he said. "How could I refuse such a gracious offer?"

So he followed me home.

"I'll draw a bath—that'll relax your leg," I said. "And a glass of wine—purely for medicinal purposes. Of course, I will need to supervise that bath— supervise closely."

And I did. And he didn't seem to mind – at all.

Something tells me I'm into something good.

* * *

t was Friday afternoon, the "countdown to Shabbat."

I was putting the final touches on my sermon for the evening and preparing something personal to say to the bar mitzvah the next morning, rushing because -- as much as I wanted to find just the right words -- I knew I had to go for a run before dinner. Running, you see, is my passion, has been since the days I was a newly-minted rabbi invited regularly to bar mitzvah luncheons, wedding receptions and fundraising dinners. Pretty quickly I figured out I had to do something or I'd turn into Jabba the Hutt. So I ran, whenever, wherever I could. The minute I had an opening in the day, I'd put on my gear and head out onto the streets of the neighborhood. My congregants thought it was a hoot to see me dashing down the street with my fleece, headband and gloves, my headphones pumping out the music and me, oblivious to the world, singing out the words at the top of my lungs. I know they did; they loved to tell me about their "running rabbi sightings" which they seemed to find endearing.

So, with the late winter afternoon sun drooping in the sky, I raced through the Torah portion, made the notes I'd need to speak later that evening, started planning what I'd say to the star soccer player who would be tomorrow's bar mitzvah. Something about "goals in life," I thought. (I know, a bit obvious but still…) Then, donning sneakers, gym shorts and a long-sleeved thermal shirt, iPhone strapped to my upper arm, headphones on, I was off, whizzing past kids and moms in the playground, strolling couples walking arm-in-arm, the occasional congregant or neighbor who waved as I passed by.

Listening to my "Running Mix" – a collection that included "Running on Empty," "Running Down a Dream," and James Taylor's "Walking Man" (okay, I took a little license on that one) -- I eased through my route, returning home, strangely invigorated and calmed at the same time. Then, peeling off my sweaty gear, I jumped into the shower, toweled off and had just enough time to dress for shul, rush through the table blessings with the family and wolf down dinner before heading off to synagogue.

That evening was cold and blustery, the sanctuary about half full. As I looked around, I realized I knew almost everyone by name and had a pretty good idea why each one of them was there. Some, I knew, came out of habit, others in need of comfort or friendship or some kind of spiritual 'something' they hoped I could provide. For my part, I knew I'd do my best to give them whatever it was they were searching for.

By now, everyone was singing a welcome to the Sabbath, turning to the rear of the sanctuary and bowing as if receiving royalty, imitating the mystics of Safed who used to dress all in white and gather in the fields outside town to greet "the Sabbath Queen." It was beautiful. But it made me wonder: When was the last time I had felt that way – when the Sabbath made me feel like a groom ready to meet my bride? I honestly couldn't remember. While I loved the music and the quiet and the warm bath of love from my congregants, when it came to something deeper, something spiritual, I wasn't feeling it so much these days.

I was just too busy setting everything up to make it right for them. Checking the sound system, rehearsing with the cantor, practicing my sermon. I was like a lover who prepares a romantic dinner for his sweetheart, lighting the candles, arranging the flowers and cooking the perfect meal but, so caught up in the details, it leaves him untouched. That was me. I made it all work. But it was for them, not for me.

Tonight, I thought, I'd love something more, not just the glow I get standing up here in front of these familiar faces, but something personal, the reason I went into this in the first place.

As the music played, I thought about my day, the people I'd tried to help, the little bit of goodness I'd tried to bring into the world. Through it all, the music played on, sweet and warm. I closed my eyes, watching the little flashes of light play on the insides of my eyelids. I drew my big, black-and-white prayer shawl a little tighter around me, trying to shut out all the noise and distractions, rocking gently to the ebb and flow of the music. Just let go, I said to myself. Like I used to do at camp, at college, at rabbinical school when I davened with my buddies. Just let go.

Then…whoa! I pulled myself back. Can't go there. I mean, if I really let myself get lost in the moment how would I be able to find the right words, the right melodies, the right page numbers? How could I be rabbi to them unless I took care of their spiritual needs before my own. That, after all, was the tradeoff, the compromise necessary to do the job. And I was willing to make it. After all, I loved what I did – almost all of it -- and felt like I was doing something important, something that made people's lives better. How many people could say that with a straight face? So as long as I put my own spiritual quest on the back burner, as long as I focused on their souls instead of mine, it all worked pretty well.

Of course it hadn't always been that way. I remember when I first got there as a young rabbi – before Sharon or Ari came into the picture. I was pretty green. Not much experience. A kid really, twenty-eight years old, barely out of school – and I knew I looked it, despite the beard I grew 'so they would take me seriously.' What did I know back then about synagogues, boards of directors, challenging congregants? What did I know about being a rabbi? Close to zero. Most of the time, I just went on instinct. Sometimes it worked. Sometimes it exploded in my face like one of those big fat cigars in the cartoons.

I remember one night during that first year at Emmanuel when a meeting had gotten a little out of hand. It had started out as a sane-enough discussion – can't remember now about what – but one that quickly got over-heated. Maybe it was me who raised the temperature with some ill-conceived comment. Maybe it was my lay leaders who stoked the fire. Whatever…like children on a playground, we edged closer and closer to one another, nose to nose, no one with the good sense to step back and ask "Where is this all heading and is it really worth it?"

Finally, one of them, a big, burly man in an ill-fitting suit said: "Wait just a minute there, Rabbi. Don't you work for us? I mean, if we tell you to do something, don't you have to do it?"

That night after the meeting, feeling hopeless, I drove back to my empty house, went immediately into the study and composed a letter of resignation, thinking carefully about every word. By about 2:30 in the morning I was done. I signed it, sealed the envelope, addressed it to the synagogue president and left it on the kitchen counter to hand-deliver first thing in the morning.

When I awoke only a few hours later, it was a beautiful day. With the sun shining in the early winter sky, I put on my gear and went for a run. It was invigorating. It cleared my head. But then I was confused. What about that letter of resignation? Did I really want to walk away? I mean: I'd worked so hard to get where I was, survived all those years of school, all those nights studying at the library -- so much invested. And besides, if I left, as my father always reminded me when I called to complain, where would I go? Another congregation where I'd have to deal with all the same meshugas? Or start back at square one as a first-year law or med student? No thanks.

As I walked through the front door, tingling from my run, the telephone was ringing. At the other end a woman I had only recently met, telling me, with a choked voice, that her mother had just died and could I please come over right away; she needed me. That was it. Called into service, I went running.

The rest of that day is a blur to me now, all these years later. I don't remember very much about it except that I was in constant motion from morning to evening. There was a meeting with the bereaved family, calls to return, a class to teach. Through it all, the letter of resignation lay on the kitchen counter, mocking me. By eleven o'clock when I returned to the kitchen, spent from the day, the letter was still there.

It was as though I'd never seen it before, no idea who had left it there. I picked it up, turned it in my hands for a moment, poised somewhere between the need to escape and the desire to forget I had ever felt so desperate. Then I placed it in a drawer under a stack of papers. I never did send it. But I never threw it away either. It stayed there at the bottom of the drawer as a promise of freedom whenever I needed it.

I guess that's the way it's always gone with me and the shul. Every time I start to wonder about my sanity doing this job, something happens – and I just know this is where I was meant to be. In an instant, the cynicism, the despair are washed away – and I'm at peace. How I wish Sharon had been able to see it that way too. But that never happened.

* *

Chapter 2:

"Losing My Religion"

Dan called the next day. I knew he would.

"Hey, Dr. Cheryl," he said into the phone, a little hint of breathlessness. "Just wanted to let you know my leg feels much better today. Must be your sterling medical expertise."

"Is THAT what you call it," I giggled. "OK, then. But you know, I think you're going to need a follow-up course of treatment, don't you? Please speak to my assistant and make an appointment at your earliest convenience."

We both laughed and made a plan for our real, official first date. This time we'd do it old school: I'd make him buy me dinner, pull the chair out, the whole song-and-dance.

I chose a dark, smoky little jazz club in Center City with great music, interesting food and an excellent wine list. I wondered what we'd talk about. After all, our worlds were so different. But conversation never flagged, not for an instant. He wanted to know everything about me: what it was like growing up in the suburbs of New York, what my family was like, how I chose the small liberal arts school I'd attended, and why in God's name I'd majored in English Lit!

"For the great job opportunities," I deadpanned. That was when I found out he'd done the same. "English Lit? That's a pretty weird major for a Rabbi-in-training, isn't it?"

"Ah, you'd think so -- but it's not! Knowing how people think and feel and act, getting to the heart of the human drama—that's exactly what you need to be a halfway decent rabbi. And that's what literature is all about, isn't it?"

At that moment, four excited strangers ran up to our table. Except they obviously weren't strangers to Dan.

"Rabbi!" the two women shrieked, then, talking over one another: "This is one of our favorite places."/"How did you hear about it?"/"Did you like your dinner?"/"We love it here."

Dan got up, hugged the women, shook hands with the men, did a three-stroke schmooze and deftly steered them away from our table towards the door. They never knew what hit them. "Sorry about that," he said. "Occupational hazard."

Then, without missing a beat, we took up where we'd left off.

That night, we stayed so long we practically closed the place down. And it quickly became "our" place—we just made sure to sit in the very back, at the darkest table so we could avoid what I came to call "Congregant Alerts." I just didn't feel like sharing him with anyone else.

In the days that followed, we fell into a wonderful, natural rhythm, in step with each other in almost everything we did: the running, the banter, the Times crossword puzzle, everything. From the time I was a kid, I had always lived in a world where language reigned supreme. And Dan loved language, literature and theater almost as much as I did. He had his limits: really depressing Scandinavian plays and weird absurdist drama were out, but otherwise he was adventurous, challenging—and fun. And we both loved music; he even made me mix tapes filled with the old classic rock he loved so much, music I didn't know but usually ended up liking. I could hardly believe my luck.

Except...

Except there was that one giant, elephant-sized "exception," the one we tried to ignore until we couldn't: the whole religion thing.

I was the child of Holocaust survivors—parents who had left behind most of their hearts and all of the people they loved in the Old Country. They had suffered losses beyond my imagining, including a young daughter who had been literally snatched from their arms and murdered by the Nazis. No wonder there was no place for God or religion in the household they built in their new American world. They were angry at the Nazis, at the anti-Semites, at their neighbors who failed to help them. But most of all, they were angry at God.

As a kid, I accepted their angry, bitter teachings about Judaism: show up at synagogue only when you had to, as at family bar mitzvahs, but make your disdain clear by coming late, sitting in the back and refusing to participate. Observe the holidays, but give them your own dark twist. Yes, the three of us went to services for Yom Kippur, but every Kol Nidre my mother made a point of coming home, taking off her going-to-synagogue clothes and having a very large cup of coffee and a pastry. Message delivered, loud and clear: There is no place for the old "superstitions" in this family.

So I grew up with Girl Scouts, ballet and ice-skating lessons but no Hebrew school. Growing up into adulthood, I adopted my own, more ironic stance: when asked about religion, I always said I was "Jew-ish – with the emphasis on the 'ish.'" Undeniably a member of the tribe, but more "Jew Lite" than anything else. This was the Jewish "legacy" my parents left me – a vacuum, an empty space.

Not long after I finished college, my father, Aaron, died suddenly of a heart attack. And then my much younger mother, who never got over losing him, died of breast cancer two years later at a ridiculously early age. Still, I never lost my "inner Ruthie". She was always with me. I could almost hear her clucking, almost see her dramatic eye-roll, the one that implicitly asked, "What are you, nuts?" My current romance only proved she was right. Clearly, I was nuts. After all, here I was, getting serious with a rabbi, for God's sake! I was relieved my mother wasn't around to see it. She never would have understood. Not sure I did, either.

Instead of making me feel ignorant (which I was) or embarrassed (that too), Dan took me under his wing. Without preaching God-stuff at me, he gave me space to ask questions and permission to challenge beliefs, even his most dearly-held ones.

Gently, kindly, he introduced me to a kind of Judaism 101 he thought I'd need if this relationship was going to go anywhere. Most of it was vaguely familiar, like the endless parade of holidays and food-fest celebrations. The rest I figured I could fake.

And I was ready to do that...because whatever he did from that point forward, I knew I had to be there with him. That much was clear. And I knew, no matter how he appeared to others, at the end of the day he would be coming home to me. I loved him for that and I loved him for the person he was when he shed his professional garb — the funny, caring, thoughtful, irreverent man who could make me squeal with delight.

And so, despite the insistent voice of my skeptical departed mother, there we were, lounging around my cozy apartment on a rare Sunday morning without appointments or religious school assemblies or weddings or funerals, a stolen Sunday when we could read the paper in our jammies and have a second cup of coffee in bed.

Dan leaned over, took my hand and said, "So I see there's a production of 'Dance of Death' on Broadway! Sounds like crazy fun, huh?"

Was he serious? This from the man who hated Strindberg and all the other dour Scandinavians. Anyway, I played along: "How did you guess? I already have tickets! And I know you'll love the singing and dancing! The kick-line finale is a real show-stopper."

"Well, then," he smiled, "Let's get the CD before we go. That way, we'll have a chance to learn the music! Maybe they even have a tune suitable for a wedding waltz. What do you think?"

I paused. What the hell? "Is this your way of proposing?"

Lifting me up off the bed into his surprisingly strong arms, he said simply:
"Yup."

"Wow! That must be the lamest proposal on record! No rose petals or string
quartets or horse-drawn carriage rides? And what about that whole "going
down on one knee" thing?"

Dan got a twinkle in his eye, then said: "Well, I can go one better. How about I
go down on two knees?"

And then he produced a beautiful light-blue box with a ring in it—a ring he
somehow knew was exactly the one I'd been eying in the magazines.

"Yes," I said. (Like Molly Bloom, yes, yes, yes.)

 And that was that. I'd never been happier.

But it didn't last long. That rosy glow hung on only about a day or so, until we
started planning the wedding and realized the time had come for us to negotiate our first official minefield together.

The timing was easy: as soon as possible. As thirty-somethings, there was
certainly no reason to wait. We'd both kissed enough frogs to know that what
we had was real. It was everything else that was so difficult.

Who to invite? I had no family, one close friend and only a couple of colleagues from the paper, so I envisioned something intimate, just a handful
of people we really loved. Dan had family and friends—and several hundred
congregants to consider.

"Really? We have to do that – we have to invite everyone? I've never even been to your Temple!"

"Then that's the first thing we need to change," he said. "In fact, the annual dinner-dance is next weekend. We'll go together and I'll introduce you to the flock. They'll love you," he reassured me. "How could they not? You'll dazzle them in that slinky black number you wore on our second date—yes, I remember it -- and entertain them with all your stories."

Unfortunately, it didn't work out that way.

We arrived at the synagogue a fashionable half hour after official starting time—late enough to make an entrance, Dan said, but not so late as to give offense. As we made our way through the room, I could feel the change in the air pressure. The men seemed intrigued, the women dismayed that their "dream husband," the one they could always count on for a sympathetic ear and a warm hug, was now taken.

Dan, of course, noticed none of this. He obviously loved these people and figured if he was happy, they would be happy for him. So he proudly ushered me around to each little knot of people, introducing me and expecting everyone to fall in love with me, just as he had. Tone-deaf to what was clearly going on, everything he did to show his joy that night only made things worse.

I didn't have the heart to burst his bubble, so I slipped away to the ladies room to use the toilet and have a private smoke. As I pushed open the door clearly marked "Ladies," I saw a group of tuxedoed men at whose center was a very drunk woman—Dina Something-or-other, one of Dan's regular groupies—with the straps of her cocktail dress dropped and her naked breasts exposed.

I couldn't help it -- I gasped audibly, very audibly. Then, as all eyes turned to me, I proceeded to do something even worse: I started to giggle. Then I laughed. Really hard.

I mean really the whole scene was so absurd. There they were, these two softball-shaped things sticking straight out from Dina's chest right into this coterie of "distinguished" gentlemen, their tongues practically hanging out of their mouths. All I could think of was my girlfriend, Candy, and how she always referred to our little town as "Hooterville." She had no idea how right she was.

Later I learned what had been going on in that powder room. The lovely Dina had just had what the classy folks in the congregation referred to as a "boob job" and was happily showing it off to anyone interested. My surprise visit — and my instinctive response -- had solidified the free-floating hostility I'd been feeling all night. Now they had met the enemy and it was me.

When I tried—gently—to tell Dan what I'd seen and felt, he took my hand ever so gently, and let me cry on his shoulder.

"I know this is hard for you," he said. "Believe me, even I sometimes feel like a foreigner in Congregation-land. But you'll get the hang of it, and they'll come to love you like I do. Eventually. I promise. You just have to be patient. Just give it a little time and you'll see."

Red-eyed and swollen-faced, I told him I really doubted it.

Then, taking my face in his two hands, as though delivering a speech he'd been practicing for weeks, he said: "Whatever happens, I promise you this: you will always come first. If this is ever a life you can't live, I'll quit immediately and find something else to do. You can count on that."

After a short pause, "I mean it."

There it was: the one thing I needed to hear. I came first, and everything would be okay in this crazy new world of ours.

Unfortunately, whether he knew it or not, it was a load of crap.

The Friday night oneg before our wedding, the one to which we'd invited the whole congregation since we obviously couldn't include them all in the wedding (could we?) -- was sparsely attended. Those who were there, made it clear that my feeble attempts to make them feel included in things were not appreciated. One attendee, a dowdy little past-president, made a special point of telling me that, even though we were hosting this communal shindig, I shouldn't expect any wedding presents since they hadn't been invited to the "real wedding."

That "real wedding" the next night, with Dan's family and rabbi-buddies, a handful of friends and a mandatory group of Temple leaders, was tinged for me by the congregation's obvious unhappiness with their new "rebbetzin." Though I tried all night, I couldn't shake it.

For his part, Dan saw none of this. For him, the wedding was intimate and warm, and we were surrounded by the people we loved.

Smiling to myself, I thought, so this is what I "bought" in Dan Chafetz: Rabbi Blue Skies, always looking for the sunshine in every moment. I tried hard to suspend my disbelief. Maybe, I thought, maybe he could read these people better than I. Maybe this was nothing more than a speed bump on the road to eventual happiness. But the truth is: I knew better. And I knew it from the start.

When it came time, not long afterwards, to move into a home of our own, we chose a small cottage-like three-bedroom as far away from the congregational McMansions as possible. Dan saw it as our haven, a first step in our lives together.

I saw it as a tiny oasis where I could have him for part of each day for myself. I was prepared to grant his congregants the rest of his heart and soul. It seemed like a reasonable compromise. But it wasn't a compromise they seemed willing to make. They wanted all of him, all the time. And as for me: they warned

Dan, without a trace of subtlety, that, if he wasn't careful, I was single-handedly going to ruin his very promising rabbinic career.

* * *

Romantics claim that couples who stay together over the years continue to see each other as they looked when they first met. I guess that must be true. Because, after all the years, when I looked at Sharon, I still saw her as the young runner at CityArtsRun. Her skin was still beautiful, her smile radiant, her body slim. In some ways, she looked better than ever. In fact, I used to tell her that all the time but she never believed me, figured I was just buttering her up.

Sure, we had our ups and downs — like all couples I guess. Like the time they called from Ari's school that we had to come and pick him up right away. (The first of many such times, it later turned out.) He had been fighting with kids bigger and older than he, they told us, and was beat up pretty bad. So I went to the school, saw Ari waiting for me in the principal's office -- with his scraped and bloody face, a shiner starting to bloom under one eye -- and brought him home. He told us he had been defending some other kid he barely knew, trying to protect him from a gang of bullies. I told him I was proud of him but he couldn't go getting into fights and that he had to find a peaceful way to resolve any disagreements. He looked at me like I was from Mars.

"The only thing these guys understand is fists, Dad. Don't you get it?"

That night after Ari went to bed with a big icebag on his eye, Sharon told me I had it all wrong, that I had to let him fight things out his way, trust him to do what he had to do.

"But Sharon, the kid's in fourth grade!" I said. "If he starts with this stuff now, where's he going to be in a year or two or three? He's going to end up the school bully."

She told me I was nuts. Just let him be.

Finally I conceded: "I'm sure you're right, dear." And while I wasn't sure at all, I knew if I couldn't at least act as if we were in agreement, it wasn't going to be pretty. Anyway, that was the way it always seemed to go with us. One way or another, we almost always found a way to come together. At parties, she still slipped her arm into mine and I liked that. Walking down the street, she would never let go of my hand. And in the bedroom, we still had that hunger for each other. We were generous with each other, protective of each other, never allowing anyone or anything to violate the private space of our "coupleness," even in the constant push and pull of congregational life.

When her friends asked how she dealt with the female attention I always got, she professed confidence in me and my commitment to our marriage vows. And besides, she liked to say, how likely is it that a man everyone in the community recognizes could get away with anything 'on the side'? He'd probably last about four minutes before he got found out.

That all held up pretty well for a very long time. Then came Lisa.

I met her on a rabbis' mission to Israel that I took in mid-March that year, about thirty of us on a bus. I noticed her right away – it was hard not to, the only woman in a large group of men. But it was more than that. She was young and attractive and, although she seemed to take pains to hide her body, I couldn't help notice it – and her. I wondered if she worked out, if perhaps she were a runner like me.

It was clear she was trying hard to be "one of the boys," making conversation, joining in the same late-night banter at the hotel bar. But she was definitely not one of us. And we couldn't help but treat her differently, making sure she was on and off the bus first, directing our remarks at her, trying to get her attention. It was kind of cute, I guess. Some things never change no matter how old we get. Like children on a school outing, we all tried to impress her and she tried hard to look impressed. But that was all it was, all she ever let it be.

One day, the two of us ended up sharing a seat on the bus on our way from our hotel to Jerusalem's Old City, a distance of only a few miles. In earlier, less troubled times, the trip would have taken only a few minutes. Now, it was well over an hour, as we navigated our way through a series of checkpoints and barricades. The sky was gray; heavy clouds scudded low in the sky.

"Enjoying yourself?" I asked.

"Enjoying? Well, not exactly, but I do feel like I'm learning a lot. And I feel good about that."

"Really? I'm surprised. To me, it seems like the same meetings with the same officials, the same lecturers as every other trip I've been on. I swear I even ordered the same thing for lunch at that place on Emek Refaim the last time I was here! Don't you feel like you've done this a hundred times before?"

"I guess…but there've been some things on this trip I thought were really kind of memorable."

"Like what?"

"Well, like that lecture on Mt. Scopus, the one on Kabbalah. I mean, I've been trying to figure out some things about Jewish mysticism for years. I even have a kind of routine…meditation and chanting and, oh, whatever…I try to do it every day. I even taught it at my shul last year although honestly I'm just a novice. Anyway, I've been to about a million lectures but I never heard anyone explain it as well as that guy did."

She paused, carefully considering her words, how open she wanted to be.

"I know you might think this is melodramatic but, for me, it was like…well, it was like the clouds opening up and the sun coming through. It all made so much sense. Didn't you feel that way too? Didn't you think it was something kind of special?"

Now I felt a bit embarrassed as I remembered playing absentmindedly with my cell phone throughout the lecture, bored out of my mind.

"Well, I guess. But, honestly, I'm not sure I really got it."

She looked up at me, quiet, maybe a little hurt.

After an uncomfortable silence, I blathered on: "I am thinking about it, though, you know...mysticism, mediation, all that stuff. But the truth is: I read the books and it doesn't really get through. I wonder sometimes if I'm just not cut out for it... but I guess I'll never know as long as I just keep faking it on my own. What I'd really like to do, what I'd really like is to find a good teacher and see if I could get comfortable with it, maybe try a little simple, entry-level stuff and see if it works for me, you know?"

She nodded as I stumbled on.

"I keep reading these books, you know, keep reading these books and I'm just not sure what it all means."

I saw her eyes drift for an instant, realizing I had just said exactly the same thing and suspecting I was being a colossal bore.

But she nodded again and smiled and, for the rest of the trip, we were regular seat-mates on the bus, talking about meditation, our favorite books, what we'd had for lunch, our families, our congregations in the suburbs (turned out they weren't all that far from each other although we had never met before), gossiping about the other rabbis on the trip like a couple of schoolgirls.

I soon realized I couldn't wait to sit down beside her on the bus each morning. I loved talking to her and getting to know her. And I did. I learned she'd grown up with money, that she'd traveled the world, went to high school in Switzerland, took cruises in the Far East, went skiing in the Alps. Not bad for a woman barely thirty-one years old, she liked to say.

But it was more than that. She'd read a great deal, had a sort of natural curiosity about the world and a gift for conversation. She laughed easily, spoke with real energy, nodding her head whenever she agreed with something I was saying. For me, the seven days in Israel flashed by in a pleasant blur.

That's where it began. But what was "it" exactly? And what did Sharon think "it" was? For the first time in our married life, I saw doubt in her eyes whenever the subject of "the Israel trip" and "that girl-rabbi" came up.

And I wondered: How could she doubt me? Sure, Lisa was young and nice-looking — very nice-looking, in fact — and separated after a terrible four-year marriage to a man who hated that his wife was a rabbi. And I liked her. That was obvious. But I liked lots of women and I'd always behaved myself.

So there was no reason for her to be jealous. But she was. And I know something about jealousy. It's powerful and toxic and once it penetrates the heart, it's almost impossible to root out.

I remember that night from my youth when I was working at a Jewish camp, a night when my "summer girlfriend" suddenly disappeared. She'd said earlier in the day that her "old boyfriend from back home" was coming up for a visit and she wouldn't be able to see me until later that evening.

Truth is: I went a bit crazy. I flew into a rage. I stormed out of the room. Who the hell was this guy? And what did she want with him?

At dinnertime, she wasn't at her usual place in the dining hall. All I could think of was her and the "old boyfriend" out together, laughing, telling the old jokes, arm in arm. I tried to concentrate on my campers but couldn't. Instead, I asked my co-counselor to take care of things for a while. I had something important to do.

I went to the parking lot. Her car was still there so maybe they were somewhere in camp. I went down to the waterfront. Maybe they were sitting on the dock, dangling their feet in the water. Not there. I went out to the archery range where couples went late at night to "be together." No dice. I covered the camp from one end to the other, my pace quickening as I became more and more agitated.

Finally, I stopped and took a breath. I stood back and – for a moment -- saw myself clearly, a madman racing around camp, crazed by jealousy. This wasn't like me, not like me at all. Time to get a grip. Time to stop and trust her and our relationship. This was, after all, an "old boyfriend," with the emphasis on "old," as in "ex." They were just friends now. She'd said so, in so many words. And I believed her. I had to believe her. So, I would wait until the end of the evening – as planned -- put my young campers to bed, knock on her door in the specialists' dorm when she returned and spend the night with her as sweetly as we always did.

At about eleven o'clock, I went to her room and knocked on the door.

"Baby, you there?" I whispered.

There was a bump, a rustle and then a pause. Finally she answered, "David? David, I can't come to the door right now. I'll see you tomorrow. Okay?"

I understood. I'm not an idiot. I knew why she couldn't let me in "right now." I heard the blood go whoosh-whoosh in my ears. I thought about smashing down the door, confronting them curled up together in her bed.

I turned and headed back to my bunk. I closed my eyes and tried to sleep but my heart wouldn't stop thumping. I couldn't shut out the images in my mind. And I knew…it didn't matter what she said. It didn't matter how she'd explain it. Things would never be the same between us.

Remembering that time, I understood the husbands who find out about their wife's cheating and go postal. I understood the fury of feuding exes who simply can't bear to look at one another, who wear their rage at each other like a hair shirt. Like blood from a wound, jealousy has a way of saturating everything -- every deed, every thought, every feeling. And now, although I hadn't done a thing to deserve it, it had found a home in Sharon's heart.

* *

Chapter 3:

"Pretty Woman"

No matter how the congregants liked to blame everything on me, I knew all had not been perfect for Rabbi Chafetz at Temple Sinai even before I came on the scene. Hesitantly (I think he felt disloyal complaining even a little about them), Dan would confide how hard it had been finding his way as rabbi in the early days. Just out of school when he'd arrived, a boy really, he'd faced not-too-surprising pushback. After all, the more hard-edged among his leadership reasoned, we hired him. He has to do what we tell him to do. Why does he have to be so damned difficult?

But, over the years, through a process of trial-and-error, he managed to figure it out. Getting to the point where he knew how to herd his congregational "cats" cost him sweat and blood. But by the time I came on the scene, I could see, he had it pretty much under control and knew how to deal them, both the men who sometimes envied him and the women who all-too-often wanted him.

He dealt with the former with what had become, over the years, a finely-tuned ability to flatter and cajole. He assigned leadership roles—explaining how crucially important they were, how much he depended on them to do whatever needed doing. Generally speaking, this worked pretty well.

The women were a more delicate problem. Many of them saw him as their "dream partner." After all, when they came to his office, he gave them his absolute attention. Hold my calls, he'd instruct his secretary. He locked eyes with them, asked gentle but insightful questions—the kind that showed he really, really understood them, sympathized with them, stood ready to solve their problems. No wonder they loved him.

Most of their issues, the ones that brought them so urgently to his office at all times of the day and night, were about spoiled children, interfering in-laws, money issues, existential angst.

The more touchy problems were marital. Weeping enough to reveal their pain but not enough to smear their make-up, they'd explain how cold and unfeeling their husbands were. Hanging in the air was the unspoken sentence: And I know you'd be different.

What was good for me, at least at first, was that they were right. He was different from other men. What was bad for me was that they knew he was mine and not theirs. And they didn't like that at all.

At first, I tried to be open and friendly. When we moved into the new house and a gaggle of Sisterhood ladies showed up to help us unpack the boxes, I welcomed them in. They're not so bad, I thought. They worked for hours unwrapping dishes and putting them away, refolding linens and making beds, arranging some of the books on the shelves of our little library. Maybe this whole community thing is okay, I thought. Maybe, in time, I'd figure out how to be more open, to tame my suspicions, to be the Ladies Home Journal version of the rabbi's wife.

But when I started hearing reports in the community describing what kind of china I had ("Can you believe she has Spode dinnerware?"), the books I read ("High-brow Literature!") and the colors and décor of our bedrooms ("Hunter green? Really?") that door slammed shut, permanently. Thank God I hadn't been caught smoking or let them into my closets – or the drawer beside my bed! (Now that would have blown their minds!)

In response to this unnerving episode, I did two things: installed the longest, thickest curtains I could find on every window in the house, and recruited my friend Candy to join Sisterhood. I knew I needed a set of eyes and ears on the 'inside.' I needed a spy in congregation-land, an early-warning messenger about trouble ahead. One thing was clear: I was in a minefield and I needed a guide to help me pick my way through without getting blown to pieces.

* * *

I'd been home from Israel about two weeks when I saw Lisa again, the last week of March.

It almost didn't happen. It was Monday and, while Monday was supposed to be my day off, this one was rapidly filling up with God-knows-what. I had penciled in the meeting of the Interfaith Clergy Council at noon but was on the verge of ditching it. I desperately needed some free time for a couple of hours, maybe go for a run or read, something to clear my head.

But then my conscience kicked in. I remembered I'd missed the Council meeting last month and the month before that and, if I expected to be taken seriously as a regular, I'd better get there today. So I headed off on the fifteen-minute drive through a surprising late-season snow shower, arriving at the old Presbyterian stone church where the Council met, walking into the meeting that had already begun.

I couldn't believe it. There was Lisa, sitting on the other side of the table, in a light tan suit, and a red-and-orange scarf. She gave me a quick smile; I felt an unexpected jolt. I'd never seen her there before; maybe she was there for me, I thought, because she guessed I might show up. Maybe. I opened my briefcase, removed my pen and notepad and turned my gaze toward the chair, all business. I took part in the discussion, hoping I wouldn't sound too stupid. Every time I looked over to gauge her reaction, she smiled.

After the meeting, I walked over to her and we kissed each other on both cheeks, European-style.

"You recovered from the trip yet?" I asked.

"Pretty much. First few days were hard, up in the middle of the night, dozing off in the middle of the day. You know how it goes. But now I'm pretty much back into the old routine again. You?"

"Yeah, actually, I'm doing pretty well. I slept for almost twenty-four hours straight when we got back and, by the next day, I was okay. Not much choice about it anyway. I think the good people of Temple Emmanuel must have saved up everything they could while I was away and then loaded it all on me as soon as I got back. I haven't had a minute to breathe since."

"Yeah, I know what you mean. It's been that way for me too."

Then she smiled and took an audible breath. Slightly flushed as she spoke, the words came spilling out, as if, had she stopped even for a moment, she might lose her nerve.

"Listen, David, I've been thinking. Remember when we were on the bus in Jerusalem and we were talking about spiritual practice and you said you'd like to find someone who could help you get started? Well, I've been thinking, maybe I could. I mean, honestly, I'm not exactly an expert but I could at least get you started. Me, I usually do about an hour of mediation every morning at my place, some simple breathing stuff and some chanting and visualization. You could do a session or two with me and see if you like it. No commitments. No hurt feelings if you decide it's a no-go. What do you think?"

We looked at each other until finally I said: "You can breathe now." And we both laughed.

Then I said: "But seriously… I want to tell you a story. A few years ago, a woman, a congregant I quite like actually, came to my office, said she wanted to tell me something, something she knew I wouldn't like but she thought I needed to hear and no one else would tell me. And so she proceeded to give me a kind of rabbinic report card, one she claimed came from pretty much everyone she spoke to in the congregation. She told me I was doing well in most things and people seemed to like me. My sermons were excellent, weddings and funerals were A+. The synagogue was running smoothly. At that moment, I was sure there was a big "but" coming. And, of course, there was. 'But…Rabbi,' she said, 'when it comes to God, when it comes to anything spiritual, we're just not feeling it from you. Somehow you come across more like the CEO of Temple Emmanuel, Inc. than its rabbi, if you know what I mean.'

I did know what she meant. And even though I'd been forced into it by my leadership who reminded me I was the leader of a $3 million dollar a year corporation and who insisted I take a course on budgets at the community college, it really hurt. So I kind of sulked around for a few days. But eventually I had to admit it. It was probably true. Bit by bit over the years, I had gotten sucked into treating the congregation as a "corporation," and myself as "chief operating officer." Somehow, I'd kind of let the spiritual side of me get lost. So I guess you could say her timing was perfect. "Ok, sure, let's do it."

We made plans to get together the following Monday at her place. It would be quiet, she said, because she would be taking her daughter to playcare and besides, she couldn't imagine being able to concentrate in her synagogue or in mine. Too many distractions.

"Wear something light and comfortable," she said. "And dress in layers. I keep the house pretty cool so you'll probably want to start off with a sweatshirt or sweater or something but I bet when you get warmed up, you'll be more relaxed in a T-shirt. Anyway, we'll play it by ear and see how it goes. See you Monday. Nine-thirty sound okay?"

That next Monday morning Sharon and I sat at the breakfast table, each of us poring over our respective sections of the paper—entertainment for Sharon, the first section for me. Ari, our teenage son, had left for school long before and a good thing too because having him at the table -- mute, daring anyone to try to engage him in conversation – wasn't a particularly pleasant way to start the day.

Sharon looked up at me for just a moment and asked: "Sleep okay last night?"

"Yup. How about you?"

"Not bad. What do you have on for today?"

"Oh," I said, pausing for just a fraction of a second, "looks like a pretty full day. Some appointments in the afternoon, a little teaching at night. Oh, and in the morning I'm going over to a friend's place to try learning a little bit about Jewish meditation. Can you believe it? Me, the great mystic! Should be interesting… And you? Anything exciting on your calendar today?"

"No," she said, "just the usual grind."

Sharon worked as an editor and sometime writer for a small, local paper more concerned about financial survival than winning Pulitzers. I knew she hated it but we needed the money; there was no way we could live on my salary alone. The only thing she really liked was when she got a chance to write herself, she would always tell me, not repairing someone else's work. Not hard to understand. Sharon had always thought of herself as a serious writer. She'd been a real hot shot in school and had a stack of published poems and short stories to prove it. But she rarely got the chance to do it – and that, I knew, rankled.

Sharon finished the article she had been reading, folded the paper and began to gather up her things for the ride into work. "Well, have a good day. See you at dinner." She walked over to me, kissed me on the cheek and walked out the door.

Why hadn't I told her more about my morning's plans, I wondered, like where exactly I was going and with whom?

I went upstairs to dress in the uniform Lisa had suggested—jeans and a T-shirt with a comfortable sweatshirt on top. I was ready.

I drove over to Lisa's place, an old house with a gravel driveway and a wild, mostly untended garden in Oakdale, an inner-ring suburb, home to a gumbo of interracial, multicultural families, sprinkled with artists and professors from two nearby liberal arts colleges. She and her now ex had purchased the place when they first moved into the area a few years earlier, a young couple just starting out life together. Now she lived there with their two-year-old daughter. I had no idea where the ex lived or if he had anything to do with Lisa or the child. I didn't even know what the kid's name was.

I had never been there before, didn't know the neighborhood at all but quickly found my way. Her directions were perfect.

She opened the door as I was reaching up to knock, invited me in with a smile, gave me a quick hug and took my coat, motioning for me to join her in the kitchen where she was just finishing her coffee. She offered me a cup. We both sipped and smiled a little awkwardly. Finally she broke the silence.

"Tell me, David, how're you feeling? You okay with this? I know it's a little bit out of your usual comfort zone."

"Actually I'm kind of excited about it…and curious…and a little nervous too I guess. I didn't sleep all that well last night I was thinking about it so much. Anyway, I'm ready to get started whenever you are."

"Okay," she said. "Come into my boudoir said the spider to the fly."

She smiled and gave me a wink, then took my hand and drew me into a small room just off the living room, what would have been, in most homes, the dining room. Here it was almost completely bare. There were a couple of hangings on the walls, a motley collection of rugs on the floor. In one corner, a small stereo. In another, a tripod with a stick of incense burning, smoke curling up toward the ceiling, shades of the late sixties. A twenty-first century ride on the Marrakesh Express.

"So listen," she said. "This is the hard part, getting started. It's almost impossible not to be self-conscious, especially for people like us who live in their heads most of the time. So here's what I want you to do. First, get as comfortable as you can. Turn off your cell phone. Take a prayer rug, find a comfortable sitting position and then let's just be quiet for a while. We won't talk. Just sit quietly, try to breathe regularly but don't force it and see if you can calm your mind down."

We sat. I squirmed as I tried to find a tolerable position, my legs cramping as I arranged and re-arranged myself on the floor. I tried to slow my breathing and calm my mind, as she had suggested, only I couldn't seem to stop the random thoughts that ricocheted around my brain.

And I guess I couldn't stop looking at her, couldn't help noticing she looked really good in her yoga pants and T-shirt. Really good.

Lisa didn't speak for what seemed an eternity. Then she almost whispered. "Lock your gaze on something in the room, David, a color, a shape, a point of light and let go of yourself, just turn off your brain so you're looking but not really seeing. Open up your heart and let the Shechinah in. Allow yourself to feel it, David. Don't think. Just be." I felt like an infant thrown into the deep end of the pool and told to swim.

There was silence. Heavy silence. The air didn't move. My ankles ached – a lot. The muscles in my neck felt tight and knotted. I rotated my head, first one way then the other. I heard sounds from outside the room -- a clock ticking, a bird chirping just outside the window, the noise of traffic coming from the street. I could smell the aroma of the burning incense and the coffee from the kitchen. I felt like nothing so much as jumping up and making a run for it.

I remembered the last time I tried meditating, a student back in rabbinical school. I thought of the sweet, young instructor patiently explaining how we were to sit and chant and relax our minds. Then, after a few minutes of silence, she asked breathlessly how the experience had gone, as though awaiting truly mind-blowing results. After a few moments of awkward silence, no one willing to pop her balloon, I answered with mock excitement: "Well, I saw God." Oy.

Now I was acutely aware I wasn't meditating at all, wasn't fixing my gaze on anything, wasn't calming my mind. Instead, here I was playing personal home movies in my head. It felt all too familiar and I knew: this was what had gotten in my way the other times I'd tried to meditate. I just didn't seem to be able to clear out the mental clutter. One image led to another in an endless parade. Monkey mind.

I closed my eyes and watched the patterns on the back of my eyelids. The video cavalcade started up again. I stood up, knew I shouldn't – an admission of failure -- but I did. I stretched and yawned. After a while, she felt me moving, looked up and smiled.

"No one said this was going to be easy. David."

"I know, but really I feel like I'm just wasting time. I'm not getting anything out of it at all."

"Well," she said, "you've hardly given it ten minutes. How about trying a little bit more patience. Not your special strength, is it David?"

Then she paused and smiled.

"Listen, I've got another idea."

She moved over to me and gently reached toward my face. Instinctively, I jumped back.

"Try this," she said, as she removed my glasses, folded them and set them in my shirt pocket, one breast grazing my arm.

Now, as I looked around the room, I really couldn't see much of anything at all

-- only blotches, fuzzy shapes of varying colors, everything indistinct. I could see the window but nothing through it, the walls but not what was hanging on them, Lisa's outline but not the features I was coming to know so well. It was as if a switch had been flipped, disconnecting me from the world. As I opened wide my myopic eyes, I felt like a swimmer in a murky, multi-colored sea.

I locked my gaze on the grayish smoke wafting up from the incense she had set burning in the corner of the room. I saw it drift, the shapes morphing as it floated upwards…now a cloud, now an eddy, now a human face. Darker and lighter gray and black and almost pure white, braiding around each other…

I heard a sound. It was Lisa speaking, very quietly. She was smiling. "Well," she said, eyes wide, "you were gone there for a moment or two, weren't you? Didn't I tell you that you just needed a little bit of patience. And taking off the glasses helped, didn't it? I had a feeling it would."

I took my glasses out of my T-shirt pocket, refocused my eyes as I tried to lock my mind back into place. What did she mean? How long had we been sitting like this? Couldn't have been more than a moment or two.

"Maybe eight or ten minutes, I think," she said, answering my unasked question. "Not bad for a novice. Not bad at all. And there's so much more we can work on to enrich the experience. But for today, not a bad start at all."

Later, I got back in the car, turned my cell phone back on and set off for the synagogue.

I honestly didn't know what to make of the whole experience. But I knew I couldn't dwell on it. Too much to do. My weekly article on religion for Neal, the owner of Sharon's paper, and absolutely no idea what to write on, perhaps something about the struggle to find God in our quotidian lives. (I liked "quotidian" – good word! – I decided I would definitely use it for the article.) A class to teach that night and nothing prepared. Numbers I had to have ready for tomorrow night's budget meeting. And in between all that, there was Lisa, eternally smiling at me from her lotus position in my mind.

I drove for about fifteen minutes before I realized I'd been on "autopilot," somehow making all the turns, stopping at all the red lights, heading in the proper direction without a moment of conscious thought. Lucky, but dangerous. Time to focus.

As I walked into the synagogue office, Kelli, my assistant, said: "Rabbi, Sharon called. It sounded pretty urgent. She said she tried you on your cell phone but you didn't answer and she figured you probably had it turned off. She's at home and waiting for you to call. And, Rabbi, she sounded pretty upset." She looked straight at me.

What now? Through the early years of our marriage, Sharon had never bothered me at work. She took pride in the fact that she could handle things on her own. But that, as they say, was then. These days, barely a week went by without her summoning me -- a note passed by someone in the middle of a meeting, a knock on the door during a counseling session, a voice calling from the intercom, "Rabbi, I think you might want to take this."

And, while once – on the rare occasions it did happen -- it might have been a busted water heater or a leak under the kitchen sink, now it was almost always about Ari and it was inevitably bad.

Ari, we had named him, we told the families, after Sharon's father, Aaron, but the truth was it was really for Ari Ben Canaan from Exodus. Perhaps that's why he seemed to have so little of the wisdom of Sharon's dad and so much of the anger and intensity of the fictional Ben Canaan.

From the very beginning, Ari did things his own way. Although our friends all said what an "easy baby" he was, Sharon and I knew how stubborn and fiercely independent he could be. Ari napped only when he chose, ate only what he liked, was toilet-trained only when he decided he was good and ready, long after his third birthday.

His pre-school teachers said he was a lovely boy but solitary, playing on his own while all the other children were busy with each other. He had amazing powers of concentration, would listen again and again to a favorite song, would take apart and put back together a wooden puzzle until he could assemble it without error or hesitation, like a Marine with his rifle.

In elementary school, Ari proved himself something less than a top student. He struggled over reading, arithmetic, social studies. He lived for recess, when his natural athleticism shone through and he was always among the first few picked whenever sides were chosen. Though his report cards were filled with C's and D's (except for the inevitable A in Phys Ed), Ari had other strengths -- tremendous dexterity, an almost mystical sense about how mechanical things worked and how to fix them when broken, and an ability to draw, far beyond his years, certainly far beyond the skills of his parents whose artistic efforts had always been limited to rudimentary stick figures.

Ari was also an exceptionally handsome child. With his shaggy mop of reddish-brown hair, the splash of freckles across his nose and cheeks and a cherubic expression — no matter what he was up to — he always started off well with teachers, coaches and parents who gave this little angel the benefit of the doubt. Sadly, that didn't usually last very long as they got to know him better.

Perhaps that's why, wherever he went, from the baseball diamond to school to the houses of his friends, people seemed perpetually clucking over Ari, as if he had personally let them down, as if they had all shared great dreams for this little "golden boy," dreams which he inevitably failed to fulfill.

He was certainly a disappointment to Sharon and me, especially me. I'd been so excited early on about how he could throw a ball or draw a picture or solve a puzzle. Now, more and more, I couldn't help seeing him as a problem, a kind of puzzle himself, a failure in school, a loner. Somehow, I couldn't shake the persistent sense — God forgive me! — that he was my personal punishment for some sin I couldn't remember committing. Now, as Ari had reached adolescence, I had to admit I was getting tired of all the irate calls. God knows, I had enough problems to deal with. I certainly didn't need any more from my own family, especially with Sharon increasingly acting as Ari's defender and enabler, taking Ari's side whenever I tried laying down the law.

* * *

Chapter 4:
"Danny's Song"

After the debacle of my entry into Dan's congregation – the encounter in the Ladies' room, the awful wedding weekend, the move into the new house -- all I really wanted was to be left alone. Was that too much to ask? So I did what I had to do. I wore big hats and dark glasses and started shopping in the next town over. If I were my own shrink, I'd probably say I was hiding, but at the time, it just seemed smarter, easier, more comfortable.

My job became a mini-refuge: no one there cared about my status as "the rabbi's wife." So I put in more and more hours at my desk, trying to work up some enthusiasm for the stories I had to write, mindless accounts of donors presenting checks to worthy organizations and politicians speechifying at schools and store openings.

I started writing my own work, too. There were things in my life I just had to say, things I had to get down on paper.

At home, it was still tolerably good between Dan and me -- as long as he played by my rules: This is my clubhouse. No congregants allowed!

We had date-night every Wednesday. We cooked together most evenings. And I was there to greet him at the door with a glass of wine in hand when he came home after one of his endless all-night meetings. Good food, good drink, great sex. I was happy enough.

But after a while, I could see Dan was not. Synagogue life was so demanding and coming home to me was no refuge. What had once seemed cute and endearing— rolling my eyes and cracking wise whenever he started telling me about his day – was now wearing on him. I could see it in the little lines, the marks of strain and worry that were starting to show on his face.

Beyond this, there was something else missing for him. He wanted something more – a family just like the one he had grown up in.

Unlike my family, Dan's had been an uncomplicated, happy one —the Jewish Cleavers, a family where Father always Knew Best and Mom stayed home and baked cookies for her two loveable kids. No sturm und drang, no shadow of the death camps, just sunshine, pick-up baseball games in the ample back yard and barbecues on the patio. That's what he wanted now   a family, a child, preferably a son.

So, slowly at first, he started the "Great Baby Campaign." Maybe it was a way to bring the scattered parts of his life together. Perhaps he thought it would change me, soften me, make me a better sounding board, a better listener. Whatever it was, the Campaign soon grew into all-out siege. He cajoled, he teased, he whined, acting more and more like a child himself.

Because we'd married later—in our thirties—I thought we'd never have to have this conversation. Actually, I dreaded it. But here it was. He wanted a baby and he wanted it badly.

"I can't," I wanted to yell. "Don't ask me to do this."

But Dan was relentless, constantly at me. At the supermarket, he'd point out the "cute little darlings" in the shopping carts! On vacation he'd find some adorable toddler and help him build sand castles, gleefully toting buckets of seawater to fill the moats he'd helped to excavate, always looking over his shoulder to make certain I saw how blissfully happy he was.

Finally, out of sheer exhaustion, I made him a deal: we'd go six months without protection, and see what happened. He saw it as a kind of God Test: would he be rewarded for his faithful service all these years? I saw it as a science experiment. At my age, I knew the odds were in my favor.

ELLIOT STROM

And yet, in the end, God – and Dan -- won. About nine and a half months after the great experiment began, baby Avi arrived. Dan said I'd fall in love with him, that my maternal instincts would take over, that everything would change.

And in some ways, it did.

I immediately fell for this red-haired, red-faced, soft and perfect little miracle. The first three months, on maternity leave from the paper, went by in a haze of midnight feedings, baby puke and sweet times when he fell asleep on my chest. How, I wondered, could a creature who did such gross things smell so sweet?

Still, I held something back. Always conscious of my parents' tragic loss, I knew how dangerous it was to love a child completely, so I made sure there was some emotional space between Avi and me, even when he was just a sweet, tiny baby.

But Dan was smitten. Every movement, every breath, every smile (even when it was just gas) was a cause for delight and it just got more so as Ari grew into a toddler and then a young boy. Dan couldn't wait to take his little miracle to the park or the pool or even to fast food—something both of us hated, but our child adored. It was the "Abba and Avi show" as Dan proudly took him everywhere—especially to Temple where Avi attended his father's pre-school and services where kids came in their jammies for "baby Shabbat." Mostly, I let them go without me. Having a child whose behavior was scrutinized by the Congregational Judgment Squad appealed even less than being judged myself.

Dan, on the other hand, was the undisputed "good parent." At least to them. To me, though, the picture was a little more complicated.

One day at the beach, when Avi was about three, I saw it clearly. I was sitting under the little canopy we'd lugged to shelter us from the sun, working intently on a book proposal of my own. It was going to be my little secret. Maybe, I thought, this will be my breakthrough, my ticket out of local newspaper hell and into a job as a real writer. My mind was swirling, cooking, focused completely on my laptop.

Dan was supposed to be watching Avi. Instead he was busy showing off for all the women on the beach—the nearly naked teenagers, the tankini-clad young mothers and even the saggy "women of a certain age." Meanwhile, our son wandered off. Adorably red-headed, wearing his "Daddy (hearts) me" tee-shirt and swim trunks with the diaper hanging out the bottom, he went off down the beach, shovel in hand, looking for something to do.

Suddenly I looked up from my writing and, panic-stricken, realized he was gone.

I ran down the beach screaming, "Have you seen a baby boy? A little boy? He's lost!"

After what seemed an eternity I found him, just steps away really, playing happily on the blanket of another family, one with four kids, two attentive parents and lots of sand toys.

I swept him up in my arms, unsure what to do first—kiss him or smack him. Dan, hearing the uproar and ashamed at what had obviously been going on beyond his notice, ran over to us and held the two of us in his arms, soothing us as Avi and I cried --me from fury and relief, Avi because his mother had obviously lost her mind.

Years later, after he started skipping school, hanging out with cringe-worthy friends and refusing to do his homework, I realized that the beach incident was just the first step in what would become a lifetime of Ari's running away from us.

As a boy in grade school, he wanted to change his name. 'Avi' was too Jewish, too strange, he said. Why couldn't he have a normal name, like his buddy T.J.? When I told him that "T.J." stood for Thomas Junior, and that Jews didn't get named after their own parents, he said, "Too bad. That's what I want. I want to be T.J. I want to be like everyone else."

Being like everyone else soon meant that Sunday school was out, replaced by endless hours of video games and socializing with kids from the other side of the tracks, kids who had never seen a rabbi and who certainly didn't know or care at all that Avi was a rabbi's son.

And who could blame him? After all, the worst parts of Avi's life came from his being the "R.K.", the Rabbi's Kid. At Sunday school, teachers held him to a different standard. When he knew something, their attitude was, of course he knew it; after all, look who his dad is! When he didn't, or when he refused to answer, or when he behaved the way all the other kids behaved, he got singled out. "Avi," the teacher would say, "I expected more from you!"

Even at public school, he could feel the eyes on him, the ever- vigilant judges holding an invisible yardstick against which he was measured and inevitably found wanting.

Year by year, he grew more taciturn and private, more remote from us. By the time he was fifteen, I hardly knew him. But the principal from his high school, Mr. Blount, certainly knew him – and he knew me too. In fact, I think he had me on speed dial. Almost daily I'd get calls asking why Avi was late, where he was, threatening him—and, I felt, me—with suspension, expulsion.

And where was his father in all this? AWOL.

When we talked about Avi, or rather when we screamed at each other about him, the subtext was clear. Avi was my job and I was failing.

Somehow we all survived to Avi's sixteenth birthday. A milestone. Desperately, I thought, if I make this one perfect, maybe we can all find our way back to being a family. So I ordered a birthday cake with my favorite picture of him on top in special frosting. I even invited a girl whose name he had recently grunted at me -- something Pirelli -- to come over. Dan, the Pirelli Girl and I set out plates, candles, and everything. Secretly, I was planning to give him the keys to my four year-old car as a super-gift, something to say, yes, I know you're a man now, and I want you to have what you want for yourself. I want us all to make a new start

He never showed up. Too busy smoking weed or something, anything to forget that he had parents and a home, or at least these parents and this home.

That was it for me. I officially resigned as his mother. Now Dan could take over. Time to see how much better he could do this job. Good luck!

* * *

I closed the door to my office, picked up the phone and dialed. It rang once, then I heard Sharon answer. Her voice shaky, she got right down to business.

"I got a call this morning from Henry Blake, the vice-principal at the school; he wanted to know if Ari was sick because he didn't show up for school today. David, he's not at school and he's not at home. I have no idea where he is and I'm starting to get worried. I don't know what you've got on for today but would you please see if you can find him. Because if you can't find him soon, I think I'm going to have to call the police. Can you do that, David? Can you? You're not doing that yoga thing this morning, are you?," contempt oozing through the telephone line.

"No. Why would you ask me that? It's not Monday."

I paused to take a breath, resisting getting pulled into the vortex of her negativity, then: "Okay, I'll go look for him now. Okay? Sharon? Try to relax and don't do anything drastic. I'm getting in the car now. I'm sure I'll find him. Don't call the police…"

She said nothing.

"Sharon, don't call the police. Let me see if I can find him. I'll call you on my cell phone when I have something. Okay? Try to stay calm. Don't call the police. Okay?"

I walked out of my study and into the synagogue office, throwing on my jacket as I went.

"Kelli, I'm going out for a while and I'm not sure when I'll be back. But I'll call and check for messages. Please don't call me unless it's an emergency."

Kelli gave me that look she always did when she could see something wasn't right, the one that said she and I both knew I couldn't function without her.

"Okay. I won't ask. Call me when you get a chance. We'll hold down the fort here."

I got into the car and sat for a moment. Where to? If Ari wasn't at home or in class, where would he be? I decided to begin at the school and check out his usual hideouts. No sign of him in back of the building or in the little wooded area just off school grounds where he sometimes went to smoke. Not in the playground. Not at the 7–Eleven. Next, I drove to his pal, Mike's, stopped the car, drew a breath, walked to the front door. No answer and no sound coming from within. He could have been hiding, I guess, could have seen me pull up and stayed quiet. Probably not. He wouldn't have been that subtle. I waited a moment, rang again, then left.

Back in the car I thought, What next? I couldn't go home and admit failure, back to face the implacable wrath of Sharon. I had to find him.

My cell phone rang. It was her.

"Did you find him? Where is he?"

"Sharon, I don't know yet. I'm looking.

"Are you in Oakdale?"

Oakdale? Why did she keeping going back to that?

"No," I said – with forced patience – "I'm not in Oakdale. I'm exactly where I'm supposed to be in my car, in our neighborhood, trying to find our son, just as you asked me to do and I told you I would do. I haven't found him yet but I promise I will. OK?" I thought of all the work I wasn't getting done as this farcical search proceeded on.

I drove back to the parking lot in front of the school and then tried to make a plan. I remembered reading somewhere that the best way to navigate a maze was to put your right hand on a wall and not lift it. That way, you would never retrace your steps and, sooner or later, you'd reach your goal. Or at least that was the theory.

So I tried the driving equivalent, turning to the right at every corner, all the while looking desperately for Ari on either side of the road.

He wasn't anywhere. Or at least I couldn't find him. What would I say to Sharon? She sounded positively unhinged on the last call and I was sure she was about to call again. I turned the cell phone off.

I made another dozen right turns until I came around again to the playground, pulled in to the parking lot and turned off the engine. I had to be logical about this. There was an answer here; I just had to figure it out. What would Ari do?

Eventually, I had to admit I didn't have a clue. My son, my only son, was pretty much a mystery to me. I couldn't begin to guess where he might be, what he might be doing or with whom. A stranger to me, that's what he was. I wiped my eyes with a jacket sleeve.

It was Ari's shoes I noticed first, his and another pair, sticking out from behind a storage shed. I knew immediately they were Ari's because they were colored vivid red. Ari had explained he wanted his shoes to be "different," so he covered his very expensive new white sneakers (that he had begged for) with ink from a red marker. Sure was different. Perhaps Ari really thought they were unique and special that way; maybe he just wanted to piss me off. In any case, there they were, Ari's bright red shoes and another pair – a more subdued blue and white – right underneath. Ari's were pointing down between the others which were pointing up. Didn't take much imagination to know what else must have been pointing up at that moment.

I got out of the car and walked around the corner of the shed. There they were -- Ari and a girl with a bright cherry red streak down the center of her otherwise black hair -- the two of them jammed up against the side of the shed, pushed up against each other, jeans at their ankles, shoes all that was visible beneath the bottom of a ratty, old blanket that didn't quite cover them.

I stood over them and watched for a moment, not knowing what else to do. They were barely moving. Then she saw me and literally jumped, clutching the blanket to her nearly naked body. Ari turned around, saw me and shouted: "Dammit!"

As quietly as I could, I said, "I'm going around the corner of the shed. I'm going to give you one minute to make yourselves presentable. And then I'm coming right back and we're going to have a little chat."

I walked back around the other side of the shed. Had I really said "little chat?" This was bad! I counted out two full minutes, then walked back. They were standing now, fully dressed, the girl's face as red as the streak in her hair, as red as Ari's shoes.

I spoke slowly, deliberately, with what I thought was admirable restraint.

"Here's what we're going to do. I'm going to drive you both back to school right now. You're going to go directly to Mr. Blake's office and explain that you were playing hooky but that you're back and ready for whatever punishment he deems necessary. Do you understand?"

They said nothing, just hung their heads. I wondered what that meant, if anything. Were they remorseful? Upset they'd been caught in the act? Or just embarrassed and angry? No way to know.

I drove them to school, marched them to the assistant principal's office, pointed to the door, indicating that they were to knock. As they waited for the door to open, I said: "I will speak to you tonight when you get home, young man. We have a lot to talk about."

I couldn't believe what was coming out of my mouth. I recognized the words and tone in an instant; they belonged to my father.

I called Sharon.

"It's okay. Well, I guess you'd call it okay. At least, he's not lying in a ditch somewhere."

She was silent.

"He's not hurt or anything. But he's in trouble. I found him and some girl I don't know…making out, I guess you'd call it, in the playground. I got them both back to school, to Blake's office. I don't know what happens next. I'm waiting outside now to see what he'll do."

Again, she didn't respond. And then, after a moment of silence, I heard her crying, very softly. I could imagine her holding the phone away from her face so I wouldn't hear. But I did hear and I knew we were now in strange new territory. Sharon did not cry easily, never had. As I waited outside the vice-principal's door, I realized I had no idea what was going to happen next with Ari, not only right now but down the road, in his life. He was like a car with failing brakes careening down a hill. I wondered if he'd manage to coast to a stop or if there would be some colossal smash-up? Would he go up in flames? And, if so, who else would get burned up along with him?

For a while Sharon didn't speak. On the other end of the line, just breathing, audible breathing. And then in one breath, choking, "I can't talk anymore now. Call me after you speak to Blake." Then, "click."

I waited on a long, high-backed wooden bench just outside Henry Blake's office. I could hear the principal's deep bass rumble and, intermittently, the quieter sounds of Ari and the girl. At least no one was yelling, I thought. A good sign, maybe. After about fifteen minutes, I heard chairs scraping and then the door opened and the two of them came out.

The girl walked right past me, her head down. Ari looked down too, staring intently at his red sneakers, then up, smoldering, into my face.

In a fierce whisper: "He wants to see you."

I walked in and sat down in the chair the vice-principal was pointing to. I had a moment to take a good look at Henry Blake. It wasn't hard to see why he'd been chosen to be vice-principal, the school disciplinarian. Perhaps 6'4"or even 6'5", a broad shouldered African-American with close-cropped, military-style hair and a neatly trimmed moustache, probably not much more than thirty-five or forty, he looked like someone who might have played tight end for his high school football team which, in fact, he had. There were two MVP trophies set out on one of his book shelves, photographs on another and the few books on the third shelf were held in place not by bookends but by small barbells at either end.

"Let me get right to the point, Rabbi. I know you know that Ari was not in school today. I know you know he was with Renee Pontarelli who's been cutting classes regularly as well. And I guess you know that this is not the first time, actually far from it. Did you know he's missed somewhere between a quarter and a third of his classes since the semester started?"

I was stunned. "No, I didn't. Why wasn't I told about this before?"

"You were. We called each time it happened. I spoke to your wife." Then he paused. "Didn't she tell you?"

I could feel the blood rush to my face. She hadn't even hinted at a problem at school (although she seemed to love to tell me about everything else she was unhappy with). That I'd deal with later. For now, I'd better concentrate on Ari and the trouble he was in.

Blake looked away, pretending to find something fascinating out the window. Then he turned back to me and said a little more softly than before, "Do you know, Rabbi, that Ari has been punished for this problem already, that he had detentions the last three Saturdays and that we warned him, if it didn't stop, we'd have to suspend him and if it still didn't stop, we'd end up having to expel him for the last months of the school year?"

I said nothing. What was I supposed to say?

Blake waited, then forged on. "I see. Okay. So let me ask you, and I don't want to get in the middle of anything between you and your wife, but I have to ask: do you think it'll make a difference if you deal with him, instead of her?"

"I don't know. He doesn't have much use for me or her, well not for me anyway. And he's not really afraid of either one of us. Well, maybe he's a little bit afraid of me."

I was quiet for a moment, thinking. Then I said, "Let me see what I can do. Maybe it'll be different when he knows that I know and that I'm going to do something about it."

The vice-principal looked me up and down. "What are you going to do about it?"

When I didn't answer after maybe thirty seconds, he said: "Alright. Let's try it that way. Now I'm going to have to suspend him, suspend him for a week. I'm sure you understand. He'll get his assignments and he'll have to do all his reading and homework and have it checked before he'll be allowed back to class. But I'll only do this if I know you're really going to make it clear to him that this kind of behavior can't continue. Are you willing to do that, Rabbi? Are you willing to get serious with him? Because, if you're not, I think we're at an impasse here. I think if you're not, and we can't turn Ari's behavior around and we can't get him to be serious about his studies, we're going to have to do something more drastic."

"What does that mean? What's does 'something more drastic' mean?"

"I don't think we need to get into that right now. I hope we won't ever. If you can get through to him, then we won't ever have to discuss it. Okay?"

Suddenly I felt that I was the one who had been called to the vice-principal's office for a "talking-to." I struggled to speak and then, in a hoarse voice, replied: "I'll do my best. But I don't know."

"Well, let's hope that'll work," said Mr. Blake, with a tight smile. "Let's hope. For everyone's sake."

That night, as soon as I came in from my meeting, I knocked on Ari's door.

"Ari, it's me. Can I come in?"

A pause. "Wait a second." A moment later: "Hold on." Some shuffling. Then, "Okay. Come in."

Ari was sitting at his desk. The goose-neck lamp was shining on some kind of text book, opened in front of him. Ari was scribbling something in a notebook, to all appearances busy with his homework, a scene to gladden any father's heart. Of course it would have been more convincing if Ari hadn't asked for a second when I knocked on the door.

I stood beside him for a moment. Then, grabbing a chair, turning it backward and positioning it in front of him, I said:

"Ari, look…I don't want to beat up on you, but I know something's wrong. I know something's bothering you. I know you've been missing school and I know you're not getting your homework done. And Mr. Blake says you're in danger of failing…"

Ari started to respond.

"No, let me finish. Then you can speak. Okay? I know school doesn't come easy for you. I know that, it never has, really. But I know you can do the work if you try. And if you need help, we'll get it for you."

Ari fidgeted, looking frantically around the room, seeking a way to stage a jail-break.

"Look, I know you're not going to be happy with what I have to say but listen to me, son, it's obvious you're in trouble. And I'm not just talking about school. To me, it looks like you're in trouble with your whole life. I mean, you never smile anymore…almost never. You don't show up for school. You don't do your homework. You don't spend time with Mike, like you used to. You just sit in your room and watch TV or play video games. And that's it. What kind of a life is that, Ari? What kind of a life? Is that the best you can do for yourself?"

I didn't wait for an answer, my anger slowly rising, in spite of myself.

"Now, I want you to tell me what's bothering you…because, because this can't go on much longer. I won't allow it to go on. Things here are going to have to change starting right now. Now, tell me, what's bothering you? What's stopping you from going to school and getting your work done? Tell me, Ari. Tell me and don't try to snow me. I want to know the truth."

Ari looked up at me, eyes flashing, in a white-hot rage.

"What do you know about my life? You don't know anything about me. I'm doing the best I can, okay? Whether you believe it or not, I'm doing the best I can. Why isn't that ever good enough for you?"

He stopped and lowered his gaze, as if finished. But then he looked at me again, seemed to get revved up and then went on. "And I don't need any sermons from you, okay? You don't have any idea what it's like for me. For you, it all comes so easy. Mom too. Well, that's nice for you but, guess what, I'm not like you. So I just do the best I can. That's what I'm doing and no lecture from you is going to change that."

"I understand," I said. "I know this this comes hard for you, Ari."

"You don't know shit about me," he replied. "You never did."

I was stunned. After everything that had happened earlier in the day, I expected Ari to be contrite. Instead, here he was angry and aggressive. I had come into his room, wanting to be gentle and understanding. But somehow this kid never gave me the chance to be the kind of father I wanted to be. It was always a battle, one-on-one, father versus son. I could feel myself getting sucked in now, getting hotter.

"Fine, then. No sermons. No sermons, just a warning. And you'd better listen real carefully to this one. If you don't go to school every day, every day unless you're really, really sick, and I'll be the judge of that…if you don't go to school every day and do all your homework and pass all your courses…"

I was on a roll now.

"And if you don't do the few chores we ask you to do around the house – and without complaining – and if you don't put your clothes away and keep your room clean, and be in by ten o'clock on school nights and midnight on week-ends – then your mother and I are going to find a school for you, some military academy where they'll watch every move you make. Make no mistake about it, young man. Your mother and I are out of patience, completely out of patience with you. You'd better get it together or you're going to be one very unhappy young man."

Ari glared at me. A long pause.

"And one other thing. I have to tell you I was shocked to find you and that girl out there behind the shed today in the...in the condition I found you in. It was bad enough you weren't in school but to be there in the park, half-naked with some girl I don't even know, some girl with a big, ugly streak in her hair...and not Jewish, I'm sure."

"Why, would it be okay if she were Jewish?" Ari smirked.

"Don't get smart with me, kiddo."

"God!," Ari shouted as he rose from his seat. For a second, I thought he was coming after me. Instead, he stormed past me out of the room, through the front door and out of the house.

I sat for a moment, trying to catch my breath. After a while, I looked out the window and saw Ari where he always went when things got bad -- sitting outside, back against the wall, smoking a cigarette. So I went where I always go when I've had enough, to my own bedroom.

From the smell of things in our room, Ari wasn't the only one smoking in the Chazen household. I looked around for the tell-tale cigarette and ashtray but she had obviously heard me coming.

"I thought you weren't smoking anymore. You promised," I said, staring hard at her.

Her eyes darted away from mine as she calculated the chances of arguing her way out of it. Then, resigned, she said: "It's not much, really, no big deal. Just a few puffs here and there when things get to be…too much."

"And they're too much now?"

"What do you think, David? Come on, just take a look around. Everything that used to be so good in our lives, well…it's just not anymore. None of it." She looked beaten. I had never seen her like this before.

"I'm sure I don't know what you're talking about."

"Don't you? Really?"

I had no answer.

"Really? Let's see now. Our kid can't seem to stay out of trouble – and the trouble just keeps getting bigger and bigger. My job sucks. And you, David, you're never around when I need you. Either you're at the shul or out doing I-don't-know-what with your little friend from the Israel trip. Isn't that enough?"

"Little friend?" I thought but bit my tongue.

She waited just a moment, looked at me and then: "Fine. I'm going to bed now. Maybe tomorrow will be better. One thing for sure: I've certainly had enough of today."

With that she reached over to her night table, took up the bottle of vodka that was sitting there, poured it into a shot glass and threw it down. Then, without a break, she poured and downed another, rolled over and, within a minute, was out cold.

**

Chapter 5:

"Doctor, My Eyes"

When it came to managing the whole Avi project, Dan was clearly getting an even worse grade than me. All those summonses to the principal's office, the ones I'd done (alone, of course) were now his. Secretly, I'd pick up the phone when I saw the school number on caller ID and listen in, getting perverse pleasure from the irony of my sensible, rational husband -- the one with all the training in human relations, counseling and sensitivity --managing to alienate this educator even more effectively than I had—and in record-setting time.

"Yes," he'd answer, with unconcealed contempt, "I DO know that Avi continues to miss class. Yes, I AM concerned about his poor performance. And I'm CER-TAIN I know the potentially dire consequences that await him. Thank-you," he'd say, voice dripping with unconcealed sarcasm, "for your ongoing concern. I'm SURE it's Avi's best interest you have at heart."

Then he'd hang up and pour himself a drink, his choice of alcohol serving as a kind of meter of just how crazed he was: Wine? Vodka? Scotch? A lot of scotch?

Between the two of us, we arrived at an understanding, a frosty truce. I re-frained from confronting him about his failures as a parent and as a husband. He stopped reporting on someone else's wife who was clearly superior to me in every way.

In terms of his long-standing promise to always put me first -- that I had given up on long ago but I knew it was gone for sure the day I broke my toe.

Yes, I know it was stupid. And it was careless and it was vintage me. I know.

Just back from a long, sweaty run, I decided I still had enough in me to accomplish one more little task in the garage before I showered and cleaned myself up.

Now, by normal people's standards, our garage was pristine: space for two cars, cabinets mounted on the walls for big-box store food bargains, bicycles hanging from the ceiling, and hooks for ladder, stepstool and jumper cables. Perfect. Or at least almost perfect.

All I needed to do to make it "perfectly perfect" was to move the old cement drainage blocks out to the street so the trash haulers could take them away. With herculean effort, I managed to drag and pull the first one out to the street. The second one, however, slipped from my hands and fell on my toe. I crumpled from the pain, let out a whoop of sheer, unanticipated agony.

Enter my gallant husband. Hearing my shrieks (not on the phone with congregants at that moment, I guess) he ran out to help me hobble into the house. Like all runners, he knew what to do: rest, ice, compress and elevate—and give me some drugs so I'd stop wailing. I leaned into him, rested my head on his taut belly, and suddenly remembered how much I had once loved him, how I had felt I could count on him when I really needed him.

"Is this better?" he asked gently. "What can I get for you, sweetheart?" Momentarily flooded by gratitude, I started to cry. Nodding—too choked to speak—I let him cradle my foot ever so tenderly in his hands. The pain that had taken up residence in my chest over the last months and even years, the deep-seated pain of his neglect and disinterest, began to ebb. In that moment, I felt cared for. I felt secure. I felt...well, loved.

"I don't want to leave you like this," he said, warming to my responsiveness. "I'll call Candy to come over—and I won't leave for my teaching until she gets here. If they have to wait for me, so be it. They'll just have to wait!"

I could not believe my ears: he WAS going to leave me after all, leave me for them. What an idiot I was!   Now I started to cry in earnest, cried so hard I couldn't breathe.   All he was aware of was the pain in my foot. What he seemed blissfully unaware of was the much deeper pain in my heart.

And the truth is: that was about par for the course. He never understood what I'd come to know: no matter what he promised, no matter what he believed in his heart of hearts, he was a fundamentally faithless man. Not with other women, at least I didn't think so. No. The magnet pulling him away from me was much bigger than any woman: it was his congregation. They came first. They were his first love, the love that had seduced him before we'd even met. Through the first blush of our passion, that other mistress had waited patiently, biding her time, knowing that inevitably, he'd return to her gravitational pull, a pull much stronger than mine could ever be.

Through my pain, I saw the truth with crystalline clarity: all those nights when he'd cancelled our plans for some perceived emergency in the synagogue or missed our son's ballgames or been so delayed at dinner time that it turned into bedtime, all those nights were agony for me. But not for him. For him, they were manna from heaven, the only thing he really needed to sustain himself. That's what he lived for. To be needed. By them. It certainly wasn't Avi. And it most assuredly wasn't me.

When Candy breezed in a few minutes later, all efficient concern, armed with tensor bandages and special salves, I could see the relief on his face: he was free to go now to his real love—and he wasn't even going to have to keep them waiting! He'd be right on time. Now I knew for sure what I'd always suspected about that old promise he had made me long ao. Me first? That was a joke — a sick joke!

**

It was Monday again, the latest in a lengthening string of Monday mornings I'd gone to Lisa's, to meditate with her and learn from her and well… just be with her. It was by now reassuringly familiar – the route I took to her place, the way we'd start with coffee and conversation, how she'd announce with great fanfare that it was time to start, how she'd light the incense, remove her sweatshirt top, settle herself on the floor and invite me to do the same, how I'd take my glasses off and say the prayer she had taught me and how I'd try to empty out my brain of distractions and not try too hard to experience something.

Sometimes I actually did. More often, I felt like I'd learned nothing since we had made ourselves partners in this spiritual endeavor. Some weeks, the time went by quickly — over before I knew it — and some weeks it dragged so slowly it felt like a kind of self-administered incarceration.

Today it was somewhere in-between. I started fitfully, unable to draw even one slow, deep breath, my mind flitting from image to image. But after a while, I drifted down somehow a little deeper into myself and emerged -- some minutes later -- feeling surprisingly refreshed. Taking out my glasses and refocusing my eyes, I could see she was already up and into the kitchen and (judging by the shrill whistle of the kettle) busy making tea.

Afterwards, we talked – about our kids and our work and the world around us. God, I loved this time with her! In many ways, it was fast becoming the best thing in my life. Sometimes it seemed like the only thing that made any sense at all.

**

The next day, just a couple of days before the start of Passover, I had to officiate at the funeral of the mother of my congregant, Miles Herman. Miles was a good-natured, decent man, a salesman for a company that sold odd lots of paper for commercial use. Miles had a large, imposing but strangely attractive wife, Fern, who would sometimes turn up in local print ads for "Rosen's – The Store for the Big, Beautiful Woman." I wondered if I was supposed to know it was her, if I should tell her I'd seen the ad and thought she looked great, but I guess I was slightly embarrassed by it so I never said anything.

Miles and Fern had two daughters, both through college and working in Manhattan in the fashion trade. Sensing his mother was near the end, Miles had called me a couple of weeks earlier to ask about Jewish funeral and mourning customs and which funeral home I recommended – "when the time comes." Apparently the time had come.

I often thought how strange it was that I was now actually considered a maven on the subject of funerals, I who had attended only one – my Bubbie's -- before I had to officiate at one as a twenty-four year old rabbinic student. ("See one, do one, teach one.") But expert I now was. So I patiently answered all of Miles's questions, offering advice, trying to read the subtext beneath the words. From the sound of it, Miles was more resigned than grief-stricken at the prospect of his mother's passing. He told me she was a wonderful woman who had led a full and happy life, had hardly been sick a day in her life and was now ready to die – so how could he complain? Indeed, I thought, how could he?

The funeral was set for two o'clock at Beckers', the big Jewish funeral home a couple of miles down the road from the synagogue. So, at 9:30 that morning, I sat with Miles and Fern and their two girls, Brittany and Mara, in my study at the synagogue. I asked them to paint me a portrait of their mother and grandmother, to help me 'see' her clearly so I could speak about her – on their behalf -- that afternoon. At first hesitantly, then with growing enthusiasm, they shared the famous family stories: how she had met her husband, Miles' father, now long deceased, at the shore, how she had secretly saved up her pennies (a knipel she had called it) to take the family on vacation when they thought they couldn't afford one, how she had decided to go to college at age seventy-three and got her degree four years later. I remembered her vaguely from the girls' bat mitzvahs but didn't have a clear image of her in my mind's eye, so I listened carefully to the stories and, in the end, felt like she was someone I had known all my life.

That afternoon at the service – in front of a large crowd of the Hermans' friends and family -- I spoke about her as if I had.

Once the chapel service was done, all that remained was to drive out to the cemetery, set her down into the earth and say farewell. But first the long drive out to Beth Israel, an old cramped nineteenth century cemetery with narrow lanes designed for horse-drawn carriages and gravestones with long-ago dates, not always in the best of repair. It was not a lovely place, not one of those modern cemeteries that look more like a place for a picnic than a burial. This one looked exactly like what it was. And it was a long, long drive from the funeral home.

As everyone lined up along the side of the wide boulevard for the procession, sitting at the wheel of my car, right behind the hearse, I closed my eyes, turned off the radio, leaned my head back against the headrest and began to hum the song that had been in my head all day, the song the radio was playing when I woke up that morning, "Casey Jones." The Grateful Dead. Just about right for the occasion, it seemed to me.

Anyway, I could see the guys from the funeral home out on the street in their shirtsleeves directing everyone to line up behind my car – a parade of some thirty or forty vehicles, quite a tribute to the deceased and to her son, my congregant. As the line began to form behind me, I noticed, immediately to our left, a second procession, this one comprised entirely of cars filled with black mourners from the African-American funeral home next door to Beckers'. It seemed like a scene from a Woody Allen picture, an outtake the director had apparently had the good sense to edit out. I laughed out loud and started humming "Dueling Banjos."

After a few minutes, the other cortege departed and went on its way, followed almost immediately by our own.

Slowly, careful to keep everyone together, our procession traveled through the old factory towns, depressed residential neighborhoods and strip malls that made up the ugly drive. When finally we reached Beth Israel, we followed behind the cemetery vehicle to the awning and the open grave where we came to a halt. Gathering up my prayer book from the glove box, pinning my yarmulke to my hair, I stepped out of the car, stretched my legs, and looked behind me. There, to my surprise, instead of the long column I expected, were only four other cars.

As we stood together waiting for the casket to emerge from the hearse, the driver of the last car said: "I don't know when it happened but, at one point, I looked in my rearview and realized the guy behind me was confused and started follow- ing the other procession. Can you imagine the scene at the other burial? 'Who knew Charlie had all these white friends!'" We couldn't help it; we laughed – and then struggled not to laugh as we laid Miles's mother in the ground after everyone finally showed up twenty minutes later. The perfect Woody Allen ending.

When I returned home in the late afternoon, Sharon was there, working at the computer. Seeing me enter the room, she quickly closed out what she was working on, spun around in the swivel chair so her back was to the screen and, looking sheepishly up at me, said: "You're home early."

"No, actually even a little bit later than I figured. I did that funeral for Miles Herman's mother today. And somehow, most of our funeral procession got lost and didn't turn up until twenty minutes later. Seems they ended up following another funeral procession. Can you imagine? Black humor at its best. Any- way, it did stretch the afternoon out a bit but I do have a couple of hours before dinner so I thought I'd go out for a run," I said. "Where's Ari? Everything quiet for the moment – or are we in crisis mode for a change?"

"He's in his room, doing his homework," her hands describing giant quotation marks in the air.

"I guess it could be worse."

I started upstairs to change, then stopped for a second and turned to face her as it hit me. "So tell me…what are you so busy with on that computer that you don't want me to see?"

She reddened. "It's just some writing," she said, "something to amuse myself when I get bored. And it's not a big secret. It's just not ready yet."

"So you'll let me see it when you're done?"

"Oh yeah, you'll see it. You can bet on that," she said, with more than a whiff of sarcasm.

When I came back down the stairs in gym shorts, T-shirt and sneakers, iPhone on my arm, headphones around my neck, she said offhandedly: "Oh, by the way, I'm going into the City next Wednesday. I'm taking a personal day. That's not a problem with you, is it?" In the Chazen household, "the City" always meant New York City, only a little over an hour's train ride away.

"No, that's fine. What are you going to do? Shop?"

"Yeah," she said. "Shop. I'll be back for dinner."

"Good. Enjoy – but don't break the bank, okay?" I was grinning. You see – of all my male friends, I was the only one who never had to worry about my wife and her shopping bills. Perpetually insecure about spending money – a product of her childhood -- Sharon would go shopping, come home with hundreds of dollars worth of clothes and makeup, agonize over her purchases for days and eventually take almost everything back. In the end, she usually ended up having little to show for her day in the city, but at least it gave her an outing, a day away from the job she hated so much. And it always seemed funny to me that, among all my friends, I was the only one who wished his wife would spend a little more on herself.

That afternoon, I ran as if trying to escape the hounds nipping at my heels – the ongoing drama with Ari, Sharon's increasing unhappiness, my confusing relationship with Lisa. At dinner, Ari and Sharon were their customary silent selves. I couldn't wait to get out of there, even if it meant going to my board meeting at the shul, not my very favorite part of the job.

The board meeting played out as it often did -- lots of talking, endless hours spent around the table because "everything has already been said but not everybody has had a chance to say it." Critical issues disposed of in a matter of minutes, trivial matters endlessly flayed.

At the helm, at the head of the table was Mel Grafman, the president of Emmanuel. Not one to mince words, an entrepreneur who always said the synagogue would be better off if it "were run more like a business," Mel himself always got right to the point.

This evening, the hot topic *du jour* was the wallpaper in the newly-renovated women's room. Some members of the Board were unhappy with the proposed color; it clashed with the painted walls, they said. Congregants had commented unfavorably, some suggesting it was so ugly they would be forced (forced?) to hold their bat mitzvah celebrations elsewhere. Couldn't the decision be reconsidered?

The discussion was animated and everyone had an opinion. I began to drift off, replaying the day in my mind's eye. Some time, over an hour later, Mel gaveled the meeting over.

When I finally walked in the door at home, the kitchen clock flashed 11:14. I knew I wouldn't be able to sleep; never could after a late night meeting. I headed up the stairs to the bedroom to change. The door was closed. The light was off but I didn't go straight in.

Instead, I walked down the hallway, turned the handle very quietly and opened the door to Ari's room. The light from the hallway floated in and settled on Ari's face, visible above the covers. He looked like he had when he was five years old -- innocent, angelic.

Impossible, I thought. Impossible that this beautiful child should be the source of so much pain in my life. Standing in the hall, the light dancing off Ari's perfect features, I remembered the day he was born, remembered calling my parents, barely able to speak, to tell them their son was now a father. I remembered lying down beside Sharon in the hospital bed and hugging her gently as she held the baby to her breast. I remembered the terror, the promise, the joy.

As I stood there over Ari's sleeping body, I wondered, where had it all gone? Now if there was terror, it was the terror of the next telephone call from school or the local police. If there was promise, it was the promise of more trouble and heartache lying inevitably ahead. And if there was joy, it was the pale and momentary joy of dodging a bullet, of seeing Ari in bed at night, at the end of a rare day without arguments, rages or rancor. Oh Ari, my son, my son, how did it come to this?

I needed to talk it out. It was all bubbling up inside me. And I had no other options. So I went back to my bedroom, opened the door and walked over to the bed, standing over her and whispered:

"Sharon, you up? Sharon?"

She groaned, rolled over to see who was disturbing her, then rolled back again, pulled the covers over her head and went back to sleep.

This was the way it had been lately – me home late from some meeting, her asleep as early as nine o'clock. When had she started thinking that was a good hour to cut her losses for the day? When had she stopped wanting to hear my voice and feel me against her at the end of the day?

It was hard to believe. Between us, there had always been something molten and raw. Years into our marriage, we would give each other a look at a party and would be mostly undressed before we were half-way home.

Now I could hardly remember what that felt like. Sharon's spark was gone – and not just in bed. On days when she wasn't working, she got up late, didn't bother with make-up, dressed in the first thing she found in her closet. As if mentally checking items off her to-do list, one by one, she went through each day—mechanically, joylessly, without seeming to give a damn about any of it.

Maybe it was change of life. Maybe her hormones were out of whack. Whatever else it was, I knew it was mostly about Ari, now the source of so much unhappiness in our lives. The brunt of it, I knew, had fallen on Sharon, not me – for years. After all, here I was living the rabbi's life, rarely home when the calls came from school or the neighbors or a disgruntled girlfriend's father. Usually, I was at a meeting or doing a funeral or in conference when Ari didn't do his homework or ended up in a fight. I was gone but she was there. And sometimes, I knew, she just got tired of being there without me.

Now I could see -- from the stoop in her shoulders to the frown lines on her face to the pills she turned to more and more – it had taken its toll. Every day was a trial. She no longer expected anything good to come and was rarely surprised.

I tried again: "Sharon?" Nothing. Then, to no one in particular, "Good night." That night, I dreamed I was leading a synagogue group traveling in the Middle East. When we all got to the border, I felt in my pocket and realized that I had none of the necessary tickets, passports or visas. The group stared at me in disappointment. I had let them all down – again.

**

Chapter 6:

"You've Got a Friend"

Six weeks after breaking my toe, I was cautiously ready to get back up and try to run again —gingerly, slowly, but with some serious residual pain. In most other ways, I had not missed a beat: I was at work the day after the break, sporting a chic bootie, ready to immerse myself in the only world that seemed to care if I was there or not. And the manuscript that I'd been working on for so long: incredibly enough, it seemed to have some interest from a potential agent.

At home things were cold and hard. When Dan walked into the room, I walked out. Avi had largely disappeared. Now our little house, the sanctuary I'd so carefully guarded from invasion from the outside, was dark and empty.

"Alone like a stone," Ruthie would have said—but she'd have said it in Yiddish. The only one I could still count on was Candy, Candy who knew my deepest secret soul and who still loved me, Candy who'd stood by me all these years— Candy who had even infiltrated the enemy camp on my behalf so she could reconnoiter and bring back intel from the Sisterhood Mafia.

In the midst of all this, Candy and I had made a lunch date at an out-of-the way watering hole, a place with great margaritas. By the time she arrived, I was on my second and puffing on a cigarette. The chill of the drink was just beginning to take effect. Maybe that's why it took me so long to notice that something was different with Candy. After I'd unloaded for several minutes on the sorry state of my child, my marriage and my relationship with the congregation, Candy shifted uncomfortably in her seat.

"Actually, Cheryl," she said, "I need to talk to you about that." Clearly on edge, Candy seemed to be looking everywhere but at me.

"I think you might have misjudged the people at the temple," she began. "You know, when I first started going to those Sisterhood programs, I have to admit I saw the women the way you did: overdressed, aggressive, competitive.

"But the more I got to know them, Cheryl, especially some of the more active ones, the more I got to appreciate them. Did you know that Dina is a really accomplished chef? She invited me over for dinner two weeks ago—almost as good as you!"

I put my drink down. Even through the alcoholic buzz I could sense that this conversation was about to take a new and dangerous turn.

"And they love Dan. Really, Cheryl, they do. They appreciate how much he does for them and they even get how much you give up for him to be their rabbi." She was warming to this; I could tell she thought she was bringing me along gently, lovingly, on this little journey.

"That's why I feel like I need to tell you something. Believe me, this is said out of love—for both of you. Please don't be mad at me." I could almost hear her gulp. "Cheryl, honey, you're hurting him. The way you are with them, with the people in the congregation, you're really hurting his career."

Et tu, Candy? You're against me now too?

Maybe because of the drink, maybe because it was just dark enough in there, I managed not to let her see the tears in my eyes.

Incrementally, her voice was starting to get more of an edge. The longer I sat silent, the more her words tumbled out.

"He's so talented, so great with everybody. And even if it's not fair, the rabbin-ate is a two-person job. They don't expect you to be old-school, baking for the onegs and singing in the choir—God knows, if they ever heard you sing, they'd be sure not to let you. But give them something. Or at least smile at them in the supermarket."

Without saying a word, I threw a handful of bills down on the table, jumped up and sprinted for the door.

***

The last days of March had trudged now into early April. It was Passover, seder night. The day before, at Saturday dinner, she and me around the kitchen table, Ari out God-knows-where. Sharon – who always took such pride in the way she ran her seders -- informed me she wouldn't cook, wouldn't prepare the table, wouldn't do anything more than show up. She hadn't invited anyone this year, just didn't have the strength to have people over. And it wasn't worth it for just the three of us.

So I could see it would have to be me to do the shopping, the cooking, the seder plate, the table, go through the haggadah, lead the service all by myself — and all this in twenty-four hours or it wouldn't happen!

It did happen. But it wasn't much. It was over in an hour. I wondered why we even bothered. I remembered the way seders had always been in the past – family and friends around the table, lots of noise, talking, joking, singing. Now, it was down to this – the three of us, sitting silent and morose, jumping up from the table with the last mouthful of food . And I wondered: Why wouldn't she do even the bare minimum anymore? Why did it always fall on me? And was this the home life I could expect from now on? It made me want to cry. It made me want to be in the shul, at Lisa's, anywhere but here.

Through the days of the holiday, I awoke each morning, trying to focus on the morning paper but endlessly re-reading paragraphs, hoping the caffeine in my coffee would still the throbbing behind my right eye. I thought maybe I could get a grip on things if I could just grab a few quiet moments. I wanted to go for a run but there just wasn't time to change, run, shower and change back again before I had to go in to the shul.

I checked my calendar. Full. Back-to-back appointments, pastoral visits and meetings from first thing in the morning until well into the evening. I needed to get away; there was no other way to get through this day in one piece. I looked again at the day's schedule. What could I drop? Where would I not be missed?

My lunchtime Board of Rabbis meeting, a two-hour slot consisting of inedible kosher-for-Passover food often accompanied by equally indigestible discussion, that time would be mine, I decided. It really wouldn't change anything if I weren't there. It wasn't my turn to be chair of the group this year, I wasn't running the show, had nothing particularly earth-shattering to add. So I called the chairperson and made my apologies.

Leaving home at a few minutes past twelve, I bought myself a salad and a drink, drove to the park, loosened my tie, removed my jacket and sat down on a grassy hill to sit in the early April sun and enjoy lunch and a few minutes of solitude. The sun's rays felt warm and good. I closed my eyes, lay back on the grass and tried to calm my over-stimulated mind.

Then I remembered what Lisa had showed me. I took my glasses from my face, folded them and placed them in my shirt pocket, let my eyes unfocus. Like a myopic with a kaleidoscope, the world suddenly looked hazy yet bright and somehow quite beautiful. Shapes and colors seemed to melt together. I was floating. I was bobbing up and down on the water, not trying to steer, allowing the waves to carry me.

"Rabbi, I thought it was you. You know, I was jogging by and it looked like you but I wasn't sure. I mean, I wouldn't expect to see you here of all places, lying out on the ground like that. Is everything okay? Are you feeling alright? I'm not bothering you, am I?"

It was Liz Weiner, a member of the congregation, a sweet and gentle woman decked out in a navy blue track suit, hair up, sweaty, red-faced, jogging in place as we spoke. How often I had seen her running along my route, slowing down to join her for a quick word before saying goodbye and pulling away.

I fumbled with my glasses, setting them quickly back on my face, and jumped to my feet.

"Oh, hi Liz. No, no, I'm fine. Everything's okay. I'm just taking a bit of break, you know, a little respite from the wars. You know how it goes." I smiled.

"Yeah, I sure do."

"How was seder for you?" Then…spinning through the invisible rolodex in my mind, "So how's…Marc? (Got it!) How are..Amanda and Brett? (Nailed it!) Everybody okay? Good, good. Well, have a good run and…have a nice day." And so came to an end my little spiritual moment in the park.

***

Spring was now finally in full bloom. And it was infectious, one of those days when every woman on the street, in the stores, in the synagogue looked beautiful, inviting. It was a wonderful, glorious, dangerous day.

Nine o'clock in the morning. I walked into the synagogue office, saw that everyone was huddled around Kelli who was passing around photos of her twin granddaughters in Texas, dressed in little, fringed cowgirl outfits. I sidled up beside her, stuck my thumbs in the top of my pants, and, in my worst Western twang, said: "Well, I do declare, ma'am, if those aren't the most beautiful little dogies in the whole dang world." Everyone laughed.

As we all stood there, enjoying Kelli's pictures, I looked up and saw that Donna Cutler had walked into the office, visibly upset. She looked straight at me and, with a bit of a forced smile, said quietly: "Rabbi, I need a moment of your time."

"Of course. Come on in. Let's talk." And, in a stage whisper to the office staff, still Lash LaRue: "See you later, l'il darlin's."

Donna was in line to be the next president of the congregation. Knowledgeable on a wide range of subjects, smart, funny and articulate, I always thought of her as the most capable of leaders. She was also tall and leggy. Dressed in a black turtleneck sweater, slacks and shoes, Donna reminded me of the old saying that New Yorkers would continue to dress in black until they found something darker. Indeed, she was the consummate New Yorker, something that, for me, always meant self-assured, seductive.

But right now Donna wasn't flirting. She wasn't smiling. Her shoulders seemed weighted down.

"Tell me what's on your mind, dear," I said.

"Rabbi, I'm really sorry to barge in like this. I know how busy you are. But, Rabbi… David…it's this budget thing that's going on. It's got me, well…tied up in knots."

The "budget thing" was real, a serious problem – declining membership, declining revenue, declining prospects for the shul. The neighborhood demographics had changed. Young families weren't moving in -- too expensive. Empty nesters couldn't afford to stay; paying for college left too little for discretionary spending. Seniors were moving to Florida. We'd been running a growing deficit for the past four years. It didn't look good.

She paused and, without blinking, looked me full in the face. It all came out in a torrent. "Here's the thing. I keep looking at the numbers and they don't add up. They don't add up now and I think it's only going to get worse. I really wonder if Emmanuel has a future, David. And if it doesn't, why am I lined up to be the president who has to face the firing squad? What are we going to do, David? What am I supposed to do?"

Now, finally, she lowered her gaze. She looked at the ground, apparently intrigued by the nap of the carpet. "You know, Rabbi, I haven't had a good night's sleep since we started talking about this thing three weeks ago." Then, she started crying, quietly.

I thought of her tossing and turning in bed. I could see her watching me closely, uncertain, trying to read my mind.

I reached over to her, not knowing what to do or say next. My hand hovered for a moment and landed, finally, on her right forearm. I stroked it with my thumb and said, "Donna, it's going to be okay. I've been here a long time and I can tell you one thing for sure: we've been through a lot before and, somehow, it always works out. I promise you: Emmanuel won't go out of business. And your presidency will be a smashing success. I mean, how could it not be with all the talent you've got?" I smiled and she stopped crying.

I could see she wanted to believe it, needed to believe it. "Do you really mean that, David? Or are you just trying to talk me down from the ledge?"

"Yup," I said, trying to look my calmest, my most rabbinic. "I'm really sure. I really do believe it. Really, it'll be okay. Now, maybe you can get a good night's sleep." I smiled again, as reassuringly as I knew how.

Her face changed. She stood up. I stood up with her. She reached toward me, pressed herself hard against me and kissed me full on the lips. "Oh you are wonderful. You really are. Anyone else can say 'don't worry' but when you say it, somehow it feels different, it feels real. David, you really are a wonderful man."

While I stood there stunned, she kissed me again, gathered up her coat and handbag, opened the office door and was gone.

I stood there, amazed. I wondered how I could possibly have assured Donna that everything would be alright when I wasn't at all sure myself. I knew the numbers too – and I had my doubts. But somehow our little dance – her questioning, me reassuring – had done the trick. And, at that moment, it hit me that I had failed to keep my door open even a crack – as I always did when I had women in the office -- while Donna was in the room.

**

That night, I got fed up waiting for Sharon to return from the city where she had gone yet again. So I made dinner for myself and Ari. We were in the middle of it when she came in the door empty-handed, looking agitated.

"Looks like a failed mission. I mean: no bags? Nothing to return later?" I joked.

"Not a very successful day, I guess." she replied, looking around the room. "Didn't find a single thing I could bring home and then change my mind about…" She took a stab at a smile, shifted her eyes away from mine.

"So what did you end up doing all day?"

"Well, just because I didn't buy anything doesn't mean I didn't shop," suddenly petulant. "I did; I just wasn't very successful. I went to Bloomie's and Saks' and Macy's and a couple of other places you don't know and I must have tried on a million things but…no luck. Very disappointing," she said. But to me she didn't sound too disappointed. She sounded angry.

"Doesn't seem like much of a day to me. I really don't know how you can look at stuff on racks and try things on all morning and all afternoon – and not find anything you like…in New York City. What, no selection?"

"Well," she said, slightly embarrassed, "I did meet someone for lunch. And that took up a chunk of the day."

"Really? Who?"

"Nobody you know," she said, "just somebody I needed to talk to. It's really not important. Okay?"

I tried to look merely inquisitive but it probably came out looking annoyed – which I was.

"It's nobody you know," she repeated.

I looked hard at her. She did her best to hold my gaze, then looked away out the kitchen window and said: "Can we just drop it? Can we?"

Surprised by the off-hand mention of a "somebody" with whom she had had lunch in New York and by her quick jump to change the subject, I wondered. Male or female? Someone I knew or a stranger? And most of all, why was she being so weird about it? Was she seeing a therapist, a lawyer, a lover? What was the big secret?

That night, after an hour and a half at the computer, she went up to bed early, leaving Ari and me alone on the bottom floor of the house together, an increasingly unnerving prospect. Fortunately he went his way and I went mine so we avoided the excruciating task of making small talk, something neither of us cared to do very much these days. At eleven o'clock, I crept upstairs and slipped into bed, as quiet as I could be, so as not to wake her.

**

Chapter 7:
"Every Breath You Take...Every Step You Take"

I called out sick the rest of that day and the day after that and the one after that, too. Food poisoning, I told them—something I'd had at lunch. Actually, it was something I'd had at lunch and it was toxic. Like Hamlet's father, someone I had trusted had poured poison in my ear and I felt like I was dying.

Even more than a best friend, Candy always had been a kind of sister to me—someone this lonely, only child could always count on. And she knew all of my secrets—even my family's deepest, darkest ones. She was the only person I'd ever told about that other one, the ghost sister, the one before me, the perfect child lost in the camps, the one torn from Ruthie's arms. That sister, the one who somehow felt more real than I ever did, had haunted me all my days; only Candy had known about her. Only Candy had understood. And now, it seemed, I was losing Candy, too.

Eventually my misery penetrated Dan's distracted fog; I broke down and told him what Candy had said. Not sure why—I guess I hoped he'd defend me, take my part, get mad on my behalf.

Instead, he looked down at his shoes, at the carpet—anywhere but at my sorry bloated face. It was clear he agreed with what Candy had said. I was hurting him. He knew it. Everyone knew it. And now I knew it too.

I could see him working really hard to find just the right words, words that would tell me how he saw the whole fiasco without making things even worse.

"I'm sorry this is so hard for you," he said. "And I know it must feel like everyone—even your best friend—is piling on. But what if there were a way to make things better: better for you, for me, for everyone? What if you could take one step forward, just one, a tiny one? Wouldn't you do it? Wouldn't you?"

Without waiting for an answer, he said: "Listen. I've been thinking about something we could do – something that might be fun and it could be a kind of small step at putting you on a different footing with the congregation."

"One step" sounded almost insurmountable at that moment, but I needed something I could grab onto.

"You know," he said, "Dina and Len Schwartz have been calling for weeks. They want to go out with us—with both of us—to a movie or for a bite. Nothing big, just a night out. And they're nice. I know you don't like Dina but I do and she's someone who could really help. She's going to be president of the synagogue next year and if she gets to know the real you, that could be a start, a first step in a better direction. So what do you think?"

Maybe all those days in bed had eroded my brain. I said yes. He almost jumped for joy! I was stunned: THIS made him happy? OK, then. Maybe he was right. Maybe I could start to turn things around. How bad could one night out be?

I found out how exactly how bad the next weekend. I decided we should start at our house—some wine, some *hors d'oeuvres*. I knew how badly everyone wanted a peak at Fortress Cheryl. Maybe a little hospitality would break the very, very thick ice between Dina and me.

They arrived right on time, Len in his usual designer jeans and logoed T-shirt, and Dina in pants so tight she must have spray-painted them on and a top that clung to her surgically enhanced breasts. Ah, yes, I recalled: I've seen those babies up close in the ladies' room! Smiling to myself, I greeted our guests at the door—hug, hug, kiss, kiss. If I was going to be someone else, I'd at least try and be someone I thought they'd like. I could see how surprised they were. "How ADORABLE!" Dina gushed. "Why, I had no IDEA this house was so super-cute!"

She walked around the room, inspecting, feeling,calculating.

"You're SO lucky! This house must be SO easy to keep clean! In OUR house—especially after the addition we put on last year—the cleaners are just working NON-STOP! As soon as they get from the top floor to the rec room they practically have to start all over again!"

She was really warming to the conversation.

"The first thing—the VERY first thing—would be to take down all these curtains! That just brings the outdoors in! My decorator did that at the shore house. Anyway, it just does WONDERS!"

I had to excuse myself. Mumbling something about finding "the boys," and getting some wine for us—something I desperately needed—I left the room and took a few deep breaths.

Len had made himself instantly at home, walking directly into the kitchen and checking out the bottles in the wine fridge. Dan seemed to think this was perfectly acceptable; he followed Len and together they chose the most expensive wine in there—the one I'd been saving for a special occasion, maybe a romantic dinner for Danny and me (does hope never die?)

Meanwhile, Dina was checking out everything in our "cute, adorable" living room, opening photo albums and making mental notes about the books, art—everything in the house. I swallowed the bile I felt rising, resisting the desire to run to the bathroom and hurl, or better yet, run to my bedroom and hide like a cat who'd just been swatted with a rolled-up newspaper.

Somehow I made it through cocktail hour. As usual, the alcohol helped. Actually, I was beginning to feel like it was helping too much, and too often.

I filed that thought away. But for right now, it was the only thing keeping me in the room, and I was grateful.

The movie seemed the perfect choice, in an ironic kind of way. It was a film about a man who was acting out a part, pretending to be someone else, someone just like me. Eventually, all his elaborate plans exploded in his face. Note to self.

I couldn't wait for the evening to end. Panic-stricken at the very idea of an after-movie coffee and conversation, I pleaded an early run the next morning; I counted on Dan to read my signals, and mercifully he did.

"Well, that wasn't so bad, was it?" he said as soon as we closed the front door behind us.

"Not bad?" I shouted. "Which part did you like best? The home invasion? The part where they raided our wine? And I'm so gratified that our "adorable little housie" pleases her Highness. Was that the part you liked best?"

Stunned, Dan fled the room with his mouth literally agape.

Too furious to say another word, I flew into our room and slammed the door. Bang! It echoed through the house, putting a final period on the evening and my one last attempt to "make it all work."

***

Every time I looked at Ari – especially these days as he grew into such an angry young man – my mind would take me on a forced walk down memory lane and I would wonder how we had ever come to this…

I'd remember how Sharon and I decided to wait on starting a family, as we explained to our families (and anyone else who had the *chutzpah* to ask) until we had the "resources to raise one responsibly," as we liked to say. But it hadn't gone as planned. Every time our income rose to where we thought we could actually afford a child, we could see the costs had risen as well. There never was a "right time" so I never really pushed it very hard.

But, by then Sharon's parents were gone and then my mother was diagnosed with ovarian cancer. Suddenly, we could hear the ticking of the great cosmic clock.

Finally, one night as we were making love, I stopped in mid-act, rolled over, then, turning on my side, cradling her head in my hand, said: "Sharon, I think it's time. I want a baby for us. I don't care if it makes sense or not. It'll probably never really make sense. But I'm ready. How about you?"

She had said: "I am too," as though she had already reached the same conclusion and was only waiting for the right moment to announce it.

We were silent a moment. Then, without a word, I pulled myself up above her and, with a clear sense of what we dreamed we were doing, set out to create a new life. Eight months, three weeks and two days later, Ari Chazen arrived – beautiful, quiet, ready for a happy world to receive him with love, as it did.

Although Sharon's folks and my mother – who had passed away two months prior -- were no longer there to share in the moment, my father and my sister were ecstatic. And my congregants were so happy for me and Sharon, it was as if they were part of our family too, at least for the moment.

The brit milah – the religious circumcision ceremony – was a busy, noisy affair.
Family came from miles away. My congregants, most of whom had never been
inside our house before, got warm welcomes from my father and sister, now
converted to host and hostesses as Sharon and I conferred with the mohel, the
ritual circumciser, in a room upstairs. The dining room table was set up as a
kind of operating theater, the sideboard laden with trays of food. The furniture-
free living room was filled with guests, a makeshift bar and wrapped gifts. As I
came down the stairs with Sharon and Ari, the house seemed like one of those
pointillist paintings, a swirl of color, Seurat's Sunday afternoon on the Island of
"La Grande Jatte," Jewish-style.

I was happy as I had never been before. All the pieces of my life seemed to
have come together at one time, in one place, and everything seemed to fit so
well. My president, a tough-minded, white-haired businesswoman, had taken
me aside just after the ceremony and said, as if reading from a prepared speech:
"David, we want you to know that we, on the Board, are thrilled for you and
Sharon. We want you to have this gift." And, with that, she handed me an
envelope with the synagogue logo on the top left corner.

"You should know that it doesn't come out of the synagogue budget – you know
how tight things are -- it comes from each of us as individuals. We're sure you
can use it, especially now. And, we want you to know that you should stay home
with your family this Friday night and the Cantor and the Rites and Practices
Committee will take care of leading services." Then she gave me a kiss that
almost reached my cheek, turned on her heel and left the room, mission accomplished.

As soon as she'd left, I opened the envelope. I counted it out: twenty-two
ten-dollar bills. Oy. Well, at least it would be nice to stay home Friday evening
instead of rushing out to services right after dinner, especially with a new baby in
the house.

During those first weeks and months of life, nothing but Ari's health and happiness mattered. The rest of the world was a blur. Sharon, too, who had taken maternity leave from the paper, now focused her full attention on our newborn son. Everything Ari did, every movement of his tiny body, every sound he made, filled her with awe. She had waited for this and was determined to appreciate it – and to win "Mother of the Year" in the process.

Meantime, I took over all the household chores – the laundry, the grocery shopping, the cooking – and was soon doing them, I thought, better than Sharon ever had. We ordered in dinner on occasion and hired a cleaning woman for the first time ever. We were busy. We were tired. We were happy.

For years, every August, Sharon and I had a summer rental for two weeks in Cape May, New Jersey, at a quiet beach community where "my Jewish people" did not often go and enjoyed the chance to sit on the sand under an umbrella, sleep and read and snack for the entire day, completely anonymous. When Ari was born, we stopped going; It was too much with a baby.

Finally, after two years away, we returned with Ari, now a toddler. We laid in a supply of infant beachwear, loaded up on sand toys, filled a soft-sided bag with his favorite treats and headed down to the beach where we set him up with plastic shovel and pail, watching as he wordlessly scooped up the sand and flung it in all directions, covering himself in dirt. It was clear: Ari loved the shore as much as we did.

One early August day in the second week of our rental, we set baby Ari up under a beach umbrella, unpacked his toys and sat down to our reading. After about a half an hour, I looked up and said: "Sharon, where's Ari?"

He was not where we had left him. His toys lay on the sand, a cookie started but not finished. No Ari. I was supposed to be watching him but something – I don't remember what – distracted me.

"Sharon, where is he? I don't see him."

We both jumped up, looked frantically up and down the beach and then, in terror, toward the ocean.

I ran down to the edge of the water. Wading furiously in, I moved left and then right in no particular pattern, my hands splashing in the water, desperately scanning both water and shore.

"Has anyone seen our baby?" I screamed out to everyone. "A little boy, about two. In a blue bathing suit. Did anyone see him?"

I turned back to look for Sharon. She was nowhere in sight although I thought I could hear her yelling in the distance.

Where could he be? Maybe someone had picked him up and snatched him away. But surely we would have heard something. Maybe Ari had simply wandered down to the beach on his own. Maybe he had walked down to get a closer look at the waves and…no, couldn't be.

Oh my God. Ari, where are you? I dived again into the shallow water, struggling to keep my eyes open, terrified to see what was beneath the waves.

Resurfacing, I heard screams coming from the shore. I knew instantly…it was Sharon. She was screaming. Oh God, please no…please no…

"David," she was yelling. "David, it's okay, I found him. David, I've got him. Look, I've got him."

I looked up -- Ari, oblivious, was cradled in her arms, smiling. Sharon was crying. A crowd had gathered around them. I ran to her, to him. Hugging them both ferociously -- the two people I loved most in the world, the two people I couldn't bear to live without -- I fell with them to the sand, sobbing.

"Ari, you're alright. Thank God, you're alright. Oh God, we were so worried about you."

Sharon had found him, happily toddling along the shore, perhaps a hundred feet from where we were sitting. That night, we broke a rule of long-standing, allowing Ari to sleep in our bed, safely nestled between us. We swore to each other we'd keep a closer watch on him in the future. But, looking back, I see now that the more we focused on Ari, the less we had for each other, the more Sharon and I began to come apart at the seams.

And the truth is: it didn't even work with Ari. Somehow, as the years passed, no matter how hard we tried, we just couldn't keep a close enough eye on our son. More and more, we could see he was slipping away, that we were losing him by degrees.

Now Ari was missing, really missing. Just weeks after he had "served his sentence," his week-long suspension from school for playing hooky with his girlfriend, Blake's office was calling to say Ari wasn't in his first class and did we know where he was?

Sharon had already gone to work and I was just leaving the house when I got the call. Thank God I was there.

After catching my breath and cursing quietly to myself, I said: "No, I don't have any idea. He's not here, that's all I know."

I thought for a moment. On the other end, I heard: "Rabbi, are you there?"

"Yes, I'm here. I'm just thinking. I'm wondering…wondering where he is."

A short pause, then: "I'd better go look for him."

Once again, I got into my car in search of our missing son, more angry this time than frightened. I began at the ball field. Surely, he wouldn't be hiding out there again! Still, I couldn't think of a better place to start. I checked behind the club-house. Not there. I drove to the 7-Eleven, walking each of the aisles in the store until I was certain Ari wasn't there, hiding behind some beer or candy display. I drove up and down the streets of the neighborhood, around the school, every avenue, every cul-de-sac, every dead-end street.

Two hours later, I drove home empty-handed. Thank God Sharon wasn't there; I couldn't face her right at that moment. I needed to be alone. I needed to think. Where would Ari go if he wanted to get away? My anger now was melting away, replaced atom by atom with a sense of dread and desperation.

Hesitating a moment, I opened the door to Ari's room and sat down at his desk. I looked at the cork board with its calendar for the month of April set in the center. Photos surrounded the calendar page – pictures of Ari striking a mock muscleman pose, Ari's friend Mike making a face at the camera, Ari and the girl I had seen with him at the ballfield – the "Pontarelli girl" -- sitting side-by-side on a park bench. I looked hard at Ari's handsome face, at his wiry body and some of the people who evidently mattered to him and wondered who this stranger was.

Then, defying everything I had always believed about good parenting, I began to rummage through Ari's drawers, looking for something, anything to help me find him. In the top drawer I found pens, pencils, magic markers and a school notebook that opened with two pages of notes on Modern European History, pages dated September 4 and September 5, followed by page upon page of draw-ings, doodles and notes to and from his friend, Mike.

In the middle drawer, I found two of my old ties I hadn't realized were missing; chewing gum and candies; ticket stubs from a movie; school yearbooks from the previous two years; souvenir pamphlets, programs and menus from our family trip to Cape Cod five years earlier; a collection of old music CDs and two plastic kazoos.

In the bottom drawer, I found an address book, beneath that a stack of men's magazines and, beneath that, a dark green shoebox. I opened the box and found three wrapped condoms, a small collection of silver dollars -- Chanukah gifts that Ari must have saved-- some letters addressed to him with "Rene" inscribed in purple ink on the back and, at the very back of the box, three perfectly rolled joints in a sealed zip-lock plastic bag.

Setting aside the contents of the shoebox for the moment, I picked up the address book and began to look for numbers to call. Quickly I found a listing for Ari's friend, Mike. I called the number; no answer. Then, in desperation, I began calling numbers at random and, introducing myself as "Ari's father," asking whoever answered if they had any idea where Ari might be. Nothing. After the fifth such call, I gave up.

Then I saw a listing for "Renee P." -- address and phone number -- and, figuring the "P" for "Pontarelli," I dialed it. A woman's voice.

"Mrs. Pontarelli, this is David Chazen, Ari's father."

"Mrs. Pontarelli is my mother-in-law," she answered, in what was clearly her stock response. "You can call me Marie." I could imagine her on the other end -- a big, loud mama with a booming laugh and a hearty appetite for pasta and cheap wine -- then felt instantly guilty for such awful stereotyping.

"Oh sure, of course. I'll call you Marie and you call me David. Listen, Marie. I'm really sorry to bother you but I'm looking for Ari and wonder if you have any idea where he is, if maybe he's with...Renee?" I pronounced it French-style, with the accent at the end.

"Actually, David, she never uses 'Renee.' She hates that name, much as her father and I love it. She likes to be called "Reenie." She spells it 'R-E-N-E-E,' like on her birth certificate, but pronounces it 'Reenie.' Anyway, that's what she prefers so that's what we all call her."

"I see. Fine. 'Reenie' it is." I was getting exasperated; why didn't she just answer my question. "But, either way, Marie, the question is: do you know where Ari is now? Do you know where Renee is? Are you sure she's in school?"

"In school? Well, of course she's in school. Where else would she be?"

"Yes, of course she would be in school -- ordinarily. But, you see, the thing is... I'm not sure where Ari is right now and obviously you know they were... playing hooky together, I guess you'd call it, week before last."

"Yeah, I heard all about that from Blake over at the school. Not too good, huh?"

"No, not really too good at all. Anyway, I just thought maybe he might be with Renee but if she's at school and he's not with her, I guess..." I didn't know what else to say. "Anyway, if you see Ari or if maybe Renee says something about him, could you please give me a call. I'm not really worried, but I'll feel a whole lot better when I know where he is."

I gave her my number, muttered a quick "thanks," and hung up.

That done, I did the only thing I could think of. I went to the liquor cabinet and poured myself two fingers of scotch. Drinking slowly, I considered my options – call the police, find out if there was some kind of number for "missing persons," wait until after school and make the same calls I had just made in the hopes that there might be something more helpful later in the day.

Two, perhaps three minutes later, as I sat with that third glass of scotch in my hand, the phone rang. It was Mrs. Pontarelli, "Marie."

"Listen, David. It's Marie. I have to come clean with you. I played dumb with you before because I didn't know what else to do."

"Oh?" A punch to the gut. "Played dumb...about what?"

"David, Ari is here…here with me…and Renee."

"What? What are you saying? He is there with you?"

"Just hold on a second. I know you won't like this but just listen. They came to me this morning right after breakfast. They told me things with Ari and you and your wife are not good and that he can't go home and he wants to move in with us for a while. He said…look I'm sorry, he said you were abusive with him."

"Abusive?" I screamed. "That's ridiculous, the most ridiculous thing I've ever heard! I never…I would never…"

"Well, I'm sure it is ridiculous…but that's what he said. And I thought it was my responsibility to…He said he just needed a place to crash for a while, to get a little space for himself and figure out what he wants to do next and I figured maybe that wasn't such a bad idea. I'm sorry to interfere – and I know you must be furious with me and my husband thinks I'm crazy -- but I'm concerned about Ari. I like him and I'm concerned about him. You know, David, he's a good kid."

I was sure my head would explode.

"I know he's a good kid! He's my son!" Then I stopped, caught my breath and then said in as restrained a voice as I could manage: "Excuse me but who are you to tell me about my son? Who the hell are you? I've never even met you before. Listen to me: I know him better than you, better than you ever will. Now you listen to me and listen carefully to what I'm telling you. I'm coming over there right now. I'll be there in ten minutes max. You have him ready and standing outside the door or there will be hell to pay. You have no rights here, lady, no legal rights, no moral rights, none. But I do. I'm his father. Do you understand me? Do you hear what I'm saying, Marie?" wrapping her name in a generous coating of sarcasm.

Marie Pontarelli didn't answer right away, then:

"Look, I know you're angry – and I don't blame you – but, forgive me, I want you to stop and think for a moment what we're doing here. It seems to me this boy is at risk. He's got some real problems and some of them are with you and your wife. So you can come over here and drag him home but what do you think that will accomplish? Don't you think he'll run away again? Don't you? You can see how unhappy he is. Why not give him some time to be away for a little while, on his own. Give him some space to get himself together. Maybe you could start talking with him about what's bothering him while he stays here for a while. And then, when you've got things worked out, maybe he'll feel ready, maybe he'll feel like he really wants to come home and be with you and your wife again. Isn't that a better idea, David?"

I had had enough.

"OK, stop. Just stop talking and listen to me. I am coming over there right now and he'd better be ready. Otherwise I'm going to call the police and have them arrest you for kidnapping. The boy is a minor. You have no right to do this, no right. I'm coming over there right now and he'd better be ready. Do you hear me? Ten minutes max."

Then, with my hand shaking violently, I banged the receiver down.

I rushed to the car and drove straight over to the address in Ari's book. He was standing outside the door, a small green plastic bag beside him on the ground, secured with a red tin tie. Ari glared at me, got into the car and turned his face toward the door. We said nothing until about a block from home, when I couldn't control myself any longer.

"What the hell were you thinking? What could possibly have been in your head? Anything at all? Or maybe it was completely empty when you made this stupid-assed decision."

Ari turned to face me, pure hatred in his eyes.

I was positively screaming now, my voice bleeding rage, hurt, humiliation.

"Listen to me, young man, you are my son, my son and nobody else's...no one else's responsibility. You are seventeen years old, not old enough to make your own decisions. The law won't allow it -- and thank God for that, or I don't know what the hell you might do. Until you are eighteen, your mother and I will decide what's best for you. You may not move out of our house. And you will abide by our rules. It's that simple. And it's my decision, our decision, not yours. Do you understand? Do you?"

The worst silence of my life. Ari turned his head back toward the car door and said nothing. Then, as we arrived in the driveway, Ari said in a voice just loud enough to be audible, never turning his face away from the passenger-side window: "I hate you."

With that, he grabbed his bag, ran into the house and straight to his room. I dropped into a leather easy chair, looked around distractedly, then picked up a book, opened it to the bookmark I'd left last time and, while my heart played out a tattoo in my chest, sat there, pretending to read.

That evening, Sharon came home from the paper, took one look at me and said: "What's wrong? What's happened?"

I tried to describe the events of the day but each time I began, I felt something catch and the words wouldn't come out. Finally, giving up, I rested my face in my hands and, very quietly, began to cry.

Sharon appeared horrified. She knew I never cried, hadn't even cried when my mother died.

"What is it? Tell me. Is somebody hurt? Did somebody die? Stop crying and tell me…right now. Please, I can't stand this."

I lifted the index finger of my right hand as if to say: Wait one second and I'll tell you.

"It's Ari," I said, my lips barely moving, as if my jaw were wired shut. I saw the look on her face. "No, no, he's not hurt. It's nothing like that. But it's still pretty bad. Sharon, he ran away today. I mean, really ran away this time. They called me from school this morning and told me he wasn't there. I called every-one, everyone I could think of."

Again, I had to stop and catch my breath.

"I called everyone until I finally got through to the mother of that little girl I caught him with at the ball field last week. At first she told me he wasn't there but then she said he was there with her and her daughter, and -- you won't believe this – he told her he couldn't live at home anymore because we abused him. Can you believe it? He told a perfect stranger that we abused him. So I went nuts. I practically bit her head off. Anyway, I went over there and picked him up and I yelled at him in the car on the way home and he's been in his room ever since.

Sharon, I don't know what to do. We've got such a terrible situation here and I don't have a clue what I'm supposed to do, what we're supposed to do about it."

I paused for a moment, looked straight at her and said: "Maybe we need a family therapist. There's no shame in that and God knows we need it. Would you be willing to consider that, Sharon? Would you?"

She said nothing and, ignoring my question, just looked hard at me. I searched her for some hint of sympathy but, as I watched, her face slowly turned from concern to what seemed like triumph. Oh my God, I thought, this is her moment of vindication!!

"Now you finally get it, don't you?" she said. "Now you know what I've been dealing with all this time. Well, I haven't been able to do anything about it, David. I haven't been a howling success with this son of ours. So now I officially turn him over to you. Let's see if you can do any better. Let's see if you can whip him into shape. God knows I can't and I'm sick of trying. Good luck. You're going to need it."

With that, she turned away and, without another look in my direction, went upstairs to our room and closed the door.

I sat there, sucking in breath. I had had all afternoon to think what I would say to her and how she might react, but this I had never imagined. Our son was hanging on by a thread and this was her reaction? This was the way we worked together to help him out?

That night, I crawled under the covers of the bed, crashing into a restless, troubled sleep. When I awoke the next morning, Sharon had already gone to work.

***

Ari's return home was short-lived. The day after I brought him back from the Pontarellis, he left for school early in the morning, the sun newly out, then returned to his room in the mid-afternoon and remained there for the rest of the day except for "family dinner" at six o'clock.

That first evening at the table, Sharon and I tried to make conversation with him. Ari answered in monosyllables. No longer visibly angry, Ari was now completely disengaged, as though his soul was elsewhere and only his body remained captive in his parents' home. It was the same the second night. By the third, I stopped trying. Our dinner together consisted of food, drink and about fifteen minutes of uncomfortable silence. It was clear: Ari was there – but no longer *there*. And we couldn't make him be there, no matter how we tried.

On the fourth day, I received an email at the synagogue. It was from Ari. It read: "I made a decision. I am going to live with Renee. Her parents are okay with this. I know I am not eighteen yet but I can't live with you anymore. Don't try to stop me. And don't go after the Pontarellis. I'm coming home this afternoon to pack my stuff. Don't try to stop me. Don't try to talk to me. Just let me go."

I was dumbstruck. I closed my office door, rested my head on my hands on the top of the desk. What was I supposed to do now? Go home and make one last attempt to get Ari to stay? Useless. Ari would never live by our rules again, that much was clear. Ari was cut from different cloth; he always had been. He didn't care about the same things Sharon and I did, didn't have the same interests or talents. Like a foundling in one of those British farces, Ari seemed like a stranger switched at birth with our "real" child. We had tried so hard to reshape and re-mold him; it hadn't worked. We had tried to accept him as he was; we couldn't.

And so, Ari had pulled away over the years, spending less and less time with us, choosing not to go on family vacations, refusing to attend synagogue and sit with Sharon except on the High Holy Days and eventually not even then. And now Ari was resigning from the family, leaving altogether. And really, he was right, I couldn't stop him. I could insist on him staying at home -- but why? I could demand he stay in school but couldn't get him to study or complete assignments or even show up to class. My hands were tied – and he knew it. It was just as it had always been: if Ari dug in his heels long and hard enough, he could not be moved.

I decided then and there to give up this fight I couldn't win. If Ari wanted to move in with his girlfriend, so be it. I would learn to accept it as best I could. What I would say to Sharon I couldn't imagine. What I would say to the synagogue leadership, my friends, my family, people in the deli, I had no idea. Just have to cross that bridge after I burned it.

It was now three o'clock in the afternoon. Ari would soon be getting home from school -- assuming he had gone at all. He would be packing his things. I decided to go home and play the gracious loser, composing in my mind the sermon I wanted to deliver to my departing offspring.

As I pulled into the driveway in the glare of the late afternoon sun, I saw a curtain move in Ari's room; he must have just come home. I paused for a moment, thought again about my message for my son, then turned off the engine and entered the house.

Ari was pulling down suitcases from the shelf at the top of his clothes closet – the big, soft-sided black valise and the multi-colored Snoopy bag, the one he had used for overnights as a child. I stopped at the entrance to his room, positioning myself like a kind of impotent colossus, hands resting on both hips, clearing my throat to announce my arrival. Ari looked up, surprised, unconsciously backing away a mini-step from the looming presence in the doorway. His eyes darted around the room. I spoke.

"Don't be afraid, Ari. I'm not here to stop you. I understand you're going to do this whether I like it or not. But, son, you've got to know - if you don't already -- that this is killing me, me and your mother. You know we've tried to do everything we could for you. All we wanted, all we ever wanted was for you to be happy. Looks like it hasn't worked too well. "

Choking on those last words but denying myself the luxury of tears, I collected myself and went on.

"I'm sorry, Ari, really I am. I'm so sorry we didn't do a better job of it, sorry you're so unhappy here. So, go ahead and move in with Renee and her parents. Maybe it'll be good for you. Maybe it'll be better for us too in the long run. I don't know. But I hope you'll keep going to school; you know how important it is to finish high school, at least. And I hope – maybe I'm completely unrealistic here – but I hope maybe we'll hear from you every now and then. And maybe someday down the road, you'll feel differently about things, about us and maybe you'll want to come home again. And that'll be okay, Ari. Because this will always be your home. And we will always be your family. We'll never stop being your family and we'll always take you back, no matter what. Because that's what families do, they accept us and love us no matter what. Even when we don't love them back."

"Now, can I help you pack?"

"No. I can do myself," he muttered, not looking up.

Ari spent about an hour gathering up his belongings, stuffing them at first into the suitcases and then into green plastic garbage bags, all of which he deposited in the foyer by the front door. He then went into his room and closed the door. I could hear him speaking on the phone. Ten minutes later, standing in the kitchen, I heard a car honk three times at the curb in front of the house. Ari went downstairs and, keeping the front door open to the balmy April breeze, dragged all his worldly goods outside. Finally, when it was all on the front step, he closed the door behind him.

I looked out the kitchen window to the street and saw Marie Pontarelli at the wheel of her red Trans Am. I saw Renee Pontarelli open the passenger door and come running to the front step of the house, look guiltily around her in all directions, then give Ari a hug. The two of them carted all the bags over to the trunk of the car. I watched as they closed the trunk, then got into the car. For a moment, it didn't move. Then, Ari got out of the car, walked towards the house, opened the front door just enough to poke his face in and call out: "Goodbye, Dad." Then the door closed and Ari was gone.

Hesitating not an instant, I went to the liquor cabinet, poured myself a scotch, downed it in one gulp, then poured another -- and another. It was more alcohol consumed more quickly than I ever had in my life and I knew I had to lie down.

**

Chapter 8:

"I Drink Alone"

More and more, I drink alone. I eat alone, I run alone, I definitely sleep alone. That slamming door was my official declaration: I'm done. I'm done with them, and Dan, I'm done with you too.

It cost me, though. At first, it felt like I was in mourning. And it took me a while to figure out exactly who and what I was mourning for.

On one level, I guess, it was for my family. Avi had left us, finally and probably forever. Yes, I know that with adolescents, "forever" is only as long as their weed-addled brains can fathom, which can be a month, a week, a day. But this felt strangely permanent. Whether or not he ever came home physically, it seemed clear in some fundamental way, Avi was through with us. I watched it happen, my heart breaking. He had come home from yet another day when he'd cut most of his classes and dissed most of his teachers, silently packed up his old bags and left. The Pirelli girl had been waiting in that rusted old wreck her mother drove, and the three of them had driven off into the sunset together. Now Avi's room was empty, silent. He had become my very own ghost child, like the one my parents had lost in the camps. Somewhere in the ether, I could feel my mother sighing.

On top of that, I was also mourning for my marriage. Starting the night of our spectacularly awful "date" with Dina and Len, Dan and I now slept in separate rooms. God knows there were now enough available ones in our "adorable little house."

So now we lived truly separate lives: he ran at the crack of dawn, left for work before I came downstairs and stayed at shul until the very last program/meeting/class was over and the very last light in the building was turned off. By then I was out cold, ably assisted by a full-bodied red or, on especially tough days, a vodka – or two.   And usually some pills and cigarettes too.

Sometimes, we ran into each other. Barely polite, increasingly distant.
Something in me still longed to reach out, but then something else, bigger
and more powerful, pulled me back. Soft and hard, soft and hard. It used to
be me who was soft, round and open and Dan who was hard and insistent,
driving and probing. If I really concentrated I could sometimes get past the fog
in my head and remember how it used to be, what it felt like to move together
and feel each other so deeply. But, really so what? All that was done.
Done and over.

***

ometime in the middle of the night after Ari left– no idea what time it was – I opened my eyes, wondering where I was. I reached up to my face for my glasses, then felt all around until finally my fingers brushed them from the end table onto the floor. Now on my knees, my hands describing wide arcs on the carpet in the pitch dark until I found them beneath the coffee table, I set them on my face and sat up on the edge of the sofa. My watch glowed luminescent in the dark; it read 2:36 a.m.

Slow and unwelcome, yesterday's memories came poking out at me -- Ari in the bedroom packing his bags, loading his stuff into the trunk of the Pontarellis' Trans Am, coming back to the door to say goodbye. Ari, my only child, was living somewhere else; he couldn't live with us anymore, he had said. Pow!

Then my mind caught on another jagged edge: Sharon. Why would she leave me on the sofa here like this? In the dark, I walked up the stairs, leaning on the banister, feeling carefully with my toes for each new riser. I remembered the woman in my congregation who had come crashing down the stairs in the middle of the night some years back and who never walked again. I remembered doing her funeral, what was it, four, five years ago? I climbed very carefully, my hand never lifting from the railing.

Outside our bedroom door, I reached for the handle and gently turned it. It wouldn't move. Had she really locked me out of my own bedroom? Unbelievable. What had I done? But then, there was no figuring what was going on inside that woman's head anymore. Over the last months, she had become a near total cipher, mystifying. Locking the door on me was no more baffling than the way she would shield the computer screen whenever I walked into the room, the way she came home in the middle of the afternoon from work just to get to the mailbox before me, the increasingly frequent trips to New York for lunch with someone she wouldn't name and refused to talk about.

We'd have to deal with all of this in the morning. In the meantime, I simply had to get a decent night's sleep. So I opened the guest bedroom door; still in my clothes and nestled beneath the covers. That night, I slept the sleep of the dead, not moving until well past nine o'clock the next morning. By then, Sharon was gone. And I never went back to sleeping in our shared bed again.

***

It was Monday, my day for meditation with Lisa, the high point of the week. (Although the bar for that was not set terribly high.) I was intrigued by what I was learning, progressing slowly in fits and starts, despite nagging self-doubt. And Lisa? Well, Lisa was great. She had nothing but encouragement for me. And I could feel something happening between us, something strong and real and, yes, a bit dangerous but fundamentally good. I didn't want to define it, didn't want to ask too many questions about it. It was enough just to feel it.

Arriving at our regular hour, I closed the car's sunroof, opened to admit the glorious spring sunshine. After greetings and a quick hug, we moved immediately to what Lisa liked to call the "quiet room." Without any conversation, I took off my light sweater, removed my glasses, got into a comfortable position on the floor and began to focus on the candle that Lisa had lit in the center of the room.

Breathing deeply, chanting in Hebrew, narrowing my focus, I felt the strain and stress seep out of me. The half-lotus position -- a source of torment for so long – was beginning to feel more natural. I breathed the way Lisa had taught me – in through the nose, out slowly, through the mouth.   I tried to focus on the mysterious, unspeakable Name of God, letting the sacred letters *yud, hey, vav, hey* dance in my head.

Every few minutes, my eyes opened and I took in my surroundings – the room, its sparse furnishings, random sounds that echoed within its walls. Despite my best efforts, I would become momentarily aware of my own thoughts or even the absence of thoughts – "a thought nonetheless," as Lisa always reminded me. Every now and then, my eyes would focus on the beautiful woman sitting across from me and I would take note of her skin, her hair, her clothes. Then I'd try again, gaze at the candle or visualize myself flying away over the clouds and then…

Dimly, I became aware that someone was speaking. I heard Lisa's voice as if calling to me in a dream. Our time was up.

Time to go back to the office.

Awkward silence. Then Lisa broke it.

"How're you doing, my friend? You okay? You seem a little distracted lately. You okay? How about we go grab some lunch and talk? You feel like playing hooky with me? " She smiled, one corner of her mouth curled slightly upwards.

I took my phone from my jacket pocket, opened the datebook, checking on my afternoon schedule.

"Yeah, I can do that. Let me just call Kelli and tell her I won't be back until later." I called the synagogue. Kelli answered, assured me things were quiet and she would "hold down the fort" until I returned. Her favorite expression.

Lisa suggested a place just a couple of blocks away, the Grove Café, a place I was happy to note I had never heard of before. Maybe we could be anonymous there and have some time just for ourselves.

Arriving separately only a few moments apart, we entered the place – a brave attempt at a hip urban art-deco design in an otherwise drab suburban strip mall – and were ushered to a booth in the back by a young woman evidently less interested in welcoming us to her establishment than in an ongoing dispute with one of the other hostesses.

Lisa took both menus from the hostess, handed one to me and recommended what she usually had for lunch. When she saw me put down the menu and close it, she took my hands in both of hers, looked up at me and said: "So, David, how are you doing? I mean really. You seem so preoccupied, so sad lately. What's going on with you? You know you can tell me."

I held her gaze for a moment, then looked away. Speaking more to the ceiling than to her, I said: "I guess things are a little screwed up lately. "

I paused for a moment, considered my options. How deep did I want to go with this?

"Listen, it's a lot of things really but mostly it's about Ari. I got a call a few weeks ago from the school that he wasn't in class. So I dropped everything I was doing and went looking for him."

"And…where was he?"

"He was with his girlfriend in the park. They were piled on top of each other behind the clubhouse, nearly naked. So I had to interrupt them, which was pretty embarrassing, take them back to school and then I had to hear from the vice-principal that Ari has been missing class pretty regularly all year and that he's just about used up his chances."

"You didn't know about this?"

"No. They've been calling Sharon and she never told me. That's a whole other story. Anyway, I tried talking to Ari but he doesn't get it. He refuses to get it. And the next thing I know: Ari's gone. I mean, really gone. Moved out. Living with his girlfriend. Gone."

I was speaking in a virtual whisper. Our faces were close together, maybe a foot apart. Lisa continued to hold on to my hands as I spoke. We just sat there like that for a moment.

Then a voice: "Rabbi, I hope I'm not interrupting anything."

I looked up, pulled my hands back in a hurry. There at the table was a face, vaguely familiar, a family member (uncle, maybe?) from last week's bat mitzvah at Emmanuel.

"Incredible," said the uncle. "What a small world. I mean, just last week we're at Vanessa's bat mitzvah and here we are again, the two of us in the same place. I mean, what are the odds? Anyway, I hope I'm not interrupting anything. Just wanted to tell you how great everything was. You know, Rabbi, you do a very nice job. I told my sister when they moved out there to the boonies a few years ago, she should join the Reformed temple. These guys do a better job with bar mitzvahs, I told her. I guess you've got me to thank for them being members. So...do I get a finder's fee?" he laughed.

"I'll see what I can do," I said, doing my best to be genial. "Anyway, yes, it was a really nice morning. Did you enjoy the rest of the day?"

"Yeah, it was wonderful. A really great party. Sorry you couldn't be there. Anyway, just wanted to say hi and tell you how much I enjoyed it."

I shook his hand and smiled again. It was now time for the uncle to move on. Instead, he stayed at the table, not moving, staring at the two of us, at me and the attractive woman with the tank top and no wedding ring on her finger. After a couple of moments of silence, I gave in and said: "Oh, this is a friend of mine, a fellow rabbi actually, Lisa Langer. Say hello to...?"

"Milt Drucker."

"Hello, Milt. Nice to meet you." Lisa gave him her most disarming smile.

Uncle Milt returned the smile and nodded in her direction, obviously intrigued. He paused for a moment, then a moment longer. Finally, giving up, he said: "Well, nice to see you both. Enjoy your lunch."

With that, he returned to his lunch a couple of booths away, pointing in our direction and speaking loudly to his companion. I knew, of course, I'd hear about this, my lunch with the mysterious woman rabbi in the revealing outfit. I knew it would get back to the folks up in my neck of the woods; such things always did. And, even though I knew there was nothing to apologize for or feel guilty about, I also knew I would have to explain, whether I wanted to or not.

**

Chapter 9:

"Free Bird"

What's the stage after denial and isolation? I'm not sure it's the 'correct' order, but for me what came next was rage—red-hot rage.

It started in the supermarket. Wearing my biggest, darkest glasses, absent-mindedly filling my basket with whatever was close at hand, I bumped into the president of the synagogue -- and I mean literally "bumped into."

"Why it's the Rebbetzin" he said jovially. Why, President Slimeball, I thought to myself. "Fancy meeting you here. You know, I've been meaning to try this new fancy-shmancy supermarket for months. I guess it's already got your rabbinic seal of approval!" Big, dumb grin, pleased with himself.

I nodded, asked perfunctorily after his family, fervently hoped he'd let me pass and waited for what I prayed would be a one-word answer. No such luck.

"Family's fine, just fine," he said. "Kids are good. Jeanie is happy. You know, she took up yoga recently. Trying to get me to join her." Maybe yoga would be a good idea for him too, I thought, as I remembered Dan's tales about the man's "anger management" issues.

"Actually, my wife says Rabbi has taken it up too--getting private lessons from that woman Rabbi in Oaklawn, I hear." He must have seen the shock on my face. He was loving this! Opening his eyes as wide as they would go, he tried his best not to show his glee. "Are you taking lessons too? Do you go with him?"

I mumbled something about being slammed at work and looked dramatically at my watch—wow, it's late—and made my escape. Leaving my basket in the middle of the market aisle, I headed straight for the exit and fled.

The minute I got home I googled her: ordained Reconstructionist rabbi. Only 31 years old (a newbie -- I almost felt sorry for her.) Newly separated (and on the prowl, no doubt). One kid, a little girl. Small congregation. Time to check her out in person.

The next day, I drove by her house. Was that my husband's car parked ever-so discretely a half block away from her very cheery, flower-festooned front step? Hard to know; there were a million white Corollas just like his everywhere I went.

Of course I had a high-def picture of what must have been going on there on Monday mornings. Downward facing dog? My hound of a husband defined the posture, letting his appetites drive him in everything he did. The combination of spandex yoga pants, flexible limbs, candlelight, patchouli and lust would be irresistibly explosive.

After what seemed like an eternity, I sped away.

In the days that followed I got more and more interested in my husband's little friend. I started following her car, watching her go from home to synagogue to hospital and back. It was eating into my work time. Actually, work was eating into my stalking time.

In truth, the drinking, sleeping and watching reality TV were all taking a toll. Just taking out the empty bottles had become a challenge. Once I'd filled our own recycle bin, what was I going to do with the extras? The neighbor across the street watched his own trash bins like a hawk. Somehow he thought the haulers weighed them or something and he'd be charged extra if anyone else's trash got in there. So I'd walk a couple of houses further. Then further still.

Finally, it all got to be too much trouble. What the hell, I thought. Let the neighbors see what's going on at Fortress Cheryl. Nothing to hide now.

All that was left was for me to quit work. That would be the trifecta of failures. Then I'd be completely free. Free to do what, I wasn't entirely sure, but free nonetheless.

***

The instant I walked in the door from lunch at 2:30, Kelli said: "Donna Cutler called. She said it's urgent and she's waiting to hear from you. She said to tell you nobody died – but she really needs to see you right away."

Walking into my office, I sat down at my desk, picked up the receiver, then stopped for a moment, distracted by the photo of Sharon and me taken on the day of Ari's bar mitzvah. I looked at the attractive couple in the picture – beautifully dressed, arms linked, gazing into each other's eyes -- and I envied their evident marital bliss. I wondered if perhaps I ought to put the picture away; it hurt me so much now to look at it.

I went to look up Donna's telephone number, then realized I knew it by heart. I dialed.

"Hi, Donna. What's going on? Are you okay?"

"No," she said. "I'm not okay. I need to talk to you. Can I come over and see you? Now?"

"Now—like, right now?"

"Now, like right now. Okay? I won't take a lot of your time. I know how busy you are. But I've got something and it really can't wait. And it's not about the synagogue this time. Listen, David, I didn't get any sleep last night and I'm kind of…well, I have to talk to someone. Actually, I have to talk to you." Then, a little bit peevish, "I know you must be busy. But can I come over now for maybe fifteen minutes of your time? I really need you."

I had a full schedule for the rest of the afternoon, starting with an appointment at 3. And I knew there was no way, whatever Donna promised, that we would be done in fifteen minutes. But what could I say?

"Okay, Donna. Come on over now. I'll tell Kelli to buzz me as soon as you get here."

I sat in my office waiting for Donna to arrive. Not ten minutes later she was there, in jeans and a T-shirt, no makeup, strands of stray hair sticking out from what she had tried to shape into a ponytail. Her eyes were red. I rose to greet her as she walked in. She closed the door behind herself, grabbed my hand and guided me to the sofa. She began to speak, never letting go of my hand, her talisman.

"Listen, David," she said. "Listen…I…Listen, things with me and Les are…" Then she became still, looked down and hid her face in her hands. Her shoulders began to quiver as she sat rocking back and forth on the sofa, crying without making a sound.

I sat quietly, waiting for a moment. Donna tried once again to speak but succeeded only in drawing a sharp breath, then gave up, still holding on to my hand. Finally, she looked up and said in a barely audible voice, "Les wants a divorce and, David…I never saw it coming. Am I an idiot or what? I never saw it coming."

She looked up at me for reaction. I tried hard not to give her one – at least not yet. I had to hear her out first.

"He said last night he wants out and, dumb old me, I never saw it coming. I thought everything was okay, not great you know, but compared to everyone else, pretty okay. But this…this took me totally by surprise. And I don't know what to do. David, I made him tell me if he has someone else – and after denying and denying, he finally admitted it. Of course he does. He wouldn't have the guts to do this on his own. So where does that leave me? I mean, what am I supposed to do?" Now she was really sobbing. I wondered who could hear her outside my closed office door.

I thought: maybe this was as a shock to her but it certainly wasn't to me nor would it be to anyone who knew her and Les even a little. It was well-known at Emmanuel that Les had his "girlfriends," generally much younger women, sometimes more than one at any given moment. I guess I had always assumed that Donna knew about them, had somehow -- as I knew some wives do -- made her peace with the arrangement. Now, I could see: she hadn't known or perhaps had chosen not to know or forgotten that she knew. Now she couldn't help knowing -- and the ground was shifting under her feet.

After a few minutes, she stopped crying and waited for me to speak. I knew there was nothing to say. She probably knew it too but that didn't change the expectant look on her face. I reached out to hold her other hand in mine and said: "Oh, Donna, this must be so terrible for you."

She said, "David, just hold me for a moment. I feel so unloved -- so unattractive and so unloved. Just hold me. Then I'll go. I know there's nothing to say. I just needed to see you. I just needed you to hold me. You always make things better somehow. Just by being you."

She dropped her hands from mine, stood up in front of me and guided my hands around behind her back. Reluctantly, awkwardly, trying desperately to maintain a little space between my body and hers, eventually deciding it wasn't possible, I held her. We stood there for a moment, saying nothing. My three o'clock appointment was surely waiting for me on the other side of the closed door.

"Oh, David," she said, swaying me slightly back and forth as if we were dance partners. "David, David, what am I going to do now? I don't want to be alone. This world sucks for a middle-aged woman on her own."

The buzz of the intercom. Kelli's voice. "Rabbi, your appointment is here."

"Donna," I said, gently but deliberately separating myself from her, "we need to talk about this. But for right now, I want you to go home and try to stay calm. Do something for yourself, take a hot bath or go work out. Just don't do anything you'll regret later. I'll call you this afternoon and we'll figure out what to do next. Okay? I'll call you this afternoon."

"Okay. But you'd better make sure you don't forget. I'll be waiting for you to call."

She reached into her bag, took out a mirror and examined herself, pulled out a brush and tried to set her hair in place. Then, without saying a word, she turned and walked quickly out the door and left by the back way.

I waited about thirty seconds, then walked into the office waiting area and greeted the three people who were waiting to see me, a couple in their early forties sitting together silently and a man, about the same age, standing by himself outside the office door, as if casing the place for a robbery. What had brought them to me was a daughter they shared in common, a young girl about to become Bat Mitzvah. It was 3:10 in the afternoon and, as I walked this unlikely trio into my office, I realized I couldn't wait for the day to end.

I looked at the three of them, the couple sitting thigh-to-thigh beside each other on the sofa, the man by himself in a chair in the far corner. It was clear: they didn't wish to be within arm's length of each other if they could help it. I knew why. The mother of the little girl had called me earlier in the week and told me the whole story.

The bat mitzvah girl's father and mother had divorced years earlier after he found her with his business partner in bed – in his bedroom. The divorce proceedings were long and painful, a stage on which they played out their deep loathing of each other. Soon after, the woman had married the business partner. Since then, the exes had had three years to disengage their lives, separate their finances, work out custodial arrangements. Now the only thing they shared in common was a love for their daughter and a sense of unsatisfied grievance. They sat and glared at each other across the room.

I began my set speech.

"I want to thank you all for being here today. It says something very positive about the three of you that you are willing to place Rachel's interests above your own. And I am confident that, if you continue to think about what's best for Rachel, and put your own hurt and anger aside for now, her bat mitzvah will end up being a wonderful day for her and, in spite of everything, for you too. I want you to let me help you do that."

A pause for effect.

"So here is what I'm asking you: Each of you has a role to play in the service. I will tell you what that role is and then count on you to accept it. You are going to have to compromise with each other for the sake of your child. That's the only way this is going to work. You have to forget about each other and focus on Rachel. You have to show her your unconditional love. Anything else has no place at this special moment in her life."

It was my best speech on the subject but, even as I was speaking, it was clear I was selling but nobody was buying. Their anger was too strong, their sense of outrage too deep. I had the sinking feeling this was not going to end well.

The afternoon sun's rays slanted into the room, lighting up a line of dust motes. They sat silent, glaring at each other, the mother sitting as close to her new husband as possible, no one willing to be the first to speak.

I waited as long as I could, then said: "So?"

The father looked directly at his ex-partner, the man who had taken his place in his wife's affections and his bed and said, without blinking, "He will not participate in this service. He is not the child's father. He has no role to play in this service. I will not allow it."

"Allow it?" the new husband blurted. "You don't get to allow it or not allow it. You're not in charge here. "

"I'm not? Just wait and see."

With that, as if he had been sprung from a cage, he lunged across the room, grabbed his one-time partner and friend by the throat and there, the two wrestled across my office floor, knocking over lamps and end tables, eventually spilling blood on the carpet.

The mother tried to burrow herself into the farthest corner of the room. I thought about intervening but feared I'd be the one to get injured. So I called out as forcefully as I could, "Stop it. Stop it right now."

I waited. The fighting continued.

"I'm not kidding. Stop it now or I'll call the police. I'm perfectly serious. I will call if you don't stop right now."

I waited an instant longer then picked up the phone and began to dial for real.

Finally, they pulled away from each other, their anger apparently in check, at least for the moment. The father, blood dripping from a carpet burn on his cheek, seized his coat and stormed out of the office. Then, without saying a word or even looking back in my direction, the mother and her loyal husband followed just a few steps behind.

As I drove home after this "steel-cage match" in my office, the story on the radio was about a local rabbi who had been convicted of hiring a hit-man to kill his wife. When a journalist asked, if things were so bad between them, why didn't he just divorce her, he said his congregation would never accept that. How bizarre! Being divorced was apparently worse for a rabbi's reputation than being a murderer!

When I told this story to Sharon, she said with a slight smile: "Do me a favor. If you ever decide it's that bad between us, just divorce me. Don't have me killed, okay?" We both laughed. Then I said: "You do me a favor. If you ever decide it's that bad between us, just divorce me. Don't kill yourself, okay?" We laughed again.

It was the first time we'd laughed together in months. Looking back on it, I'm not sure it was all that funny.

***

For the last two months I'd begun to feel like Lisa's star pupil, getting gold stars from her every Monday morning. But today it wasn't working, none of it, not chanting, not focusing, not breathing exercises. Nothing. Every time I began to bear down a bit, I could feel anger bubble up in my soul and get in my way. I had been stuck for one full hour -- almost to the minute – something I could only know if I'd been riveted to my watch…which I was.

It was an old story with me. "David is full of energy. He finds it hard to be quiet during nap time" my kindergarten teacher had reported – and little had changed in the intervening years. Now, as an adult, I could at least sit still for a few minutes at a time. But calming my spirit, that was something else altogether.

I tried to compose myself, sitting on a rug in Lisa's prayer room, but it wasn't going well. I was angry at Ari; why couldn't he get himself a life like everyone else's kid. I was tired of his excuses, tired of his lies. Above all, I was tired of Ari – his rage, his cruelty, his ingratitude. Tired – and very angry.

And I was angry at Sharon. Why had she locked me out of our bedroom? Why did she seem to hate me so much?

In the end, though, I was angriest at myself – and from this there was no escape. This anger, this self-contempt followed me wherever I went, from meeting to hospital room to pulpit. I couldn't get away from it.

Now I had come to Lisa's to unburden myself of all that anger but it wasn't working.

Maybe that was because there was something else going on between me and Lisa that had nothing to do with meditation, something that always seemed to get in the way. Every time I walked in the door and she wrapped her arms around me and hugged me close, every time I left her place and she took my face in her hands and kissed me on both cheeks, I felt something considerably more than metaphysical. And I wondered: Wasn't she feeling it too?

As I closed my eyes and tried to chant, all I could visualize was her holding me, her breath on my face, her fingers stroking my shoulders. I pictured raising my face to hers, kissing her, pulling her T-shirt out of her yoga pants and reaching in. I wanted her so much it was like being fifteen again, my heart thumping as if ready to burst through my ribcage. No wonder I wasn't getting anywhere.

She picked up on my restlessness.

"You seem so distracted, David. What's on your mind? "

I debated how honest to be. I temporized. Yes, I was having trouble concentrating. It was about Ari and about Sharon and about work too. Surely she knew all the strain I was under. Surely she must know how hard this all was for me right now?

"Yes," she said. "I know all that. But, David, I have to ask you – and forgive me if I'm off here -- is there something going on between you and me, something we haven't talked about, something…well, that might be getting in the way here? I'm feeling it and I suspect you must be feeling it too."

OK. She had named it. It was on the table. Now what?

"Listen, David," she said. "Listen, I understand there's a special kind of closeness we share here. But, David, I think we've been pretty clear all along that this is… well, a spiritual closeness. It's not romantic. It's not sexual – or at least it's not for me, David. And it's not for you, right?"

"Right," I lied, completely deflated.

"Because, you know," Lisa picked up again, "people are always asking me, my girlfriends are always saying: 'What do you two do alone in your house together every Monday? Is it really mediating? Or is there something else you want to tell us about?' And I reassure them and laugh at their jokes because I know – whatever they think – that we're always on the up-and-up with each other.

But I have to tell you: I know what they mean. It is pretty strange for a man and a woman – especially a single woman and a not-so-happily-married man-- to be behind closed doors together every week and not…you know, cross the line."

"And we've never crossed that line, have we?"

"No we haven't – and I want to make sure we never do, because if we ever did, I think that would be the end of everything, David. That would ruin it all. And I never want that to happen."

"Is it so easy for you to keep it safe?"

"I didn't say it was easy. I'm just saying it won't work for me any other way."

As much as I wanted her, I knew what I had to say, at least for now.

"Well, obviously it's not easy for me either. But I know it too. I know we have to keep it platonic. And I think what we do here – the hugging and everything – that's okay. It's just two friends being affectionate with each other. Right? I'd hate for us to be so hung-up we couldn't do that without having to worry it would lead us into…well, into, you know…something inappropriate."

I stopped. "Am I making any sense here?"

"You're making perfect sense, David," she said "What you said, that's exactly the way I see it."

She stopped for a moment, took a breath, then looked straight at me.

"We're not like most people. At least that's the way it seems to me, David. You and I can make this work without getting sucked…pulled into…some kind of romantic relationship with each other. You are a very nice-looking man, David Chazen…"

I grinned – God help me! -- like a four-year-old getting praise for helping Mommy.

"And I do care for you, quite a bit actually. But I'm very comfortable with us being friends – but without 'benefits.' I'm very comfortable with that. And as for you and your marriage, David Chazen, well, I don't know much about it but I think you either need to work on it or get out. Just don't use me, don't use us to avoid having to deal with her because, I promise you, that won't work.

I was devastated – but I knew she was right. All the way home, I thought: either I've got to give Sharon and me one more chance or give it up and move on with my life. Tonight, I decided, I'd take one more shot at it. Desperate times call for desperate measures.

Arriving home in the mid-afternoon, long before she'd be home from work, I set about preparing a textbook romantic dinner. I decided to make *coq au vin* for dinner, set out a bottle of champagne I had picked up on the way home, covered the table with our best cloth, set candlesticks and flowers from the supermarket and got to work in the kitchen. Sipping wine as I worked, I followed the recipe with a couple of added flourishes. A little more spice. Always the way I liked it.

When Sharon came in through the door at nearly seven, the smells permeated the house. I handed her a flute of champagne – she had always loved champagne! -- and, before she could speak, said simply: "Here…drink this. I'm sure you need it."

At dinner, we talked about something more than our respective problems for the first time in weeks. As she drained her first glass of champagne, then set to work on the next, she grew more animated. It felt a bit like…well, a bit like old times. For dessert, I had picked up a Dutch chocolate cake, her favorite. As I brought it to the table, she looked at me with one eye cocked and said: "You looking to get lucky tonight, sailor?"

I just smiled and said: "Never crossed my mind."

After two bites of the cake, she said: "Come on. Let's skip coffee." We went upstairs to the bedroom where she took control. When it was all done, she rolled over beside me and said: "God, I needed that." I laughed. She said "I'm not kidding. I really needed that. I've been so tense lately."

As I lay in bed, hands clasped behind my head, Sharon went into the bathroom where I could hear her washing up, putting on pajamas and brushing her teeth. She was humming some tune I didn't recognize. After a few minutes, she came out of the bathroom, got into bed, turned on the television and was soon engrossed in some reality show. At about ten o'clock, the program not yet over, she turned to me and said: "I think it's time for you to go back to your own room." Then, as if remembering something she wanted to be sure to mention, she propped her head up on one arm, and said: "I hope you don't think this changes anything." She said it so matter-of-factly that I forgot to be angry. Then she rolled over again and fell fast asleep.

That night, I dreamed about Lisa. I was in the hospital, alone in a giant ward with maybe a hundred beds, an image out of a children's classic I used to read to Ari years ago. She came in to me in a nurse's uniform, smiled as she placed a thermometer in my mouth. Then she lifted up her skirt and raised herself over me on the bed, naked underneath. As she hovered over me, I awoke with a start to see Sharon standing mutely just inside the doorway to the room, no longer asleep and clearly fascinated by the noises I was making in my sleep.

***

After the debacle of our "romantic dinner," I poured myself into my work just as I was now pouring myself a scotch at the end of every work day. Perhaps it was escape, or maybe just plain comfort. Mostly, it was survival. More and more, my work felt like treading water; the moment I stopped, I was certain I would get dragged under the waves.

Rising earlier and earlier in the morning, up most days before sunrise, running, reading, catching up with email. More phone calls than ever. More hospital visits, breakfast meetings, evening meetings. More visits to our Hebrew school to drop in on the kids and teachers. Racing from one thing to another, often going hours at a time without having to think about the mess I was making of my life.

At night, I dropped into my solitary bed, exhausted, sometimes stopping to strip off my clothes first, sometimes not. My sleep was rarely uninterrupted. I would awaken once, twice, three times or more with some crazy fragment of a dream dangling on the edge of my brain. Often, I'd find myself unable to go back to sleep at one or two or three o'clock in the morning and would end up playing endless rounds of spider solitaire on the computer.

One morning, after a particularly restless night, I awoke at 9 a.m. -- completely disoriented – and checked my date book. First up: a ten o'clock meeting with Steve Kurwitz, a major player in the congregation whose son had just become engaged. I'd have to hurry if I was not to keep Steve waiting, and I knew I better not!

At five minutes before ten, I walked into the building. Steve was already there, a large, well-dressed, not-quite-handsome man, chatting up the women in the office, smiling, showing photos of the bride- and groom-to-be. As Steve saw me enter the office area, he marched directly over to me and drew me into a big bear hug, practically lifting up off the ground, slapping me on the back repeatedly with both hands. I kept saying: "Mazel tov, Steve, mazel tov." Steve kept saying: "I am so happy; I feel so blessed."

After several rounds of this, I gently freed myself from his embrace, straightened my jacket, smiled weakly and invited him into my study, saying: "Sounds like we have a lot to talk about." Steve followed behind me and, pulling off his suit jacket and, folding it and setting it beside him on the back of a chair, found a place to sit on the sofa.

As I watched Steve make himself comfortable, I wondered why he had come to see me in person this morning. He had called last week to tell me his son had gotten engaged. All that remained was to pick the date and the time and the family could then go ahead and make arrangements and I'd make plans to see the bride and groom. Nothing complicated about it. As a rule, this was all done on the telephone, at least that was the way it usually went. Instead he asked to come in and see me. So why the personal visit -- and on a weekday morning at an hour when most people had to be at work? I was sure I wouldn't have to wait long to find out.

An enormously successful businessman, Steve had branched out from private dentistry to manufacturing dental prostheses to real estate and then to more speculative investments everyone seemed to know about but must have been sworn, on pain of death, not to reveal to the rabbi. However he had managed it, Steve had done very well for himself, moving years ago out of his home in the same subdivision as Sharon and me to a "country estate" on a private road somewhere up in the rolling hills. There had been a great deal of curiosity about Steve's new home, heightened when the synagogue had it as its *pièce de résistance* on a "home tour" fundraiser several years before. And that wasn't the only way the Kurwitzes had leveraged their good fortune for the benefit of Emmanuel, something I remembered every time I walked into the "Steve and Elaine Kurwitz Chapel."

Steve and his wife drove matching black Audi R8s, invited friends and business associates to the shore for weekends on their boat, had recently begun to collect vintage cars and, whenever I called to ask a favor, seemed to be traveling somewhere exotic. "Not bad for a neighborhood dentist," Elaine loved to say with a laugh. No, not bad at all.

Steve and Elaine had three boys, all with names beginning with 'J,' all of whom had become *b'nai mitzvah* at Emmanuel, all now in their twenties and living and working in Manhattan.

When Steve had called last week, saying: "I've got some good news," I had assumed it would be Jason, the oldest. Instead, it was Jared, the next in line. Jared, I guessed, must be about twenty-five, twenty-six by now. The best I could recall, he had gone to school for communications at Boston University -- and had moved down to take a job with a sports management company in New York immediately after graduation, a job Steve had had something to do with finding. Jared had been a very good athlete in high school, captain of the lacrosse team as a senior. Handsome and cocky, he always presumed a certain closeness with me, an intimacy that always put me slightly on edge.

"So, Rabbi, it looks like my Jared has found his *bashert*, the one he was meant to be with."

I smiled. "That's wonderful, Steve. Tell me about her."

"Well, miracle of miracles, she's Jewish. Can you believe it? Jared with a Jewish girl? So I guess we ought to give thanks to the good Lord for that." Although this was clearly supposed to be funny, the best I could do was a pale, little smile.

"Anyway, Jamie's from the Island, at least she grew up there. Her parents moved out to Arizona -- Scottsville area – about ten years ago. Has a couple of brothers. And she works at an advertising agency in the city. Anyway, she's a 'perfect ten.' She's got her own money, she's a knockout and she's Jewish. Oh, and she thinks Jared is God's gift which is perfect because he does too. Anyway, that's our Jamie and we're already in love with her."

"So… as soon as Jared and Jamie made their announcement, I got busy talking to her parents about the wedding. It turns out they're actually very nice, very reasonable people. And they want to make the wedding." Steve spoke those words with fingers marking quote marks in the air.

"I mean, can you believe it? In this day and age, they don't want any help from us; they want to do it on their own. I said to them: 'Look, we can certainly afford to help. Why don't we just split it?' But they said it was easier if they did it themselves without a conference call on every decision. So…what could we say?" He beamed like he'd just won the lottery. "We told them go ahead."

"Anyway, Rabbi, that's what brings me here. The kids went ahead and picked a date and booked a place in Manhattan, the Plaza, could you guess? And, of course, after Jared and I told Jamie about you and your silver tongue, she and her parents agreed that we all want you to officiate."

"Well, that's great, Steve. I'm very flattered." Visions of a night in a suite in one of the better hotels in the city at the expense of Steve's new in-laws danced in my head. "So what's the problem? Is there a problem?"

"Well, I don't know, David. Maybe not. I hope not. You see, when I called last week and told everyone in the office here about our news, your secretary said that Saturday might be an issue, something about a service that night, something she said you're usually at. So, David, I'm asking you. Would you check the date and then tell me that it's okay, that you'll be there no matter what. I know for me and Elaine – and for Jared – it's really important that you be the one to do it. After all, you bar mitzvahed him. You bar mitzvahed all three of the boys. And you did Dad's funeral. You're very important to us David. We need you to be there."

He smiled broadly. "David, check your calendar for Saturday night, September 23 and let me know we haven't got a problem here."

Of course I knew immediately what date they had selected -- Selichot, the Saturday night service just before Jewish New Year, the one that introduces all the High Holy Days, something I could never miss and, anyway, a singularly inappropriate time for a Jewish wedding no matter who officiated. I looked in my book although I already knew what I'd find there, and sure enough, Saturday, September 23 was the evening of Selichot.

Summoning up my courage, I looked up and said, "Steve, I'm afraid we do have a problem. It's Selichot. We have a service here, it's the big lead-up to the Holy Days and I really can't miss it."

"David, please don't tell me this. I'm sure you don't absolutely have to be there. Why can't the Cantor do it and you can be there with me and my family. I'm sure they don't need both of you for a service that maybe twenty-five people come to when I'm asking you to be there with me and Elaine and our family and friends on the most important night of our lives."

Like a drowning man grasping for something to keep him afloat, I asked: "Steve, how firm is this date? I mean, surely there have to be other dates available."

"No," Steve said firmly. "There are no other Saturday nights available in the whole fall. Do you have any idea how hard it is to find an open Saturday at the Plaza, especially less than six months away? I mean, the only reason we got this one is because somebody else backed out two days before Jamie's parents called in, a broken engagement or something....No, David, you can't just say: 'Aren't there other dates?' There are no other dates and we're lucky to have this one. This is the Plaza we're talking about here!"

I knew I shouldn't ask but..."Well, what about another place, another hotel?" I could see from Steve's face that this was not a direction he wanted to go in.

"No, David, this is what the bride wants. This is what she's been dreaming of since she was a little girl, to be a bride getting married at the Plaza. And I don't think anybody -- not me, not you -- is going to change her mind. You know what I mean?"

"Yes, of course I do. But it's not..."

"I'm sure you do," Steve interrupted, clearly agitated and tired of being diplomatic. "You're a bright guy, David. But let me make it crystal, okay? And I don't like to have to say this, but let me lay it all out for you. Elaine and I are your biggest contributors here at Emmanuel, biggest by far. You know that as well as I do. Yes, we have plenty of money and we're happy to give it to the synagogue but, remember, we don't have to. Do you have any idea how many asks I get in the average week? But I always thought it was important to support my synagogue and I have. And you accepted that money with a smile. And in all this time, David, think carefully, have I ever asked you for anything, anything you wouldn't do for anyone else? Well, now I'm asking...asking a favor for me, for all I've done for you and this place over the years. I'm asking you to do this for me and my family. I want you to think carefully before you answer, David, because to me it's that important."

I knew what the answer had to be but I just couldn't give it. There was too much trouble in my life already without adding this disaster-in-the-making. I knew I'd eventually have to say no. I knew how Steve would respond. And I knew how it would eventually blow up in my face, but somehow I just didn't have the courage to go there right at that moment.

"Steve, you know how much I care about you and your family. And you know how much I appreciate what you've done for us here, more than anyone. And I never, ever want to say no to you. But, Steve, this is kind of asking the impossible." Steve scowled. He did not want to hear that word.

I backtracked. "Well, not 'impossible' exactly, but very, very difficult. And I, uh, I need some time to think about it. Okay? I just need to think this through very carefully and then we'll talk. Okay?"

"As long as you understand what's at stake here, David, you can think it through all you want, all you need to. But, in the end, I trust you'll see the big picture and do what's right. I'm confident you will, David. I know you're a smart guy and you'll do what makes the most sense here for everyone."

He grabbed his coat and started for the door. "When will I hear from you?"

"I'll need…forty-eight hours. That should be enough. And then I'll call you. OK?"

"That'll be fine, David. I'll look forward to hearing from you so we can go ahead and tell everyone that our rabbi will be there with us on the most important day of our lives." And, with that, he sped off out of my office.

**

The next morning, I tried to focus on the Kurwitzes and the Plaza and the wedding. But all I could think about was Ari. I knew he was at the Pontarellis' house, in their basement. I wondered: Did they share a bed, he and Renee? Did her parents allow it? Was he going to school, passing his classes? Was he happy with the choice he had made or was he regretting it but too proud to admit it? A swarm of questions buzzed around my head, questions with no answers. How was I ever going to get through the day?

I moved through the office with a quick hello to the women there, then sat in my study, pen tapping out a rhythm on my desk, unable to get started. Messages, emails, the voicemail light flashing on my phone, like a chorus of demands from a brood of needy children. I moved to the door, shut and locked it, turned out the light. For a few moments, I sat there, "The Thinker," holding my head in my hands. Then, as if acting on secret instructions, I removed my jacket, tie, shoes, socks, shirt, lifted the glasses from my face and sat cross-legged on the floor in the middle of the room in trousers and an undershirt. It felt liberating. I could hear the hum of the air conditioner as it strained to hold back the stifling heat of the mid-May morning, as I closed my eyes and began my own little "hum." Ommm.

I could feel my chant as it vibrated through my body. Waves of darkness and light poured through me. I rocked back and forth as though floating on the waters of the sea, drifting with the tide, in and out, forward and back…

I sensed something scratching at me. Let me be. The scratching wouldn't stop.

"Rabbi…Rabbi, are you there?…Rabbi? Rabbi?" God, how I hated that voice yanking me from this world of quiet and peace.

"Rabbi, are you okay?"

"Yes, Kelli, I'm okay. What is it?"

"Rabbi, I'm really sorry, really sorry to bother you. Are you sure you're okay?"

"Yes, absolutely sure. What is it, Kelli? What is it?"

"It's Mel Grafman. He's on the phone. He said he needs to talk to you. And,

Rabbi, I don't know what you were doing in there but I saw you had turned out the light and I had a feeling you didn't want to be disturbed. So I tried to put him off but he wouldn't hear it. He said he needs to speak to you now, it's an emergency. So, he's waiting on the line. Rabbi, are you up to…do you want to take it? Can you talk to him now? Or should I make some excuse for you?"

Silence, me trying to answer, no words coming out.

"Rabbi, I hope I did the right thing here. I hope you're not mad at me."

"No, Kelli, I'm not mad. You did the right thing. I'll talk to him. Just give me a second."

I picked myself up from the floor, moved over to my desk and, looking at the pile of clothing folded neatly on the sofa, picked up the phone and said with audible annoyance: "What is it, Mel, what do you want?"

Things with Mel and me had been heading steadily downhill of late. The truth is: Mel and I had never really liked each other much, were very different people, I guess you might say. Somehow, especially lately, I found just about everything about Mel to be annoying. Not a good way for a synagogue president and rabbi to be with each other. But there it was.

"What do I want? I want to talk to you. I want to talk to you in person. I'm concerned, David, concerned about you and your, ah, your state of mind."

"My state of mind?"

"Yes, your emotional state, your…state of mind. I need to talk to you and the sooner the better, preferably today. David, we need to talk. I'm worried about you. I'm, I'm concerned."

"Alright, Mel. Come in this afternoon if that's what you like." My earlier "ominduced" serenity completely evaporated, I said: "Sure, Mel, come on by and we can talk about my state of mind. I'll look forward to it. Should be fun."

"Yes, well, yes. I'll come by at two?"

"You do that, Mel. You come by at two. I'll look forward to our little *tête-à-tête*"

There was a part of me that still floated somewhere overhead, a part of me that looked down from the heights, saw myself sitting half-undressed at my desk, in conversation with the man who signed my paycheck -- and knew, even if dimly and incompletely, that I was starting to come unglued.

Some time later, Kelli called on the speaker: "Rabbi, it's Mel here to see you. Should I show him in?"

I looked at the digital clock on the desk; it read precisely 2:00 p.m. Mel was nothing if not prompt.

"No, Kelli, I'm coming out to meet him now."

I walked out to the main office, executed a facsimile of a smile, then asked Mel to come in.

Mel didn't bother to smile back. The right side of his mouth seemed to twitch intermittently, a tic I had never noticed before. Had it always been there? He proceeded to lick his lips as though a child trying to summon up an appetite for a dish of liver or spinach. And then, in a voice more sorrowful than angry, he explained that he was very worried about me, and that he wanted to tell me what was on his mind and would I please not interrupt until he was completely finished. I nodded my head.

Mel laid it all out, all of it, everything he (and, he assured me, everyone else) was talking about – my distractedness, my failure to listen in meetings and personal

conversations, the irritable tone I had assumed with almost everyone, my growing tendency to close my office door when I was there by myself, my drifting off
during services, the unpolished way I presented myself in the community. This
was not the David he – and everyone – had always known, not the man they had
hired so many years before with such a sense of promise.

Mel was aware of certain "things" going on in my life. He wasn't sure what it
was all really about and he recognized that it wasn't his (or anyone else's) business, but it was pretty evident that things were not good at home. Sharon
had not set foot in the synagogue in quite some time. It was known in the community that Ari had moved in with a girlfriend, not Jewish. And I should know
there was a lot of talk from the leadership – and, to be frank, the entire congregation – about my relationship with a certain "Rabbi Lisa Langer," an attractive,
young woman I had been seen with quite a bit lately.

Now, Mel explained, he had always felt it was none of his business or the congregation's business, what I did with my private life. But that was only true as
long as it stayed private, and as long as I managed to keep up the professional
standards everyone had come to expect of me over the years, neither of which
was currently the case.

Then he turned his head so that he and I were face-to-face, locked eyes with me
and would not let me loose.

"David, I say this as a friend and an admirer. I think you're in trouble. In all the
years I've known you, I've never seen you like this. So, I want to make an offer
to you. It's an offer, you should know, that comes not just from me but from all
of us, all the directors. It's an offer but I guess it's really more than an offer. It's
a request, a strong request. Anyway, whatever you want to call it, I hope you
take it in the spirit that it's offered because it comes out of concern for you and
nothing else."

He took a breath.

"David, we want to ask you to take some time off, to get out of the synagogue for a while, I'm not sure how long, two weeks, maybe three, as long as it takes you to clear your head. Maybe take a trip, maybe just stay at home, I don't know, but do something to get yourself together or, David, I'm afraid we're all in big trouble here. David, are you listening to me? David?"

There was a long moment of silence and then, increasingly aware of the look of pain and pity on Mel's face, I allowed the full force of the question to penetrate. It did, finally, when I allowed it to, like the sharp jab of a pointy object.

"You want me to take some time off? Take two or three weeks off? Leave everything, all my responsibilities here, leave everyone hanging and hope they're okay when I get back? Is that what you're asking me? Because, if you are, Mel, you can forget it. This is my job. I'm the rabbi of Emmanuel and I'm needed here. I'm not going anywhere. I'm fine, just fine, thank you very much. You don't have to worry about me. And whatever's going on in my private life, Mel, well I guess that's why they call it 'private,' isn't it? So I'd be really happy if you didn't mention it ever again. Now you can go back and tell everyone they can rely on me, rely on me one hundred percent. Just like they always have."

Mel was visibly shaken. The blood had drained from his face, leaving it the color of something left too long in the freezer. He had never seen his rabbi like this – so angry, so (call it what it is) crazy. Without another word, he picked up his coat and literally backed out of the office, unable to unhitch his gaze from mine as he left.

***

"I quit my job," she said, as I walked into the kitchen from work. She was bent over the counter, absent-mindedly finishing off the last of a bag of stale potato chips in the fading light of the day.

I said: "What?" but it really didn't surprise me. I knew what she was like at home, could only imagine how she was at the paper. I wondered what they must be thinking at work about the obvious changes Sharon was going through. The change was striking. After all, while others had come and gone, put off by the poor pay and lack of benefits, Sharon had been their stalwart -- writer, thinker, planner, always the one to figure out the right story, the right angle, the right approach. Never mincing words, she was clear about her journalistic standards and insisted that everyone adhere to them. She was highly-regarded in the community, knew everyone and how to get them to open up and tell her something at least approximating the truth. She was strong and ballsy, creative and well-organized, demanding and forgiving. And, on top of all this, she was clever, funny and attractive; of course they loved her. Why wouldn't they? But now, now that she could barely drag herself in to work, now that poison seemed to ooze out of every pore?

"You what?" I asked again.

"You heard me, I quit my job. I've had it up to here," signaling with her leveled hand a line across her eyes, exactly where she'd had it up to.

I considered a number of options. Practical: How do you figure we cover our expenses every month? Incredulous: Are you out of your mind? Compassionate: Oh dear, you must be so unhappy to do something like this. Petulant: Don't you think I'd like to quit my job too? In the end, the only thing that came out of my mouth was "Really?"

Like a teacher working hard to be extra patient with a particularly dim-witted student, she looked at me and said: "Yes, really...really and truly. Why are you so surprised? You know how much I hate it. The paper is losing money. Our writing staff has been slashed to nothing and I'm doing almost everything myself. And besides, the pay stinks and I detest the boss. I think that about covers it. Or do you want me to go on?"

"I know," I said. "But how do you propose we pay our bills if you stop working? (Apparently, I'd gone with practical, after all.) Surely you don't think my paycheck can cover all our expenses? You know as well as I do it's not enough. And we've got college coming up for Ari, at least I hope we do."

"I'll do something. I'll find temp work. I'll work at farm stand or wait tables or clean houses. I'll figure something out. But I just woke up this morning and I got out of bed and I knew, I mean I just knew I couldn't walk into that crappy little office one more time. So I picked up the phone and I told Neal the truth. I said I've had it. And I have. So I'm done."

Incredible, I thought. After almost twenty years working in the same office, for the same boss, she just picks up the phone (the phone, mind you!) and says: "Sorry, I've got other plans. I won't be in today – or, by the way, ever again." Incredible. Even more incredible was that she had made the decision without any input from me. I was stunned and hurt.

"Sharon, that's just not fair. I would never have made such a decision without talking with you about it first. We're supposed to be partners, husband and wife."

"Now he remembers," she laughed out loud.

"My God, Sharon," I said. "Don't you think I wish I could quit my job too? Don't you think I'd like to just run away sometimes? But I don't. I don't because I have a sense that I owe something to you and to Ari."

She raised one eyebrow a half an inch, doing her best to suppress a cramped and nasty smile.

"Yes, to Ari," I said. "He's part of this family too even if right now he's a little mixed up. Anyway, my point is: I don't walk away from my commitments because I'm a grown-up. And it would be nice if you acted like one too. You can't just up and quit and let the chips fall where they may."

"I knew it," Sharon said. "I knew you'd get up on your high horse. Listen, David…I don't want to play games. It's too late for that. Listen to me: I just can't do it anymore. And if you'd been paying more attention lately, if you hadn't been rushing off to séances with your little girlfriend, maybe you would have known this is what I had to do. And maybe, just maybe, if you hadn't been so self-absorbed, maybe Ari would be right here living with us instead of with that girl.

"My God, you just don't get it, do you? You always think it's someone else. It's me or it's Ari or who-knows-who. But, maybe it isn't, David. Maybe it's you. Consider that for a moment. Maybe it's your fault and not anybody else's." And with that, she retreated to her room, to her pills and her vodka and her solitude.

My mind raced around crazily. I thought of those experiments where they put a frog in water that is slowly brought to a boil. As the temperature rises, degree by degree, the frog never senses the danger and so he never jumps out and saves his skin. Unlike the frog, though, I knew it was time to jump before I got cooked.

So I did. Right into my car, driving off to the one place I could always go, to the one person who understood me, who always took my side, who didn't blame me – at least not exclusively -- for the epic screw-up of my life.

Cutting in front of anyone slowing me down and ignoring every speed limit along the way, I headed straight for Lisa's. In less than twenty-five minutes, I sat in her driveway, looking into the front windows for signs of life. There was movement in the bedroom. I could see shadows flickering against the drawn blind and knew it was her.

I knocked on the door, once then again, then heard the padding of her feet as she came quickly down the stairs and opened the front door. There she stood before me in a man's plaid flannel bathrobe that probably once belonged to her ex-husband.

Obviously startled by my turning up without warning on her doorstep, she seemed to be searching for words, then took a really good look at my face, took my hand, led me inside and said: "Come in, baby. Come in and if you feel like crying, that's okay too."

That's what I needed. I needed to be somebody's baby. I needed someone to soothe and comfort me and let me know everything would be alright. I needed to stop trying to hold everything together – and doing a pretty lousy job of it.

Without another word, Lisa gathered me up in her arms. Leaning on each other, we stood locked together in her front foyer. As I tried to speak, she put her finger to my lips, shushing me, took me by the arm and led me upstairs to her bedroom where she babied me as tenderly as ever I had ever been -- gently, tenderly, kissing, touching, building in intensity into a final release, until I cried out like a child.

***

My cell phone chimed the opening bars of Beethoven's Fifth; it was "home" calling. I opened my eyes to bright sunlight, jumped to attention, quickly tried to identify the room I was in and where my phone was. Grasping in all directions, I found my glasses, quickly put them on, then searched around for the elusive phone. Four rings, five…finally I found it lying on the night table next to the bed and said in a scratchy voice, "Hello."

It took me a moment to realize it was Ari on the other end, his voice clipped and agitated. "Dad? Are you alright?"

"Why, what time is it? What's the matter? Why are you calling?"

"Why do you think I'm calling? I'm calling because we're all crazy worrying about you. Dad, where are you? Are you alright? What's going on?"

"I'm fine, Ari, completely fine. Don't worry. I'm just...I'm in a hotel room. I had to get away for the night. I had to be on my own for a little while. Things just got too crazy around the house. Of all people, you ought to understand that. But, Ari, why are you calling? Where's mom?"

"She's here with me. She called me, told me you ran out last night and never came back and she needed me to come over right away, to help her find out where you were. So I did. I came home...I mean, not permanently but for right now. Dad, are you really alright?"

"Yes, of course I am. Why shouldn't I be? I just needed a little time alone. Anyway, I slept like a baby last night – which I desperately needed – so I'll just shower now and throw my clothes on and I'll be home in an hour."

"Okay," he said. Pause. "Dad, why do you need an hour to get home? How far away can you be? Don't shower, just come home...now."

Calculating the distance from Lisa's house, I said: "Alright. I'll be there as quick as I can, no more than forty-five minutes."

"Dad, we need you here now."

"I know, Ari. I heard you. I'll be home in forty-five minutes, like I said." I hung up, then turned to Lisa, couldn't begin to label the look on her face.

"Look," I said, "I've got to get home. Ari's there. They're frantic, wondering where I am. I'll call you as soon as I'm alone, I promise. But I gotta go."

Which, after retrieving my clothes from the chair in the corner of the room, licking my fingers and smoothing down my hair and slipping my feet into the shoes I finally found under the bed, I proceeded to do – and made it home in thirty minutes.

They were waiting for me, sitting at the kitchen table, coffee mugs pressed to their lips, not talking, Sharon in her usual sweatpants and T-shirt, Ari in what might have been his night clothes with a hoodie. As I walked into the room, Ari stood up but stayed at the table, Sharon didn't bother to stand -- he apparently relieved, she clearly furious.

Attempting to take control, I said: "OK. I'm fine. Just like I told you. I'm fine. Take a look. I just needed some space after yesterday."

Nobody spoke.

Finally, Sharon broke the silence. "So that's how it is, is it? I say one thing you don't want to hear and you just pick up and run – and you don't even bother to let me know where you are. It gets a little sticky and you're outtahere, just like that? And when were you going to call me and tell me where you were and what you were doing and when you were coming home?   Or were you just going to stay away forever, you gutless…?" The rest drifted off into murmuring.

I said nothing. What could I say? I let her vent. I knew her well enough to know it would only make her madder if I tried to respond.

"You have nothing to say to me? Nothing? You stay out all night and your son – who you already chased out of this house – has to call you to find out whether you're dead or alive and you come in with nothing to say except you're fine, everything's perfectly fine? That's it?" she said, as if explaining to an invisible jury.

She didn't pause for long.

"So you stayed in a hotel last night? Is that what you did? So now I'm wondering: can I check out too whenever I don't like it here?" She let that thought percolate a moment, then, newly energized, asked: "And which hotel did you stay in? The Carriage House, the Sheraton, where?"

"What difference does it make?" I responded. "I stayed in a hotel and now I'm back and I'm sorry if I made you worry but I did what I had to do. Now I'm home. And I'd be happier if I didn't have to get the third degree from you. You may have noticed I don't bother you for details when you go in for your famous lunches in New York City, or what you're always working at on that damned computer, do I? How about you doing the same for me and just cut me a little slack?"

"No, actually, now that I think about it," she said, "I do want to know where you were. I want to know which hotel? Why won't you answer me? What's the big secret – unless the big secret is you didn't stay at a hotel at all last night, unless the big secret is you were somewhere else, with someone else. Is that why you don't want to talk about it, you who always love to talk about everything? What's the real story, Rabbi? Where were you last night – as if I couldn't figure it out."

I worked very hard not to let my expression change, not to be the guy caught in a lie.

"Well," I said finally, "I'm not going to stand here and be interrogated. I told you I stayed in a hotel and I did and I'm not going to talk about it anymore. If we're going to talk about anything, I'd rather talk about you threatening to quit your job. That's where this whole thing started and that is something worth talking about."

"I didn't threaten to quit my job. I quit. I told Neal I was through and I am. So there's really nothing to talk about."

Through this whole interchange, Ari sat at the kitchen table, wincing with each verbal grenade. I was baffled. Why did he care, he who had chosen to leave this place, he who said quite clearly that he detested his parents and wanted nothing to do with us? Why was he here at all? To protect his mother? To referee between the two of us? And I wondered if maybe Ari felt a gravitational pull home in direct proportion to the level of discord between his parents.

"Well then, fine," I said, giving up. "I'm going upstairs to change and then I'm going to work…because, unlike others in this house, I do still go to work…even though sometimes I'd just as soon not. Are we done here? Are we?"

Ari looked pleadingly at me. Sharon looked away, spent. I went upstairs, did my best not to slam the bedroom door and took the longest and hottest shower I could stand, hoping to rinse off the residue of the last twenty-four hours.

**

Chapter 10:

"Another One Bites the Dust"

In a way, it was interesting, kind of like my own personal science experiment: how much could I shrink myself without actually disappearing? How much alcohol, how many sedatives could my body take before it just gave out? Stay tuned: horrible pictures at eleven.

I was glad my son wasn't here to see his mother erasing herself from the world. I don't think my husband even noticed.

Oh, Danny. More and more lately, I've been thinking back to our early years here. I remember taking Avi to services, proud of the handsome little red-headed boy who held my hand and sat in the pew beside me. For a time we were both happy to be there, happy to bask in the love of that handsome man on the pulpit, the one who would look down at us with such affection in his eyes.

But the memory of that time quickly gives way to the harsher reality that came so hard on its heels: the judging faces, the harsh words, the harsher silences.

Now all I could think of was endings. All I could think of was a "hit list" of everyone who was making me so miserable.

I'd start with that awful synagogue president. All that would be left of him is a greasy trail.

And, of course, my buxom buddy Dina: all she'd leave behind is those two extra-large silicone mounds—ironically, the very best parts of her.

Then there's Rabbi Yoga-girl: spandex and lotus-blossoms, strewn across the floor.

Ari, my son, I don't know how to reach you. I know you love me but I can't help feeling you'd be better off without me. You fired us as your parents and maybe you were right.

And you, Dan. What would be left of you? A soiled, empty, white robe, the one you wear on the High Holy Days to suggest purity, and a giant, over-sized basket of empty promises.

All this leaves me incredibly weary and very, very sad.

True confession time: the only part of the religious year that ever meant anything to me was Yom Kippur. The idea of taking stock of myself and trying to change for the better always seemed so hopeful to me.

But now, today, on this my own private Yom Kippur, I take a hard look at who and what I've become. And what do I see? The girl who ran as fast and far as she could from her immigrant parents, the woman who aspired to be a real friend, a loving wife and a selfless mother, but, in truth, never managed to make it work very well – not any of it.

So here I am with my own "Hit List" and now, today, it comes to me with perfect clarity that the only name that really belongs on it is mine.

And what finally will be left of me? Just as in the prayerbook, "Dust and ashes, dust and ashes."

**

It was Friday evening, Shabbat, end of a week of cold and icy silence between us. It was Shabbat and I was leading services, although – with everything I was going through -- my head, my heart and my soul were miles away.

At seven o'clock – a half hour before the start of services -- I closed the door to my office, turned off the lights and, draping myself in tallit and prayer shawl, began to rock forward and back, sole to heel, lifting myself just a bit off the floor at the end of each rocking motion. Humming a *niggun* – a wordless melody -- I gathered the folds of my prayer shawl tightly around my body and head until I saw nothing but what lay straight ahead and above me out my office window: a dusky, graying sky.

Suddenly, I felt a sharp sting at the corners of my eyes. I took off my glasses, wiped my eyes with the back of my sleeve, imagining how stupid I would look if anyone could see me now. Drawing the tallit tighter against my head, I looked back up into the sky again and whispered, "God, where are you? And, more to the point, when are you going to give me a break?"

"Rabbi, are you in there? Are you okay? Rabbi, it's time to start."

It was the cantor, knocking on my door, dragging me back to my previous coordinates of space and time.

"I'm fine, Cantor, just fine. Everything's okay. I was just…just having a personal prayer before we started. I'll be right out."

"Oh, sorry…"

I lowered my tallit from my head, relaxed its fit around my body, put my glasses back on my face and set out to the sanctuary to begin services, prayerbook in hand.

That evening, quite unexpectedly, I really felt my prayers as I hadn't in a very long time. The Hebrew words, mere rote for months on end, suddenly seemed laden with meaning. The music of the chanted melodies raised me up. I felt strangely, happily disconnected from my usual routine, swaying through the final hymn, blissful, at peace. Thank you, God. Thank you. Thank you for this gift.

As the cantor sang, signaling the end of services, I felt especially grateful for his offer earlier in the day that he would cover services the next morning, to let me take a Shabbat off and "just rest up a bit," as he put it. "Looks like you need it," he had said.

It was then I saw their faces, the faces of my congregants -- confused, staring at me, mutely asking what was wrong with me. It made me wonder too. I reached down and ran my thumb along the zipper of my pants. Closed. I fished with my tongue in the spaces between my teeth. Clean. Had I forgotten to clip my yarmulke to my thinning hair, ascending bareheaded on the pulpit? No, covered. So?

Hard to say. It seemed to me I had been just fine during services. The cantor and I seemed to have our cues down. Okay, maybe I had gone at a bit more leisurely pace than usual. Maybe there had been fuller pauses between the prayers, a longer-than-usual time for silent meditation…Okay, maybe a lot longer. But that was exactly why it had felt so right! That's what had made it all work. I hadn't rushed it, hadn't been distracted, hadn't been stage-managing things. That was good, right? Not judging by the looks on their faces.

Later, at the *oneg* – the social hour after services – everyone seemed to be keeping their distance. They were watching me, waiting, for what I couldn't guess. I looked over at Mel Grafman who was conferring in hushed tones with Donna and a couple of the other leaders. They huddled, heads together, looked over at me every few seconds. Something was up. One thing I knew for sure: I didn't want to stick around to find out what. My lovely, little spiritual bubble had burst. Time to get out of there. Time to go home.

Home to Sharon…not the beautiful girl I'd fallen in love with so long ago but the one who holed up in her room all day in the same stained powder blue sweatpants and T-shirt, whose skin was growing as grey as the hair she had now stopped coloring, whose eyes seemed to be looking out over great distances but seeing nothing at all, who didn't shower much anymore, who barely ate and whose days consisted of two- and three-hour naps punctuated by Judge Judy and home improvement shows on cable.

On my way home, I thought seriously about stopping off at the Westover for a beer or maybe something stronger. The idea of finding a back table, away from everyone, sounded appealing. Appealing, but unrealistic. I knew that the chances of sitting there quietly, urecognized were close to nil. I could just imagine the reaction to seeing the rabbi drinking alone at the Pub on a Friday night. Alert the media! So I kept driving.

Pulling into the driveway, my shoulders hunched, I sat for a time without moving, engine running, radio playing, humming along. After about five minutes, the song finally ended, I pulled the car into the garage, turned off the engine and closed the garage door behind me.

The alarm was beeping as I entered the house. That's strange. Why would she put it on? Didn't she know I was at services and coming home right afterwards? After entering the code "SHAR-Enter," I hung up my coat and put on the kettle for a cup of coffee. I noticed some smudge marks on the refrigerator door and brought the silver finish back up to a shine with a rag. By then, the kettle was shrieking. I removed it from the burner, spooned out two measures of coffee, poured the boiling water into the French press, then went to put on pajamas while the coffee steeped.

Up the stairs past her room. Usually, I could see a thin strip of blue-grey light shining out from under the door, the glow of the TV. Tonight it was dark and quiet. No light, no noise. She had probably gone upstairs after whatever "dinner" she had thrown together and couldn't be bothered turning on the set.

Another slide further down the slippery slope.

What made me open her door I can't say for sure. No idea what made me check on her, when for so many nights I had gone straight to my room and let her be, no strength to fight with her or listen to her crazy talk. This time I opened the door and looked in. Instantly I knew something was wrong -- no sound of Sharon's loud, whistled breathing, of her shifting under the covers, nothing. Quiet. Too quiet.

I went over to her, pulled down the covers bunched up over her head. This wasn't normal sleep — her breathing was too shallow, her tongue loose in her mouth! I called to her, louder, then louder still. I shook her. No response. I smacked her across the face. She moved and then moaned ever so slightly but, even then, didn't open her eyes.

It was then I noticed the bottle of pills and the vodka and, in one motion, leaped over the chaise lounge to the phone, dialed 911, and shouted "Send someone here quick. My wife won't wake up. I think she took something. Please…get over here now. We're at 422 Holden Lane in Fentonville. Please. Please hurry."

The rest of that night I felt like an actor without a script. I had no idea how many pills she had taken, how long she'd been lying there, if she'd left a note. I couldn 't find her Blue Cross card – or mine -- no idea of how to reach her doctor at this hour. And, most of all, no real understanding why she'd done it. "Completely bushwacked," I muttered to the EMTs when they arrived. "Never saw it coming."

Once in the hospital, catching up with her behind the curtain in #6, flashing my bravest smile at the emergency room doc, I said: "Well, at least I know she's okay now, now that she's here in the hospital, under your care."

The doctor's face betrayed concern and a trace of annoyance. "Actually," he said, "right now I'd call it touch-and-go. Excuse my candor, Mr. Chazen, but there's no way to be sure right now how this will end up."

I couldn't believe it.

When I finally left the hospital and drove back home, when I hoisted myself up the stairs and dropped my body down on my bed, there was nothing left in me at all; I had used it all up, every drop of myself. As I drifted off to sleep, I kept thinking: Touch-and-go. Touch-and-go. That was the last thing in my head until morning.

**

As the Saturday morning sun crept through the slats in the window blind, I woke up, disoriented. Grabbing my glasses from the end table, I looked around the room. Here I was in our old bedroom – after months in the guest room -- and Sharon wasn't there. The sun was up. I had slept without interruption, without dreaming for the first time in months.

Then, as though cueing up the camcorder in double-fast mode, I spooled through the events of last evening: the quizzical glances of the leadership at services, coming home to find Sharon splayed out on the bed, eyes glazed, alive but just barely, the frenzied call to 911, the arrival of the ambulance, the frenetic activity of the EMTs, leaving her in the hospital, the physician's "touch and go."

I was shaken to my roots. Things between Sharon and me had not been good in an awfully long time. But this…this was something else. I knew she was deeply unhappy but I never imagined her capable of this. I knew I had better get over to St. Theresa's – and quickly. But first there were calls to make.

The first was to my father in Florida. He was stunned by the news. Over the years, especially after my mother's death, I had chosen to share little about my marriage with him. When things were good with me and Sharon, it felt like gloating to this once happily married man now widowed. And when things were bad between us – as they had increasingly become -- I didn't want to burden him with my troubles; he had enough of his own. So my news that morning came as a total shock to this man who wanted nothing to shake his conviction that, even if he wasn't happy, at least his children were.

He said: "Call me as soon as you get back from the hospital, son. I'll be waiting to hear from you. I love you."

Then I called Mel Grafman. I had to tell him something. Eventually, people would find out Sharon was in the hospital. Too many doctors at St. Theresa's were congregants. Too many colleagues, community members, friends going in and out. I knew I had better tell him something but the less said, the better.

"Mel," I said. "Listen, something's happened, something you should know about. Sharon's had, well, a bit of an accident. She's in Emergency at St. Theresa's. And I don't really know how long she's going to be there but I thought you should know. And I won't be around the building much until we get things figured out."

Mel, of course, pumped me for more. After all, I had told him next to nothing. And, although he didn't know it then, not all of what I had said was entirely true. What had happened to Sharon was no accident. It had been a conscious choice -- desperate but conscious. And, although Mel pressed me to say more, I said: "Mel, look, this is kind of private. I appreciate your concern, really I do. But I hope you'll trust me that this is all I can say right now. Okay?"

Then Kelli, at home.

"Kel, hi, it's me. Sorry to bother you on a Saturday but, look, something's happened and Sharon is in St. Theresa's for observation. She's had a bit of an accident and they want to keep an eye on her for a while. So I'm probably not going to be in to the building on Monday, not sure yet about the rest of the week. Can you run interference for me until I get this together? Okay? I'll let you know when I know more."

She started to ask a question. I cut her off.

"Kelli, please don't ask, not now. I promise I'll get back to you when things are clearer, okay? If anybody calls for me on Monday, I'm taking care of an "urgent family matter" and will get back to them as soon as I can. Got it? Good. I'm sure everything will be alright."

It was time to get over to the hospital, to Sharon, to talk to her and see what could be done. An overwhelming prospect. I must admit: for the briefest of moments, I thought about getting into the car and just driving right out of town and never coming back. Rabbi, Run.

But, of course, I wasn't about to do that. I was going to shower and shave and dress and get to the hospital ASAP. Which I did.

When I got there, I went in through Emergency but found she had been transferred to the psych ward since last night. I knew my way there, had been there any number of times through the years to visit congregants. On the elevator up to the third floor, I checked in my cell phone for the security code to the locked ward, got off the elevator, entered the four digits that opened the bolted door with a loud buzz and went looking for a doctor to talk to about Sharon's condition before I went into her room. Eventually, I found a middle-aged doctor with graying sideburns and glasses perched on his nose, baggy brown trousers, a sloppy deep-blue sweater with a large stain in the front – a shrink straight from central casting – and asked about Sharon.

The doctor looked up from his charts, focused for a moment on me, seemed to comprehend suddenly who I was and what I wanted, then asked: "And you are the husband?"

"Yes, I'm her husband."

"OK. Good. Let me bring you up to date. She is stable for the time being and not in any immediate danger. But she did take a lot of pills. She wasn't fooling around. She took a lot of pills and drank a lot of alcohol and she came very close to killing herself. Thankfully we got to pumping her stomach in time.

Anyway, right now she's pretty sedated and I want to warn you, she's not looking too good. But I'm sure that's what you expected, Mr. Chafetz, didn't you? She's been through the wars these last few hours. So…I'm sure I don't have to tell you. Be gentle with her. She's in a very precarious state. I know you understand that, don't you?"

Well, of course, I understand, I thought. Out loud I said: "Of course. Thanks."

As I arrived at the entrance to Sharon's room, I saw Ari sitting on the floor just outside her door, dressed as he was when I last saw him at the house. When had he gotten here? How had he even heard about it?

I went to hug him but quickly gave that up as I saw him recoil.

"Ari, what are you doing here? I mean, how did you know about this?"

"The police called probably right after you left last night. Mom had something in her wallet that said to call me in the event anything happened to her."

A blow to the gut. There was so much I wanted to say. All that came out was: "OK, son. I'm going in."

The door to Sharon's room was slightly ajar. I knocked softly, then entered. She was alone, sitting in a chair beside her bed. She looked like hell. Her hair was uncombed, matted clumps poking straight up as if she were the victim of electric shock. Her face was ashen. Her eyes stared off into space, focusing on nothing, disconnected from the world. It was "Night of the Living Dead." I turned away, feeling sick to my stomach.

"Sharon, it's me. I'm here."

She finally noticed me standing there, a flicker of recognition in her eyes. "Sharon, the doctor says you'll be okay. You're going to be alright."

She looked up. And her eyes narrowed. She fixed on me for a moment with sudden intensity – as though squinting down the barrel of a sawed-off shotgun, then said quietly but with utter conviction: "Do you have any idea how much I hate you?"

I felt like I'd been struck with a blunt object.

She waited a moment, then said, suddenly lucid: "You heard me right. I hate you. You're the one who pushed me to this – you and your stupid life, you and that little slut of yours. God, do I hate you."

I paused, tried to take a breath and hold back my tears. "Sharon," I said, "how could we have let it come to this? There used to be so much love between us. I just don't know. I can't..." And then I couldn't go on.

Sharon was silent, her eyes never shifting from mine. It was clear she wasn't about to dignify my words with a response. Then she turned away, eyes aimed out the window, the conversation clearly terminated.

After a long, painful, silent moment, I said: "I'll be back later. Can I bring you anything from home?" No response. I turned to go, asked Ari if he wanted a lift back to the Pontarellis. He said no, he wanted to stay with his mother.

By now, I needed to get out of there – and right away. I thought for a moment. Then it came clear. I would head over to Holden State Park – just up the road from St. Theresa's. I figured I could run on the trail that led towards Mt. Joy, in the park's interior, then hike up that hill if I felt strong enough and try to figure out what to say, what to do before I went back to see her again.

I went out to the car for the extra set of jogging shoes, shorts and T-shirt I always kept there, changed in the men's room on the first floor of the hospital, got back in the car and headed over to the park.

Power-walking up the hillside, huffing and puffing, I took a break at a bench in the first of the hill's rest areas. Sitting alone, no one in sight, I tilted back my head, closed my eyes and began to hum a *niggun*, the same wordless melody I'd been singing to myself when my prayers were interrupted in my office before Shabbat services last night.

I sang it once, then again. As the refrain came around, I got up off the bench, stretched out my arms, looked to the top of the peak – barely visible from where I stood – and resumed my melody, only now with greater feeling.

Slapping time to the music on my thigh, dropping lower on the verses, louder on the refrain, I began to speak to the sky as though the words had been placed in my mouth – and perhaps they had.

"*Ribono shel Olam*, Master of the Universe, I beg you: Give me strength. Help me get through this. Give Sharon the will to recover. Bring my son back to me. God tell me what to do. Show me the way."

I waited. Silence. More silence. Then, when I could stand it no longer, I started singing every Jewish song I could think of, until I came to my favorite, *Kol ha-olam kulo*, "All the world is a narrow bridge and the main thing is not to be afraid." Yes, I thought, that's it. No matter how bad things look, everything is in God's hands so I only need to let go and let be. That's why I haven't been able to get that song out of my head for the last two weeks. I'm sure of it.

I looked down to the parking lot and the cars and the grass and the trees far below, every object in sharp relief, distinct and somehow perfect. And it seemed to me I understood now everything I needed to know.

Later that afternoon, I went back to the hospital to see Sharon again. This time, Ari wasn't there. I walked into her room. She was in bed, watching TV on the monitor suspended from the ceiling in front of her.

"Are you feeling any better?"

She shot me a contemptuous look and asked: "What do you care?"

"You *know* I care, Sharon. Please don't be that way. You know I care. I always have. How are you feeling?"

"I feel like shit, if you really want to know. And most of all I don't feel like talking, especially to you. Let's not pretend that everything's okay between us. Let's not pretend that it isn't you who's to blame for my being here, okay?"

"Okay, I know you're angry. But Sharon, forget about me, you've got so much going for you, so much to live for. Don't you see that?"

She looked hard at me without speaking for a moment, then said very quietly: "Don't bullshit me. And don't give me any of your sermons. Don't tell me how wonderful my life is because I'm not buying it. How about we approach this another way? How about you turn around and leave by the same door you came in and stay out of my life? Do you think you could do that? Do you think you could just for once leave me the hell alone?"

"Sharon, what can I do? Do you want a divorce? What do you want from me?"

"Absolutely nothing," she said, closing her eyes and shutting down in front of me, as if I were already gone.

Maybe it was time for me to leave, to give her a little space. We could pick this up another time when things weren't so dark for her. I'd come back and we could pick this up more rationally tomorrow.

With that, I bent over her awkwardly to plant a kiss on her forehead before she could squirm away. "Please feel better," I whispered before heading out the door, out of the locked ward, out of the hospital and out into the world.

***

Monday morning, I got to the office before anyone else. That way, no questions from Kelli or the other women in the office.

At about 9:15, Kelli knocked on my door, opened it a crack, asking tentatively: "Rabbi, are you alright?"

"Yes, Kelli, I'm fine. Really fine. Why, what's up?"

"What's up?? Well, I'm sure you've just had the weekend from hell. And I'm worried about you – Sharon and you. How is she doing, David? Is she alright? Are you alright?"

"She's fine, thanks, just fine." As though she had asked about the weather.

She stood there unmoving, started to speak, shook her head, looked up again at me and then, obviously giving up, said: "Listen, David, you should know Steve Kurwitz is here...in the main office waiting... and he wants to speak to you. David, are you up to this? Can you do this now? Should I tell him to come back later?"

I said: "Of course. I'm fine, really I am." Then, louder to make sure Steve heard me, "Of course, please ask him to come in."

Steve approached me warily; no hugs and back slaps this time. Did he know what had happened over the weekend, I wondered?

"Come on in, Steve. Happy to see you. Come have a seat. How are you guys doing? And how are the young bride and groom-to-be?"

"Well, Rabbi, if you don't mind my getting right to the point, that's exactly what I'm here about. You told me last week that you'd think about my request and get back to me. 'In forty-eight hours,' you said. But you didn't. So, Rabbi, tell me now. We can't wait any longer. We have to make plans. Have you found a way to make this all right?"

My mind shifted into gear. What exactly was it Steve had asked me? Seemed so far away now. Something about a wedding, about the timing of a wedding? Couldn't quite remember. But I knew it was something important to Steve and I kind of liked Steve or at least appreciated what he'd done over the years and I certainly didn't want to tick him off or have him go away mad and have some kind of major public scene over this. Whatever it was, I knew I wasn't in any mood for a fight. Not today. Maybe not ever again.

So I smiled at Steve and said, "Steve, you know I can't say no to you. I'll be happy to do it. Tell Elaine and the kids we're on and we'll do it your way. Would have been back to you sooner but some...family complications this last weekend."

Steve jumped up out of his seat. He lifted me up off the ground in a big bear hug and said: "I knew you'd come through, David. I told Elaine you would. This is the most wonderful thing you could ever do for me and my family, David, and I promise I'll never forget it. I can't wait to tell Elaine that you'll be there!" As he got to the door, he turned around, and with a slightly embarrassed smile, said: "God bless you."

As soon as Steve was gone, I remembered what the issue had been -- a wedding slated for Selichot evening. Oy. But, really, how could I say no? Well, I couldn't and now it seemed I hadn't. I'd have to explain it to Mel and the others. Maybe they'd understand. Maybe they – who worried about money more than anything else – would decide it was best to do whatever the Kurwitzes wanted.

Maybe not. But, suddenly I could see I'd done the only thing I could have done. It just wasn't worth fighting about and creating bad feelings. No, this was better, better than standing on some principle that meant nothing to anyone. The cantor would do Selichot. I'd be in New York and do the Kurwitz wedding. And I felt okay about it. More than okay. I felt good I could make someone so happy. Maybe I should do it more often. I hummed a little bit more of my *niggun*.

***

There was one person, of course, I couldn't seem to make happy at all.

Sharon eventually came home under the care of Dr. Melnick, the psychiatrist I'd met in the hospital. He insisted that Sharon give up all her medications, every last pill in her medicine cabinet and take only what he prescribed. Her job, he said, was to get well mentally and physically, so she had to walk every day outside for at least forty-five minutes, eat regular meals in the kitchen sitting down at the table, do all the things she had previously enjoyed – listen to music, watch television, read the paper, write. She was to come and see him for a fifty-minute session every other day for now. Cindy – despite some evident but unspoken new friction between her and Sharon -- was her driver for these one-on-ones with the shrink. And Sharon and I were to come in together for what he called "couples work" once a week until "things got better."

At home, Sharon had few visitors. Cindy would come like clockwork every other day, bearing stories and the latest gossip. Ari visited fairly regularly in the afternoon, after school, and was always gone before I got home. I had no idea what they talked about but I was grateful that he came.

Beyond Cindy and Ari, she was pretty much on her own. She had lost all contact with the "girls" from the office, although she never told me why. She certainly didn't have any friends in the congregation. And my attempt to "fix her up" with Donna, well…that hadn't been too successful either. The truth was: Sharon was someone who didn't "work and play well with others." Maybe the legacy of being the only child of parents who always warned her away from anyone outside the immediate family. Maybe it just was who she was.

In a sense, I was solitary now as well, at least in my own home. Having gotten used to having the place to myself while she was in the hospital, it was an adjustment to share it now with her. But really it didn't feel like sharing. Looking like the corpse she had almost become, gaunt and vacant, she wandered around the house, never acknowledging me unless forced to. Between sessions with the doctor, she made the occasional meal for herself, took long, steaming-hot showers, watched endless hours of TV, went to sleep early and stayed in bed until I left for the shul in the morning. For my part, after a short-lived return to our old bedroom while she was still in the hospital, I was now back to sleeping in the extra room.

What mostly seemed to occupy Sharon was her work at the computer, something that she did now for hours a day. This seemed to be the one element of Dr. Melnick's program that she did with any enthusiasm. When I begged her to tell me what she was so busy with, she told me sharply that it was none of my business. When I mentioned it to the doctor at one of our couples sessions, he said he'd suggested that Sharon do some journal-keeping to help get her thoughts and feelings in order. Whatever he or she called it, I could barely get to our shared computer anymore.

At one point, I did get on the machine long enough to compose a letter to our congregants, telling them the bare minimum about what had happened and asking their patience if I was at home more than usual helping to take care of my family. Although that seemed like the right thing to say, and I meant it when I wrote it, it never worked out that way. I simply wasn't able to take care of a family that seemed not to want my care anymore. And so, as she pulled further and further away, I replied in kind.

I went into the office for several hours every day, left the house whenever I could find an excuse and prayed for a congregational emergency on Thursday mornings so I could beg out of our sessions with the shrink. I was happiest when I didn't have to step around her, didn't have to struggle for words to say at the dinner table.

No idea really what my congregants thought about all this. Nobody seemed to want to talk to me about it. After all, if the rabbi's wife had taken an overdose of pills and ended up in St. Theresa's getting her stomach pumped – as everyone seemed to know -- and if she hadn't been out of the house in weeks that anyone could see, and if the rabbi himself seemed to be teetering on the edge, perhaps they ought to be just a little restrained and allow him and his family a little privacy. Perhaps.

***

Sharon and I were now near total strangers in the same house. About the only time we did speak was when we had to endure our joint therapy sessions. Between the long silences and bitter recriminations, it didn't take the doctor long to figure out there was little good left between us. When he asked us when was the last time we had enjoyed each other's company, we looked at each other quizzically. When he asked when was the last time we had 'made love,' Sharon laughed out loud.

So the doctor prescribed what he called "sharing days," times when we were to do something together just the two of us – go out for coffee, see a movie, dine together at a favorite restaurant. Although I tried at first to comply, Sharon -- not wanting to be blamed for sabotaging our assignment -- 'worked to rule,' obeying the letter but not the spirit of the doctor's law. Soon I stopped trying as well. So we went out for coffee, sat and stared at each other, checked our watches and, at the requisite hour, went home. We watched a movie on DVD, then went to our separate corners in the Siberian vastness of the house. We went out to dinner together, made occasional comments about the quality of the food or the service, then retreated to our separate bedrooms as soon as we got home again.

After a number of these assignments, Dr. Melnick suggested that, since we had "done so well," it was probably time to see if we could "rekindle our passion for each other." This would not be easy to do, he said, but if we could manage it, it might draw us closer together in other areas of our lives. When the doctor first broached the idea, I could see the pained look on Sharon's face. Before I could respond, she said: "No way. Can't do it."

Patiently, the doctor explained that, if we waited until we felt better about each other, it might never happen. "And one thing about physical intimacy," he said, "it often has the power to bust open a stopped-up relationship, like nothing else can. " Not the best image, I thought. It sounded like drain cleaner -- but I got the idea.

Sharon gamely argued some more until finally agreeing that she would go along with it one time and, if it was no good – as she was certain it would be – we wouldn't have to do it again.

Our window of opportunity: the week before our next appointment with the shrink. He wouldn't prescribe when. "Not good for romance," he said. (Romance?) It was up to us. So, as the days passed, I waited on Sharon and Sharon ignored me as before. Finally, the night before our next session with the doc, I said: "So, are we going to or not? We told the doctor we would. Are you willing to or not?"

"I'll do what I said I'd do. Come on, let's go," like it was time to wash the floors or re-organize the kitchen pantry.

And with that she marched up the stairs. Following behind her, I saw her pull her belt out of her pants and loosen up her shirt as she walked toward the bedroom. Staring off into nowhere, she went to the bed, pulled down the covers and turned out the light. As she yanked down her sweatpants and then pulled the covers back up over her nakedness, she said: "OK, I'm ready. Are you?" I was not. I thought of the infertile couples I had counseled over the years, how the men always complained they couldn't perform on cue. Didn't do much for romance, they said.

She said: "You'd better get yourself ready. Don't think I'm going to do that for you."

I tried my best, spooling through all my steamiest fantasies. Nothing doing.

After about five minutes, it was clear it wasn't going to happen. I opened my eyes. She was staring at me in obvious disgust. "I'm not surprised," she said. I guess I wasn't either.

That was the end of our "sharing days," and the end of our joint sessions with Dr. Melnick. From that point on, she refused to go. And I didn't complain. The result was predictable: worse than strangers now, we had become adversaries, no longer able to remember what had ever attracted us to each other in the first place.

***

The rockier my road at home, the more I turned to my growing spiritual life for strength.

I awoke every morning, immediately taking up my copy of the *siddur*, the prayer book, from the nightstand beside my bed and launched into morning prayers. I especially loved the ones called "daily miracles," the blessings that thanked God for the ability to see, to walk, to dress myself, all the little acts of starting a new day that might otherwise go unappreciated. I often found myself stopping with these prayers, looking out into space, losing track of time, losing track of myself. Then a wordless song would find its way to my lips and with no conscious intention, I would sing it quietly over and over. If only I could share this with my congregants. If only they could see what I saw, feel what I felt. I wondered if perhaps I could.

It was Friday evening early July, still bathed in bright sunshine even at that hour. At five minutes before our starting time of 7:30, I wrapped myself in my prayer shawl, took my copy of the *siddur* and headed out into the sanctuary. Stepping out from behind my lectern and down into the center aisle, I began singing the Hasidic melody I couldn't get out of my head. *Ya-ba-bim-bam, ya-ba-ba-bim-bam.* Quietly at first, then rising steadily to crescendo, I wordlessly invited my congregants to join me, raising my head and tilting it toward them as the refrain came around. And they did join in – or at least it seemed they did, until, after a while, I became aware that I was the only one singing. The others had stopped at some point and they were looking at me some confused, some concerned, some annoyed. I reached down as if adjusting my cufflinks but really snuck a peak at my watch, was stunned to see that we (I?) had been singing the same melody for almost half an hour. I looked up from my wrist, grinned sheepishly and then said, "Shabbat shalom everyone. Now that we're really ready to pray, let's begin our service on page 77."

With that, I drifted up the stairs to the lectern and launched into the prayers of the service, a chief with no braves, a captain with no crew.

Although at the end of services, I always went straight from the sanctuary to the social hall to greet everyone, on this lonely night, I pronounced the final blessing, then headed straight out the back door of the sanctuary and into my car. Couldn't get away fast enough.

As I pulled out of the parking lot and into traffic, I remembered there was something I had planned to do once I got home, something I had to check out once I was certain Sharon was asleep. In the days since she had come home from the hospital, Sharon had been passionate about one thing only – the writing she was doing at the computer. Now, suddenly, in the last few days, I realized she hadn't been at the keyboard at all. As consumed as she had been before, now there was nothing. What was going on? I had to see what she was doing and I didn't much care if it violated her privacy. To my way of thinking, she had pretty much lost that privilege, having used it not so long ago to make an attempt on her life.

Arriving back home, I crept quietly up the stairs and stood outside her room.
No light. I pulled the handle, opened the door a crack and listened. The quiet,
rhythmic sound of her breathing.

I climbed down the stairs and went searching on the computer to figure out
what she had been working on. I clicked on the icon marked "Sharon" to scan
her personal files, looking for a name that might be the mystery file.

At first, nothing unusual, the same titles I vaguely remembered seeing there for
so long. But then I noticed a new folder marked simply "Reb." What in God's
name was "Reb?" Rebel? Rebound? Reboot? I could see that the file was quite
large and that the last entry in it was a week and a half ago.

I double-clicked on it. A message came up "Enter Password." You're kidding
me. Sharon writing something she's protecting with a password? Since when
did she even know how to do that? So I tried everything I could think of – the
name of her elementary school, her mother's maiden name, all the passwords I
knew she used…Nothing.

I tried again. Our old telephone number, her social security number (I had
told her a million times never to use it but…who knows?), the password we had
invented combining our first initials together, "SAD777." Sharon and David –
sad, sad, sad.

I was now officially out of ideas. No way to open it, no way to enter. I was
locked out of her files, just as surely as I was locked out of her life.

***

With my new priorities at work – focusing on the essentials, avoiding the fruit-
less hours of emails, telephone calls, personal discussions, late-night meetings -- I
now had plenty of time to go for a run in the woods or to sit on a park bench in

town watching the men play checkers. I had given a thousand sermons on the importance of "stopping to smell the roses," but I'd always been in too much of a hurry to listen to my own advice. Now, as I went through the streets of town, I noticed the sounds of the birds, the way the clouds hid the morning sun and then suddenly opened to reveal its light, how a mother would speak softly to her baby in a stroller, calling out her name as if in song. For the first time in my life, I didn't miss a thing.

At the same time, it was clear not everyone saw things the way I did now: when a congregant flashed me a look of annoyance for declining to meet with her – as nicely as I knew how -- when Mel Grafman called to beg me to please, please be at the Executive Meeting that night, when members of my staff pursued me from the back door of my office to the car before I could pull away. For most of them, I could see, it was incomprehensible. I was incomprehensible.

But for me, it was a relief. I felt a whole lot more focused, more purposeful trying to get closer to God and not letting the minutiae of my former rabbi's life get in the way. Still, there were certain meetings and appointments I just couldn't avoid. That Thursday afternoon in late July featured one such unavoidable session, a meeting with the young couple I was marrying on Selichot evening at the Plaza in New York – Jared Kurwitz and Jamie Royce.

The young couple had come in from Manhattan for several days for a shower Jared's mother was making for the bride, so they had time to meet me in the middle of the day. Our appointment was set for 2:30 in the afternoon. I got to the office at two o'clock, took out my file marked "Weddings," gathered up the materials I would share with them – the readings, resources, music…everything – and laid them out on the coffee table.

At five minutes past three, they arrived hand-in-hand at my door, entering to apologies, the traffic had been impossible. Sitting across from them over the coffee table laden with my wedding materials, I gave them a good long look. Jared seemed remarkably unchanged from when I had seen him last – at his younger brother's bar mitzvah -- only taller, more chiseled. It looked like he must have been a regular at the gym. And Jamie was, well, striking – as beautiful as a model, just as Steve had said, blonde, tanned, and poured tightly into her outfit.

Together, they made an exceptionally handsome couple. I had a feeling they were also bright, successful in their careers and filled with a sense of entitlement.

Anyway, we made small talk for a few minutes and then I suggested we talk a little about the ceremony. I laid out their options. Jamie had strong opinions she wasn't shy about sharing. As a feminist, she said, there was no way she was going to circle around Jared in the service. She wasn't going to sign a *ketubah*, a Jewish wedding contract, unless it was egalitarian. And she wanted them both to break a glass at the end of the ceremony. Jared, for his part, was quiet; he just sat smiling and shaking his head, bemused. When I asked for his opinions, he said he knew better than to try to stand in Jamie's way when she had made up her mind about something. "If that's what she wants," he said, "it's better just to let her have it."

"Fine," I said, stifling the urge to take Jared by the shoulders and shake him hard. "As long as you both agree." I made some notes for myself and then said: "So, we've agreed there's to be no circling, a modern *ketubah* and you're each going to break a glass, yes?" They nodded.

"Good. So, let's move on. I want to learn a little bit about the two of you – how you met, what attracted you to each other, what makes you want to be together for the rest of your lives. Tell me the Jared-and-Jamie story."

Without looking at her husband-to-be, Jamie began to talk about how they met (introduced by friends), what they did on their first date (drinks at a bar in the Meat Packing District), when they knew they wanted to get married (on a Royce family trip to Jamaica in which Jared had been included), when they moved in together (about a year ago).

With nothing more than an occasional "true" or "right" or "uh-huh" from Jared, Jamie continued to detail their strengths (communication, she said, and unself-ishness), and their challenges (sometimes they argued over silly, petty stuff, she said, but they always got over it.) When finally she stopped, I turned to Jared and asked, "How does all that sound to you? How do you see your relation-ship?" To which Jared replied that he and she were pretty much in synch.

"That's great," I said. "It's great that you see things eye-to-eye." All the while, I kept thinking, Run, Jared, run. Get away from this girl as fast as you can.

Instead I said: "Okay, you say you sometimes argue about silly stuff. I guess every couple does. Tell me, what was the last thing you guys argued about?"

With that, the atmosphere in the room chilled. They looked at each other, visibly embarrassed. It was clear they hadn't expected to be having one of those discussions. This was not a therapist, after all; it was only the rabbi. For a while, there was silence, a silence that grew heavier the longer it continued.

Finally Jamie said: "Well, I'm not sure I really want to talk about it. It's kind of personal," as she tried her best to smile.

"Okay, fair enough," I said, ready to move on to a more comfortable topic.

"Actually," Jared said, "maybe, Jamie, it's not such a bad idea if we do talk about it. It couldn't do us any harm and I'm sure it'll stay private, right Rabbi, what we say in this room stays here, right? Like Vegas." He smiled bravely.

Before I could reassure them, Jamie turned to him – as if cornered – and said okay, fine, they could talk about it, but she didn't want it to get too personal. Some things were just private and nobody's business. Shocked at how quickly she'd retreated, I smiled at her and said: "Of course, you get to decide what feels comfortable and what doesn't. Just remember, the more honest you can be with each other here, the more we'll get out of our time together. So…tell me, what was the last thing you argued about?"

Again, Jamie jumped in: "It was about who was going to write the thank you notes for the engagement gifts we've been getting. I thought Jared should write the thank you notes to his family and I would write the ones to mine but Jared said he thought that was something the bride should do and he didn't think he should have to do any. So we did argue about that – but, in the end, we worked it out, didn't we, Jared? Just like we always do."

Jamie looked at me and then over at Jared. Jared didn't respond. Then he shifted in his seat, turned to face her directly and said: "Jamie, you know that wasn't the last thing we argued about."

She looked back at him, her eyes wide opened now, pleading "don't go there."

"The last thing we argued about was just last night and it had nothing to do with thank you notes."

She stared at him fiercely as though she might gouge his eyes out.

Jared looked over at me and, smiling a bit awkwardly, said, "Rabbi, it was about, well…it was about something intimate. I asked Jamie to do something and she didn't want to do it and I couldn't imagine why she wouldn't want to do something that would make me happy and, well, we got into a pretty big argument about it. And in the end, although we made up, we didn't really settle anything."

Jamie stared at her husband-to-be, stunned that they were having this discussion in the office of this rabbi she barely knew. She started to speak several times but each time she opened her mouth, she closed it again and said nothing. Finally, after a long, awkward silence, she turned from Jared to me and said: "Rabbi, you said before that we wouldn't have to talk about anything I wasn't comfortable with. Well, I'm telling you now that I don't want to discuss this. I'm not comfortable with it. Not a bit. So can we just move on to something else? Can we?" She was almost in tears.

"Of course we can," I said. "Of course."

And so we did. We talked for a few minutes about a variety of safe topics -- their shared interests, their plans for the future. We went through the motions for about ten minutes until I said: "Well, I think we've started an important discussion today we'll want to continue. So, when you know you're going to be in town next, let me know and we'll plan on getting together. Thanks to you both for coming in. And, Jared, say hi to your parents for me, okay?"

We shook hands, Jared looking like a child who knew he was about to be punished, Jamie looking positively ambushed, as I led them toward the door. "Have a good day," I said to their fleeing backs, noticing that, while they had come in holding hands, they were leaving as far apart as the narrow hallway would allow.

I had nothing else on my calendar for the rest of the day. Or at least I was pretty sure I didn't since I had misplaced my calendar earlier in the day and hadn't gone looking for it yet. Anyway, I headed home.

I wasn't all that hungry, although I hadn't had anything since a slice of dry toast in the morning. But I knew I'd better have something to eat or I'd wake up hungry in the middle of the night just like I had the night before. So I looked into the refrigerator and took out what remained from last night's dinner – a half-eaten hamburger and a baked potato. Standing at the open refrigerator door, I pulled each from its tinfoil wrapping, bolted them down cold, listening all the while for the telltale sound of Sharon's presence in the house.

Thankfully, I heard nothing.

So I trudged up the stairs to "my" bedroom. I lay on the bed in the semi-darkness, knowing it was hours too early to try to fall asleep. Pulling myself up into a half-lotus, I began to draw deep breaths through my nose and out my mouth but couldn't find any serenity. Too much "monkey mind."

Eventually I must have lain down and fallen asleep because somewhere in the early hours of the morning, I awoke. I had been dreaming, the dreams more real, more gripping than usual. This night, my dreams were about my old classmate from rabbinic school, Brad Solberg.

Brad had been a member of my class, bright, creative, sweet, slightly awkward. Brad was married to a pretty, little girl who taught yoga and carried her own mat with her wherever she went. Brad was always the first to read the latest book, the first to experiment with the new drug, the first to try, well…just about everything. There was even talk among some of our classmates that Brad and his wife spent their Saturday nights – while the rest of us were busy with a burger and a movie – at parties where guests were expected to throw off their inhibitions along with their clothing and their marriage vows. Nobody really knew quite what to believe.

What was clear was that Brad was slowly falling away from his studies, his teaching, his classmates, drifting more and more into a kind of netherworld inaccessible to anyone but himself. He came less and less often to class. When he did, he seemed to have one foot in and one foot out, speaking to no one in particular, dressed in some weird outfit. Eventually, we heard that Brad's wife had left town and returned to her family in Boulder and, at about that same time, Brad simply disappeared altogether.

Two weeks later, there was a story in the paper about a young rabbinic student who had been found walking nearly naked, barefoot, disoriented and confused, down the center lane of the interstate. When the authorities went to retrieve him, he led them on a chase up and down embankments and overpasses and eventually jumped from a bridge, breaking both legs in the fall. According to the article, the young man, Bradley M. Solberg, 24, was now resting comfortably in Good Shepherd Hospital.

A number of us had gone over to visit him but had been turned away -- it was never clear if by the authorities or Brad himself. A few days later, we heard that he had checked out. Nobody was really sure where he had gone. And no one ever heard from him or spoke to him again.

Through the years, I thought of Brad from time to time. Although we had never really been close, I was haunted by his descent into the void. I guess I had always thought of him as the most "God-intoxicated" person I had ever met – but also the most screwed-up -- and so his story seemed a kind of cautionary tale, reminding me not to stray too far from the straight-and-narrow of work, studies, family and responsibilities.

Anyway, Brad had now returned to me in dreams -- hovering in the air like a Marc Chagall figure, smiling at me as though he knew a secret he would share only if I agreed to join him. I was dimly aware of waking up after each dream fragment, tossing and turning, then returning to sleep where Brad waited for me again. Through that whole night, I just couldn't shake him. When, after the fourth or fifth such dream, awakening at 4:33, I decided to stay awake and see if I could elude Brad that way. But even half-awake, even there in the dim light that breathed into the room from the hallway, even there Brad continued to hover…and smile…and invite.

***

Next morning, as I sat down in the bedroom after my morning prayers and stripped off my sweaty clothes, I began to formulate a plan of attack for the day. I would go in to the synagogue, catch up on the most pressing items, then go to the park for a bike ride. Excellent. Then I'd come back home, do a little meditation in the backyard and make dinner for myself. Something light. If I felt up to it, I'd drop in at the religious school teachers' meeting tonight; if not, maybe just stay home and read. A good day and a good plan, it seemed to me.

I took my time in the shower, let it play on my body, turning it as hot as I could bear, focusing the spray on my achy lower back. Stepping out of the shower, I realized the phone had been ringing – probably for some time. Where was the answering machine when you needed it? I went over to the phone, saw it was coming from a "Personal Caller." OK, I thought, let's see who "Personal Caller" is. As soon as I heard her voice, I wished I'd ignored it. It was Lisa. I had been avoiding her since our…indiscretion. The truth was: I was uncomfortable speaking to her, uncomfortable thinking about her, uncomfortable with what we'd done, didn't want to be reminded of it. Our last communication had been a message I left on her machine that Sharon was ill and I wouldn't be coming on Mondays anymore.

"I'm glad you picked up," Lisa said. "I've been wondering if I'd ever hear your voice again."

I hesitated, said nothing.

"Please, David, don't hang up. I know you want to but please don't. Let's just have a normal conversation like old friends. Cause that's what we are, right, we're old friends who have a history together and who haven't spoken in a long time, so it's time to reconnect, okay?"

Slightly smiling, I said: "Okay, old friend, how are you?"

"Well, David, I'm fine, I guess. Everything's okay, except of course that you and I haven't really talked to each other since you tore out of my house that morning. And how about you, David? How are you?"

Ignoring the sarcasm, I said: "Well, actually, I'm doing pretty well. Don't know exactly why I should be. But I am -- probably more at peace with myself than ever. I wonder…does that make any sense?"

She paused for a long moment, then said: "Well, David, honestly, no…it doesn't. From where I stand, it looks like your life's a mess. And I think you're too smart not to know it. So how can you say you're at peace? You're living in a giant shit pile and you don't seem to think there's anything wrong. No, David, actually…it doesn't make any sense at all. I have no idea how you're coping. Who do you talk to when you…need someone to talk to? I know it's not me. I know I haven't heard word one from you in weeks and, frankly, knowing what I do about you, I can't imagine who it is if it's not me."

"Well," I said, "it's not you and I guess it's not really anyone. I honestly haven't felt the need. Actually, I seem to be doing okay by myself and, when I feel things getting a little out of control, I've been turning to, well, you know, a Higher Source and that's been enough for me."

"Ah, so that's it, is it? It's you and God now, on a first name basis? Sorry, David. I know you too well. You want to play at being some kind of mystic but I don't buy it."

I started to set the phone down. Didn't need a lecture from Lisa or from anyone else. I heard her fading voice calling from the receiver as I was just about to set it back down – but then I started to feel guilty. So I raised it back to my ear and said: "Lisa, I'm sorry you don't 'buy' it but it's true. It's for real. I've been trying to use all the negative stuff that's been happening to get a new start in life. You know I wasn't very happy with the way things were so I just I've been trying things a different way. I'm focusing more on what's important and trying to avoid all the stuff the makes me unhappy. So far it's been working okay."

"But David," she said, more desperate now, "I understand you cutting out the things about your job that you don't like and the toxic relationships. But, David, why would you cut me out? Of all the things in your life, I thought you and I were good. So, tell me, David, why did you cut me out? And don't hang up the phone. Don't hang up until you tell me. I think you owe me that much."

"Okay. You want the truth? The truth is that I realized something after Sharon's trip to the hospital. When I got home and the house was empty – there was no

Ari, no Sharon – when I got home and the house was really empty and it was just me, it suddenly hit me that I liked being alone with no one to answer to, no one to look after and no one to distract me."

"Distract you? Distract you from what?"

"No, that's not what I mean. I mean I like being able to do what I want when I want. Don't you see? If I want to read, I read. If I want to pray, I pray. If I want to run, I run. If I want to have dinner at three in the morning, no one's gonna stop me. I feel liberated. And the more I think about it, the more I realize that's what I need in my life. I need less time stuck in messy relationships and more time by myself."

"Messy relationships?" she said, as though smacked in the face. "You and I are a messy relationship?"

"No, no…that's not what I'm saying. Listen to me, Lisa, and don't get defensive. Listen, I appreciate everything you've done for me. I really do. I don't forget how much you've taught me. I don't forget how you took care of me when things were bad. And, the truth is: the night we were together, well that was probably one of the sweetest ever. But, Lisa, I can't stay there. It was just too weird. And too dangerous, much too dangerous. So I've moved on. I know I owe you big-time but that still doesn't mean I'm going to jump every time you call. I'm sorry but I have to be honest with myself and with you."

Honest I was. And I had probably put more words together in one conversation than I had since I found Sharon barely breathing on her bed weeks before. I hoped that Lisa, who probably knew me better than anyone else in the world, would understand. It took me a few moments of silence and a couple of times calling her name to realize that she had, at some point, hung up the phone on me. Another bridge in flames.

***

It was another Tuesday evening, a class on Jewish mysticism and Kabbalah – something I was pretty excited about. So, without notes, I began to explain about the Zohar and its purported author, Rabbi Simeon bar Yochai, about the 16th century mystics of Safed and the Kabbalah. I was kind of free-associating but it was okay because I actually did know something about the topic – and they seemed to be with me. At least, no one got up to leave.

After an intense hour-long session, I set out for home. First thing I did as I walked through the front door was head straight for the computer and check for Sharon's recent activity. Nothing new on "Reb." Still inactive.

I trudged upstairs, walked past Sharon's bedroom, entering my own room. I hadn't seen Sharon in a few days, hadn't even bumped into her in the kitchen or passed by her on the stairs. Like a ghost fading from the world, Sharon kept getting paler and less substantial until she seemed about to vanish altogether. Seized by an inexplicable desire to see her face, I opened the door to her room and peered in...

If this was sleep, it was the deepest I'd ever seen.

Sharon's eyes were closed. She lay under the blanket with only her bare feet showing out the bottom, a nearly drained bottle of Grey Goose on her night-stand alongside an empty bottle of Percocet. Her wrists, neck and face were ice-cold, tinged slightly blue, her pulse weak and faint, her breathing intermittent and shallow.

I tried to wake her, shaking her at first gently then more forcefully, but nothing... no flutter of eyelids, no blurted-out fragments of words. Just stillness.

It was clear. She had done it, exactly as she said she would – gotten drunk, then swallowed every last one of her pills and lay down to die. I guess it was no surprise. She hated her life, she always said. She wanted out. And this time, she warned, this time she'd get it right.

I picked up the phone and hit 9, then 1, then another 1, missing that simple sequence not just once but twice. Finally, I got through. "It's my wife," I said. She's in bed and she's cold and she's almost not breathing. Please, come as quick as you can."

***

The hospital staff was as sweet and comforting as could be. I heard someone say: "That's the rabbi." They held my hand, put their arms around my shoulders as if we were old friends and, when Sharon was pronounced, they told me the news in the gentlest whispers. I cried. What else could I do? They cried with me. The social worker sat with me for about an hour in silence and then suggested I might be better off going home, there was nothing more I could do there. Did I have someone I could call so I wouldn't have to be alone?

Who did I have? Lisa was out of my life. My father? Then it struck me – Ari. His mother is dead and he doesn't know it. I knew I had to call Ari at the Pontarellis' place, somehow find a way to tell him. Maybe he could meet me at home and we could comfort each other, or, at least, I could comfort him. Whatever… I had to call and tell him. Then it would be up to him.

I called the Pontarellis. "Yes, hello, this is David Chazen. I'm really sorry to call so late but I need to speak with Ari. It's very important. Actually, it's an emergency. Otherwise, I wouldn't call at such an hour."

Then, Ari on the phone, groggy: "Hello. Dad, is it you? What's going on? Do you know what time it is?"

"Ari, listen to me, I have talk to you. It's important. Can't do it on the phone. Stay right there, I'll be right over." And, before Ari could protest, I hung up.

I zoomed over to the Pontarellis, ignoring the posted limits along the way. Ari was waiting for me at the door, looking puzzled, stunned, frightened. Leaving the key in the ignition, I jumped out of the car, slammed the door and ran to him, took him by the shoulders, looked into his clearly petrified face and said: "Son, I have something to tell you, something really terrible. Ari, listen to me. Your mother took a whole bottle of sleeping pills and she drank almost a whole bottle of vodka and, Ari, listen, I'm sorry but this time she's really done it. I mean, she's… taken her life. And, Ari, I'm sorry. I'm so sorry."

Silence. And then the muffled sound of Ari crying so softly I could barely hear, perhaps wasn't meant to hear.

Then, "Oh my God, I can't believe it. This can't be real."

"Well, it's true, son, she's really done it this time. And there's nothing we can do about it except cry. So, if you want to cry, honey, go ahead and cry. It's really okay. I've been crying too."

That night we both slept in the bed in which Sharon and I had spent nearly all our married nights, until just a few months ago when our marriage had ended in everything but name. Now it was irretrievably over in every way. She was gone. I was a widower. A widower! I heard Ari tossing and turning, then I rolled over, put my head on the pillow and heard nothing else until morning.

***

I awoke the next morning, thinking "Yesterday my wife died," like that guy in the Camus novel I'd read as a teenager. She had taken a whole bottle of pills and as much of the vodka as she could get down, almost the entire bottle. Not a cry for help, not a plea for attention. This time, she really wanted to die.

I looked over at Ari, asleep with a pillow over his head, all balled up in the sheets and blankets, like a little boy. Best to let him sleep a little longer.

I knew somehow – from all the times I had counseled others – I had to get busy. There were 'arrangements' to be made. I called the folks at Beckers' Funeral Home. They told me how shocked they were, then said to leave everything to them. I should go do what I had to do.

What was that? I wondered. Exactly what did I have to do?

I called my father who let out a wail that pierced my heart. I asked him if he could make the calls to the rest of the family; I just couldn't do it myself.

Next I called Kelli and told her quite simply, without waiting for her inevitable meltdown, that Sharon had taken her life, and I needed her help in getting the word out to everyone in the community – everyone from the synagogue, my colleagues, the other synagogues in the area, the community people, everyone who would want to know. Oh, God, and Cindy. I almost forgot about Cindy. She would be devastated.

What next? Of course, I knew I'd have to make some decisions soon – when to have the funeral, whether to have it at the funeral home or at the synagogue, how many days of shiva…My head hurt. I couldn't think.

Minutes later the phone rang. It was Phil Becker, the patriarch of the Becker family, calling to offer condolences and to assure me that there was nothing they wouldn't do to help. "Nothing," he emphasized. I thanked him and said I knew I could always count on him.

"But," Phil continued, "I have to tell you, David, we do have a slight glitch, a little problem making the arrangements just yet. You see, the coroner's office is refusing to release the deceased, uh, Sharon, from the hospital until they have a look at her."

"An autopsy."

"Yes, an autopsy. But I'm sure it won't take long and we can get moving on this right away. I'm sure the sooner we take care of this, the better it will be for you, David."

I tried really hard not to think of autopsies. "Yes, of course."

"So, I'll call you when I've heard that they've released her. In the meantime, why don't you plan on coming over here this afternoon and we can take care of everything we have to do here. And, David, I want you to know, I want you to know that Beckers' will be taking care of everything, I mean the expenses, all of it, David. "

"Oh, no, Phil…" I sputtered.

"No, that's something we very much want to do. We all hurt so bad for you, David. Please let us do this."

Finally, after a few more refusals and a few more reassurances, I gave in and hung up after we had decided I would go over to the funeral home at one o'clock in the afternoon.

For the moment there was nothing to. I padded into the kitchen, scooped out coffee into the French press and started the water boiling, while I sat and slowly let it percolate through that this was for real, that Sharon really was dead, that I really was alone now.

I decided I had better wake poor Ari so he could go with me to the funeral home. I shook him, feeling heartless for dragging him from his slumbers. Ari looked around, confused. What was he doing at home again, and in his parents' room? Then I could see the light of memory slowly fill Ari's red-tinged eyes. I went to hug him and, remarkably, he let me.

"Oh, Ari, I'm so, so sorry. I so hurt for you." Then, incredibly, we rocked in each other's arms for a long time until, finally, I said: "I'm sorry I had to wake you but I need your help. I have to go to the funeral home this afternoon and I want you to go with me. Can you do that?"

"Yes, of course."

"Okay, get dressed, I'll make you some breakfast if you want and then we'll go over to Beckers' together. Okay?"

That afternoon, Ari and I drove over to the funeral home. The usual somber faces of the Becker family and staff more pronounced than ever, reminding me where the world "funereal" came from. Phil gave us both hugs. Ari cried into Phil's massive chest. I began to wonder what had ever made me think it was a good idea for Ari to come with me.

We sat together for a few minutes in Phil's small, spare office, Phil again saying how shocked he was, how he really couldn't believe it when he heard the news. "Such a beautiful girl," he said. "So much to live for. She really had it all – a wonderful husband, a terrific son, a successful career. Sure doesn't make any sense to me."

I said it didn't make sense to me either. Ari just sat still, visibly fighting back the tears. Then down to business. We decided in short order that we would do the service in the synagogue, in the sanctuary. As Phil had said, "no way we can accommodate everyone in our chapel here." I was emphatic that I wouldn't officiate or eulogize. Phil, slightly raising one eyebrow, asked who would do the service and who would do the eulogy. "The cantor will do the service…and who will do the eulogy? Well, I haven't actually figured that out yet…"

Without missing a beat, Ari said simply: "I will."

"No, honey, you can't do that. How can you be expected to speak about Mommy in front of all those people?" Me trying to save Ari from himself – as always.

"Why not? Not smart enough, not good enough with words? Maybe I'm no rabbi but I can do it, Dad. Don't worry, I know I can."

"I didn't mean that, Ari. I know you're capable of doing it. I would never doubt that. It's just I don't know if you can do it...emotionally. I mean how are you going to do this without, without breaking down? Have you thought about that?"

"So I break down. So what? I mean really, Dad, who's not going to get it if I cry a little at my own mother's funeral for God's sakes?"

I was stunned, and, I had to admit, impressed. Ari was right. Let him talk. Let him do it. He knew her as well as anyone, loved her probably more than anyone. Let him do it. That'd be fine.

I turned to Ari, seeing him suddenly more as a maturing young man than a petulant little boy and said: "You know what, son, you're right. You do it. You'll do it better than anyone else could."

"And when do you want to schedule the funeral, David?" Phil asked.

"I'm thinking maybe tomorrow in the afternoon. I think everyone who needs to come in from out of town will be here by tonight or tomorrow morning at the latest and, frankly, Phil, I don't want to wait. I just want to do it and get it over with."

Phil again raised an eyebrow.

"I mean...it's so difficult waiting. I think it would be better for everyone and more respectful of her if we did it as soon as possible. What do you think, Ari?" Ari agreed.

After we pinned down a few more practical details -- who should go in the limo, where and when and for how long should we sit shiva, when we should do minyan services each evening – Phil said: "Okay, one more thing we have to do, gentlemen. We have to go into the next room and select a casket. Are you ready?"

Phil looked at Ari who looked like he was ready to bolt. I said: "I think you and I can do this together, Phil. Ari, why don't you stay here and we'll be back in a few minutes."

"No, I'm coming with you."

I looked at Ari long and hard. "Right again," I said, "right again. Of course we'll do this together."

We settled on a simple wooden casket with a minimum of flourishes. "Simple is better," I said. Ari and Phil shook their heads in agreement. We got out of there in about ten minutes, all of us looking relieved. Finally, Phil said: "Don't worry about anything now, David. I'll take care of all the details. You just go home and leave it all to me." Thank yous all around, more hugs, then into the car.

At home, the answering machine was blinking rapidly, signaling urgent messages. I pressed 'play,' listened to two calls from congregants who were "shocked," then walked away and into my bedroom. I knew I just couldn't stand any more condolences. From downstairs, I could hear Ari playing the rest of the messages, one by one. I could picture him writing down the names and the phone numbers and the messages, patiently, one by one, on the yellow lined pad beside the phone.

In the late afternoon, the doorbell rang. I could hear the muffled sounds of Ari speaking quietly to a female voice, then someone busy doing something in the kitchen, silverware and pots clanking. At six thirty, Ari knocked on my door and said: "Come on, let's have some dinner. Mrs. Grafman left us something I just heated up. Looks like enough for about a hundred people. Come on. No point in starving ourselves."

After dinner and more calls that Ari fielded, I said: "I'm going upstairs to read and maybe see if I can fall asleep." After a futile stab at reading, I turned off the light and, without thinking too much about the day I had just lived through or the one I was about to have, I drifted off to sleep.

In the middle of the night, 2:14 a.m. according to the bright red digits of my clock radio, I was suddenly awake. I heard Ari breathing deeply beside me, soundly sleeping. I wondered if perhaps this was all Ari had ever wanted – to sleep in his parents' bed, something we had denied him as a child. Fine, I thought. He finally gets his wish. This way he'll get the sleep he needs. With that, I rolled over onto my side and returned to dreamless sleep.

***

The sanctuary was a sea of faces as Ari and I walked into the room, filled to over-flowing with the caring and the curious. I scanned the rows, saw my father and sister close to the front, thought I saw Lisa on the far side of the room, sitting with a few of her congregants and there, in a corner of the sanctuary, was Renee Pontarelli and her parents. Draping my arm around Ari's shoulders, I walked alongside him, reassuring him he'd do okay, he'd be okay. Ari looked down at his shoes, feeling for his notes in his jacket breast pocket every few seconds. Escorted by two ushers from Beckers, we walked -- two condemned men -- from my office to the front row of the sanctuary.

Vaguely, I felt the presence of hundreds of eyes behind me, heard the buzz as Ari and I settled into our seats, then the hush as the cantor ascended the steps to the pulpit to begin the prayers of the service.

The cantor's rich tenor quivered with emotion. Behind him, muffled sobs, noses blowing. I wondered at the depth of emotion around me. Was it real?

How? Sharon had had so little to do with these people, this place, rarely attending services after our first few years here, coming along with me for simchas and social occasions like a child forced to take her medicine. She was not a beloved "rebbetzin" – a role she rejected and a term she reviled. And I thought: she would have hated this.

Ari had taken the eulogy out of his pocket, had smoothed it out on his lap and was reading it over, as if cramming for finals. My mind wandered from Ari to the cantor to the people across the aisle, eventually to a parade of memories – our meeting at CityArtsRun, our first date at the club she loved in the city, the day we moved into our place on Holden, the day she "propositioned" me from her car on the highway. But then, inevitably, it lurched into images of her moping around the house in her pajamas in the middle of the day, the flare of her nostrils and the outrage in her eyes as she attacked me for being a pitiful excuse for a husband, until finally it all ended in the now-frozen vision of her pale face, almost blue, no longer breathing. This was how I'd always think of her, I knew, Sharon splayed out on the bed, looking like an extra in a horror movie.

More than anything, it all seemed so not really real -- not really my congregants crowded into the sanctuary, not really me sitting there in the front row, and certainly not really Sharon in that wooden box that sat at the front of the room.

Somewhere in the midst of this reverie, I realized the cantor had stopped singing. All eyes turned to me, expectantly. Instead Ari slowly rose from his seat. He looked around, as if searching desperately for someone to stop him before it was too late. Then he folded his pages back again and walked up to the pulpit. Without looking up at the rows and rows of semi-familiar faces, he began:

"Good afternoon." Not a sound in the room. Utter rapt silence.

"My mother's life was not an easy one.

Nothing ever went easy for her.

And she was lonely a lot of the time.

As a young girl, she was raised by parents – Holocaust survivors -- who taught her never to trust others, to rely on yourself, because you never knew, you just never knew what people were capable of.

She never had a brother or a sister, and her only really close girlfriend from school moved away when she started junior high school. So she walked to school by herself, ate lunch by herself, went home by herself. And, since both of her parents had to work to make ends meet, she came home to an empty house at the end of the day.

To her great credit, instead of feeling sorry for herself, she worked on enriching her life – with music and art and dance -- and with the pursuits of the mind, especially reading and writing. I wonder how many of you know she wrote poetry and short stories from the time she was thirteen years old. I'm betting not many -- because hers was a very private world, a world she would allow very few to enter.

My dad did for a long time. I know how much he loved her, how hard he tried to pull her out of her dark and lonely world and how hard she tried to reach back to him, even though it wasn't easy.

And I know how much she loved me. She didn't always say so – not in so many words – but she showed me in a hundred different ways every day. So I never had to wonder.

Still, in the end, me and my dad weren't enough for her. Her poetry and her stories weren't enough. No one and nothing was enough for her. We saw her – my dad and me – sinking deeper and deeper into sadness every day.

It was so hard for us, because we loved her and we knew we were failing her. And it broke my heart. It broke our hearts as we watched her drift away from us into a place full of sadness and pain.

Now she is gone and she is not coming back. And all we can do is cry."

For the first time he looked up.

"But maybe we can, maybe we should do more than cry. Maybe we can look around sometimes and see the sad and lonely people around us. Maybe we can reach out to them and care for them and make them feel they're important, that they matter to us. Maybe then they won't be driven to do something desperate, something tragic like my Mom. And, if we can do that, if we can help them believe that life is worth living – even when it's sometimes really sad and painful – then that's probably the best tribute we could ever pay her. And don't we all owe her that? Don't we?"

With that, he picked up his notes and sat back down back beside me in the front row. I looked at Ari, seeing someone I had never seen before. Then, kissing him on the top of his head, I said: "I am so proud of you, son."

The rest of the day was a blur, a fast forward dance in black and white -- the casket, accompanied by eight friends, rolling out the back of the sanctuary to the hearse; Ari and I escorted out of the sanctuary and into the limo as the crowd returned to their cars; the mostly silent ride to the cemetery, my arm around Ari all the way; the lowering of the casket into the ground; the heavy thud of earth on the casket lid; the quiet ride home; the washing of the hands at the front step; the interminable hugs, kisses, tears and awkward words of condolence; the compliments to Ari on his eulogy; the evening service with worshipers jammed into every corner of the house. And all the while, everyone eating, drinking coffee, telling stories and laughing, until finally, at about 9:30, after my father and sister said their goodbyes and returned to the hotel, the house emptied out and only Ari and I were left.

Standing in the kitchen, leaning over the counter, I looked at Ari and said: "I was blown away by you today, blown away by what you said...and the way you said it – absolutely blown away. I mean it, Ari. It was perfect; no one could have done better. She would have been proud of you. I know I am, so very proud."

"Thanks, Dad. But, really, it just kind of wrote itself. I mean, I sat down yesterday and the words just seemed to come by themselves – probably the same way you told me the words of your sermons sometimes do. Anyway, I hope everyone heard it."

"Well, of course they heard it. Didn't you hear how quiet it was in there? Didn't you hear from everyone all day telling you how amazing it was?"

"Sure, but that doesn't mean they really got it, or that they'll remember it...or that they'll actually do anything about it, you know, like, change their ways."

I reflected for a moment on my own experience sermonizing to these same people through the years, thought perhaps I had complained about them to Sharon in exactly the same words – and wondered who had stolen away our impossible child and left this wise and mature creature in his place.

"Well, that's a lot to ask. I mean, for most people..."

"Right, but if they don't, if all they do is compliment me on how well I spoke, then they're missing the whole point, aren't they?"

"Of course, Ari. Of course you're right. But let's give them the benefit of the doubt. Let's hope maybe they'll be a little nicer to each other in the future..."

With that, I slid around to the other side of the kitchen counter, reached out to Ari and hugged him. Ari said quietly: "Thanks, Dad." And then: "I think I'm going to bed."

"Goodnight, son. Goodnight. I love you."

He started to respond, then simply nodded his head up and down and started up the stairs. But before he had gotten half-way up the staircase, I took a big breath and called out to him, "Ari, could you come back for just a minute. I want to, I want to say something to you. I know you're tired but, could you give me a minute. It's important."

Looking confused, he walked back down the stairs toward me. I pointed to the sofa, motioned for him to sit down beside me.

"Ari, listen, I want to tell you a story. It's a story about you, Ari, you and me from a long time ago. Ari, do you remember when you were a little boy, we used to go down the shore for two weeks every summer? Well, one year, when you were about two years old and barely walking on your own, we were down on the beach on blankets. I was reading. I don't know what your mother was do-ing. But suddenly I looked up and you were gone. I looked all around for you. Couldn't find you anywhere. And, Ari, I went nuts. I mean I went completely crazy. I ran up and down the beach in every direction, calling out your name. I ran into the water and started looking there. My head was filled with crazy, awful thoughts. You'd been kidnapped. You were under the water. You were gone, horribly gone and we'd never see you again. And then your mom called out to me. She had found you a bit further up the beach, completely calm, just checking things out. I remember running over to you and calling out your name and holding you so tight I almost crushed you – and you looking up at me with a little smile on your face, completely unaware of the terror you had put us through.

Ari, I have to tell you: that really scarred me, scarred me forever. And here's the thing. Later on, much later on, when you grew up, when you were at school, when you became a teenager, every time you went out with your friends and wouldn't tell me where you were going; every time you disappeared after school and we didn't know if or when you were coming home; and when you missed school and we had no idea where you were and when you…when you moved out of our house to the Pontarellis, Ari, I have to tell you: it felt the same way it felt on that beach. It felt like I was losing you. It felt like I would never see you again. And all I wanted to do was scream out your name and hold you and never let you out of my arms.

I know you didn't understand that, Ari. Really, how could you? I know to you it must have looked like me being controlling and trying to, I don't know, to limit your freedom and stop you from growing up and being your own person. And I know you hated that. But, Ari, it was never about me not trusting you. It was just me being so afraid I was going to lose you. I loved you so much, love you so much, Ari. And, after everything that's happened, I just need to ask you to accept my apology – I guess that's what this is – and forgive me for being such a crazy, over-protective parent. But know, Ari, that it was always out of love. That's all it ever was. It was always just because I love you so much and don't ever want to lose you. And that's the way I feel right now. I just don't want to lose you, Ari.

So, it's okay if you stay with the Pontarellis as long as you need to, and grow up the way you want to, the way you need to. I won't interfere. I promise. Just don't disappear, son. Don't disappear. Because that I just couldn't bear. Especially after today."

His eyes wide, he just nodded his head, looking straight up at me. Then he turned and gave me a quick hug, broke away, then came back for a longer hug, a tighter hug and said, very quietly: "I'm not going anywhere, Dad. Promise."

***

The phone rang at precisely eight o'clock, Joan Grafman, Mel's wife, on the line -- words of condolence, an offer of help. What did I need? Food? Did anyone need a ride back to the airport? What could they do for Ari? Did I need to be driven anywhere?

As soon as I set the receiver down, another call much like the first. And so it continued through the morning. After about an hour reciting the same answers – thanks, I was doing okay, I didn't really need anything right now but I'd be sure to let them know if I did, I thought there was probably enough food for dinner and for everyone at minyan this evening (and probably for the entire community for the next six months, I thought but never said.)

Against my better judgment, I had said it was okay to begin *shiva* at two in the afternoon. The thought of having a house full of people from so early in the afternoon to what, nine? ten? It was too much. What had possessed me?

I headed downstairs to the kitchen, got myself coffee and something to eat (no shortage there!) Then, throwing on shorts and a sweat suit and gym shoes, I headed out for a run (proscribed during mourning, I knew well, still…), closing the door quietly so as not to wake the still-sleeping Ari.

It was a beautiful mid-summer day – warm, sunny, clear. I checked my watch and started out along my usual route.

I moved quickly, smoothly, but didn't miss anything along the way – the houses and cars, the people walking their dogs, the shingles that had blown off roofs in the last storm, the children playing in their yards. The world just keeps on going, without much of a hitch, once we're gone, I thought. As of two days ago this world had a place in it for Sharon Chazen. Now she was gone. And everything looked just about the same. Everything would continue on. I would continue on although I wasn't at all sure what that would look like now.

I picked up the pace of my run, moving now as fast as I could. After a while, my thighs ached, my shins screamed and my chest felt like it was going to explode. But it had been a while since I'd really let it out and, in a strange way, it felt good. As I reached the end of the route, I slowed down, gasping for breath, letting the tension ease in my thighs, the bright pain melt from my shins. I continued to walk for another few blocks, then turned the corner and was back on my own street again. Time to go home, shower, change and prepare to meet the onslaught.

I had barely finished showering and dressing when the doorbell rang. It was Donna, newly and publicly separated from Les, bearing something in a bright orange casserole dish. Though it was still fairly early in the morning, she was dressed as if for an evening out. She stood contritely at the door, waiting to be asked in.

"Good morning, David. How are you, my friend? I mean, really how are you? May I come in? I know it's early but…"

"Of course, of course, forgive me…come on in."

Stepping over the threshold of the door, she set the dish down on the front stairs, leaned toward me, smelling of Chanel Coco – the same scent Sharon had always worn – and offered her open arms to me. "Come here. Give me a hug. I think you need it. I know I do," she said. She hugged me tight and long, letting go only when I finally broke the embrace.

"Oh, David. I am so sad for you. I can't imagine how hard this must be. You must feel so lost and alone. So, look…I'm just coming by now to make sure you have something to eat…and then I'm coming back later when everyone else is here. But I want you to know that you can count on me for whatever you need. You know you have a friend in me so…whatever you need, you just let me know and I'll make sure you get it. Understand?" She smiled.

"I do, Donna, I do…And, honest, I won't hesitate. I'll call if I need anything. You can count on that," I stammered.

She looked at me tenderly, then spreading her arms open to me again, said: "Come here, David. Come here. You know how much I care about you." A quick hug, then she slipped back out the front door.

That afternoon, just before two, I heard talking outside the front door. They were congregating there – who knew how many? -- waiting for the official start of shiva. At two o'clock precisely, the doorbell rang; in came about a dozen women from the synagogue, among them Donna who immediately took charge of setting the table, organizing the food and the house. This she continued to do throughout the afternoon and evening until the last of the many visitors had left at 9:45 that night.

***

The week of *shiva* -- the longest of my life -- was winding down. The crowds, the noise, the food…it was all finally ending. It had been even harder than I had imagined. The only saving grace was the time I'd taken each day to run outside in the sunshine, to read, to talk to Ari – who seemed, at least for this one week, to be back in the house and in my life again.

On the seventh and last day of mourning, I woke Ari up from a deep sleep and the two of us took a walk around the block before breakfast, symbolizing our re-entry into the world. As I walked alongside my prodigal son, out in the bright sunshine, I felt strangely invigorated, freed from captivity, even if it was the captivity of well-meaning friends and family. It was time to go back to work, to the synagogue, back to my real life. It was time to "move on" whatever that might mean.

I got to the synagogue early, before anyone was there, closed the door to my office, sat down at the desk and surveyed the mound of mail Kelli had placed there. Methodically, I sorted out the seemingly important from the trash, opened whatever seemed essential and began to build a small pile of letters for follow-up. Then I swiveled to the computer screen and opened my inbox, wincing as I saw 343 emails to review. (How is that even possible?) Outside my door, I heard the office begin to stir; I decided to go out and face my "comforters."

They were lavish in their condolences, all of them. They felt so bad for me, Sharon was such a good person, they couldn't imagine how hard this was for me, was there anything they could do? Coffee? Danish? Cake? Maybe it would make me feel better?

"No," I assured them, "I've certainly done enough noshing this last week. But, you know what, a cup of coffee would be great." They knew how I took it. I said thanks then returned to my office and tried to figure out how I was ever going to get back up to speed again. Of course the truth was: I hadn't been "up to speed" even before Sharon's death, hadn't been "up to speed" for months beforehand, still…

I looked at my email, then – on a whim – called my father who had gone back home to Florida on the fifth day of *shiva*. No answer. I decided to call home to see if Ari was around. No answer there either. I guess I just felt like talking to someone. I thought for a moment about calling Lisa but, then remembered our last conversation. Probably I owed her an apology. In fact, I was sure of it. But it just wasn't in me right now.

Needing to hear a human voice, I began listening to voice mail messages. Naturally, they all began with condolences. I tried to move through them as quickly as possible, doodling on a notepad, then realizing I hadn't been listening at all, no idea what the caller was saying. This was pointless. What now?

There was absolutely nothing on my calendar, nothing I needed to do. And so, without really thinking it through, I got into my car, went home, upstairs to the bedroom, turned off the lights and pulled the covers over my head. "What am I doing here?" I wondered aloud?

And, with that in my head, I fell asleep. It was 11:30 in the morning.

I awoke to the sound of the doorbell ringing repeatedly. Grabbing my glasses, I looked at the clock – 8:05 p.m. it flashed. I had slept away almost the entire day! Jumping out of bed (where was Ari?), smoothing out my clothes and hair, I moved quickly toward the front door. Got to stop that racket.

Through the glass pane in the door, I could see it was Donna -- dressed (surprise, surprise) in black jeans and a black sweater, Donna with a bottle of wine in one hand and glasses in the other. I opened the door. She smiled at me, stretched her arm out to me, offering the bottle: "Beware of Jews bearing gifts." I could see that she wasn't wearing anything beneath her cable-knit sweater. Was I not supposed to notice?

"So…may I come in?"

I escorted her into the family room, trying to figure out if I should offer her a seat, if I should sit myself. Eventually we both sat down, Donna set the bottle and glasses down on the coffee table, turned to me and said: "David, I've been so worried about you. I know what happens. As long as *shiva's* going on, the house is filled with people and then, when it's over, the house gets quiet and empty. Am I right? And you get lonely…and you need company…and, well, I thought it might as well be me. I'm on my own now too since Les moved out; I'm sure you know that. So here I am with my bottle of wine – and a pretty good one too, from Les's private stash. I figured maybe you and I could just talk and enjoy the wine and just…have a nice evening. I'll bet you haven't had one of those in a very long time, have you?"

Struggling mightily not to let my glance slip down below her face, I said: "I certainly haven't."

"Well, David, you deserve it. And I guess I do too. So tonight, let's make a promise to ourselves, shall we? We won't talk about the synagogue and we won't talk about my marital troubles and we won't talk about poor Sharon. We can talk about anything else – but nothing that's going to make us feel shitty about our lives. Okay? How about tonight we just talk about stuff that makes us feel good." She smiled, opened the bottle, poured a full glass for herself and another for me, handed me mine, raised her own to clink against mine and said: "Here's to things that make us feel good. We've earned them, both of us, haven't we, David?"

There wasn't a whole lot of subtlety to Donna's act. I knew where it was headed – if I let it, if we kept talking, kept drinking. I knew for certain it would be a mistake. Here I was only days after my wife's death, drinking with a completely unpredictable – probably unstable -- woman, a congregant, separated but not yet legally divorced from her husband, a woman who liked to enjoy herself and who liked to talk about it afterward. No, this would certainly be a serious mistake.

Then I thought, well...maybe we'd just finish the bottle and then say good-night. There was no harm in drinking a little good wine; no harm in a little conversation. So we drank and we talked and she moved over next to me on the sofa, started gently rubbing my arm, slid her thigh up against mine. I thought: We're both adults. We're both unattached. I haven't had any loving in months, the better part of a year. And, if I did it with Lisa when I was married, why shouldn't I do it with Donna now?

The bottle was now empty. Donna took me by the hand and led me silently up the stairs to the bedroom where she undid the buttons on my shirt and said with a smile: "Why don't you take care of the rest, okay?" She stood up, lifted her sweater up over her head and I saw what I'd been trying not to look at all night. She shimmied out of her jeans, looked over at me and said: "Come on, you first." And then, as I removed the last of my own clothing, she took her thumbs, hooked them on either side of her panties – black, of course – and stepped out of them. As if she had all the time in the world, she moved over to the bed, lowered herself on top of me and proceeded to rock back and forth gently, slowly. Tilting her head slightly back, she took control. After a few minutes, she let out a hungry yowl and then was quiet.

I climaxed just after her, without a sound, then dropped off to sleep.

***

It was a beautiful September day, the summer still burning brightly, unwilling to let go and give way to autumn. High in the upper seventies, bright sunshine. I went out to pick up my morning newspaper, filled my lungs with air and said, echoing the words of the prayerbook, "Thank you, God, for returning my soul to me."

It was only a few weeks after Sharon's death. Ari had gone back to the Pontarellis, although he had left the house with a hug and a promise – since fulfilled -- that he would come by regularly. I was seeing Donna almost every night, although I wondered how long before it became common knowledge, if it hadn't already. I was running longer, faster and better than I had since I ran for my high school track team so many years ago. And when it came to condition of my soul, there I felt a new but wonderful sense of calm at the heart of everything. After all the years of feeling like a hypocrite -- advocating for mindfulness while ignoring it myself – I felt that my "walk" and my "talk" were finally in sync.

It was Shabbat morning – and I was ready for it, really ready, not just to act out a part but to really throw myself into it. I had done all my prep work the day before -- chanting Torah, studying the text so I knew it from all angles. It was the Shabbat just before High Holy Days – Rosh Hashanah was coming up on Friday evening -- and there was time for everything that mattered, time for prayer and study and discussion, time for being with my community and with God.

My chanting of the Torah portion went smoothly. And the Torah discussion, a serious look at the preaching of Moses to the Israelites just before they entered the Promised Land, spoke to my own heart. It was quite a morning. Afterwards, about half of my little group remained in the chapel, crowding around me, hugging me, thanking and congratulating me on a memorable morning. I thanked them in turn, then slipped away as smoothly as I could. Other fish to fry.

I checked my calendar. The rest of the day was – thank God! – all mine. No obligations, no responsibilities. I knew what I would do, how I would use this wonderful gift of an afternoon and evening just before the High Holy Days, tending to my own body and soul, seeing if I could somehow get myself ready for the coming Days of Awe.

I returned home, changed into shorts and a T-shirt, treated myself to a light lunch of yogurt and berries and then, with a bottled water clipped to my belt, set out by car to Mt. Joy. By now, it was early afternoon. The sun was almost at its peak in the sky. Slathering myself with sunblock, a baseball cap on my head, already dripping with sweat, I set out for my hike up the mountain.

Looking up, I could barely see the peak atop a path that disappeared in the still-lush growth of the late summer. I knew from experience that it would take at least two hours going up, that I would need to stop along the way a few times for water and rest, and that when, finally, I reached the summit, it would be faster but almost as hard on my knees and shins for the two hours coming back down.

I also knew that, if I approached it in the right spirit, I would get more than a great work-out -- if I could just get my head in the right place, if I could just open up my heart.

I didn't look at my watch as I began, didn't want to know how slow or fast I was moving. I had nowhere to go and nothing to do except keep my eyes and ears open to the world around me, to drink it all in. I took my time, stopping regularly for swigs of water along the way.

I had taken a little pocketbook edition of Psalms in Hebrew and English. Stopping regularly to read my favorite ones in both languages, I asked God to let the words speak to me. There was no one else there, no one else crazy enough to be out in the mid-day sun, so I read aloud, at full throttle and without a trace of self-consciousness.

There was nothing but the placing of one foot in front of the other, nothing but the looking and smelling and savoring. I felt like a man in love -- in love with that mountain, with the world, with God.

When finally I got back down to the bottom of the mountain, the sun was dipping down towards the horizon, bathing the world in an orange-pink glow. I rewarded myself with my last couple of sips of water as I sat panting on the hood of my car in the now-empty parking lot.

The air inside the car was fiery hot. Hoping to cool things down just a little bit before driving home, I opened up the car door, rolled down all the windows and waited for the air to circulate and the temperature to drop. Immediately, I heard my cell phone paging me with its insistent call from the front seat. Of course, I thought, that's why I felt so peaceful this afternoon – no calls. No wonder it had felt so good.

Okay, let's see who's been looking for me. I pushed the voice mail icon on the phone and, then, with the name "Steven Kurwitz" on the dial, my glorious idyll came to a sudden and screeching halt. Oh my God, I thought, as my stomach leapt up, this isn't the evening of the Kurwitz wedding in New York City? I can't be that stupid, can I?

I looked at my calendar just as I had looked first thing in the morning before I left for services. No, nothing scheduled after Shabbat services. The day was mine; it belonged to me. But then why was Steve Kurwitz calling me on a Saturday late afternoon? That didn't make any sense. I went back to the calendar. What was the date of the Kurwitz wedding? I did a search for it and there it was – Sunday, September 24, the next day, at eight in the evening at the Plaza in New York.

Then it all came flooding back. I remembered the conflict with Selichot, Saturday evening. I remembered how I didn't want to officiate at first but how I'd finally agreed to do it. So it couldn't be tomorrow. It must have jumped on my cell phone's calendar from Saturday to Sunday – no idea how. Oh my God. Oh my God! -- what must be going on at the Plaza, with the starting time drawing near and me not there? And what can I possibly do now with the service set to start in what, like a half-hour, the city at least an hour and a half away and me in sweaty running clothes?

My mind raced over every possible thing I might say to Steve Kurwitz while they all awaited my arrival in their tuxes and gowns. Was there maybe time to get into the city, even if I'd be terribly late? No way, too many miles, too late in the day. Was there anyone who could substitute for me last minute who wasn't far from the hotel, a colleague who could get over there in a hurry and fill in? But then, they wouldn't know the bride and groom and, and…oh my God. This really is a disaster!

My mind raced faster, playing out possible dialogue in my head. I picked up the phone, dialed Steve's number and before Steve could finish asking: "Where in God's name are you?" I said: "Steve, before you say anything, I want you to know that I'm okay. But I've just had the most harrowing experience."

I went on talking, talking right over Steve, talking without pausing, knowing that, if I stopped for a moment, Steve would pounce and it would all be over.

"Steve, I've just lived through a nightmare. And, oh my God, I'm so sorry I'm not there with you but I'm glad just to be alive. All I can remember is that I was walking on Mt. Joy after services, just before I was going to pack up the car and come into the city. I was going for a short walk on the mountain when these guys came up to me, three of them, and asked me did I know what time it was, and then they jumped me and they had me on the ground and they were kicking me and, Steve, I must have passed out because when I came to, they were gone and my wallet was gone and every part of me was aching and I was bloody and really messed up something awful. I don't know if I broke anything but I know I've got to get to a hospital and I've got to call the police but as soon as I came to, I thought about you and the kids, and, oh my God, Steve, I can't even imagine what you must be going through there. "

There was a long pause. Strangely, Steve did not speak. So I went on.

"Obviously, there's nothing I can do right now. I have to get to a hospital and there's no way, even if I set out now, that I could get to Manhattan in time anyway. Oh, Steve, I'm so sorry. I don't know what else to say, but I'm really, really sorry."

With an audible mix of anger, distrust and pity, Steve said: "Alright, David, I'm glad you're okay. I really am. But now what are we supposed to do here? Everyone's ready to start. Everything's in place except the rabbi. Who's supposed to do our ceremony for us? What are we supposed to do now if you aren't here to do it?"

I had an answer for this too.

"Here's what I've been thinking. Did you invite the Judge and Nancy to the wedding? Is he there?"

"The Judge" was Sam Silverberg, a member of Emmanuel and a family friend of the Kurwitzes. As a justice of the peace, Sam had done hundreds of weddings over the years, even – as he so liked to tell anyone who would listen -- kept his robe and wedding service materials in his car just in case he was needed. "Marrying Sam," as he liked to call himself, could do the ceremony. He even knew the groom if not the bride. It wasn't the best solution but it was a solution, perhaps one that could get us through this in one piece.

There was a pause on the other end. Then Steve said: "But, David, you told me you needed special permission, that you have to be registered in Manhattan if you want to do a wedding here. How do we know Sam is registered? How do we even know he can do this?"

"I'm sure he can," I said. "He's done lots of New York weddings over the years so he must have a registration number. And, if he doesn't, Steve…and I don't like to have to suggest this but we could do it if there's no other choice…he could do the ceremony and then he could bring the license home to me and I could sign it tomorrow and no one would ever have to know that I hadn't actually done the ceremony myself."

"Seriously?" Steve blurted out.

"No, wait. Hold on a moment. I know it's not the best thing but it's an answer and there's not a whole lot of choice right now. Look, Steve, I know you're upset, I know you are. And I don't blame you. But here's a way out of this. I think Sam can do it and by the end of the day, the kids will be married and you can party and have a great evening and it'll all be more than okay. And I'm sure I'll be okay too when they get me all bandaged up and everything."

"Yeah," said Steve, "yeah, I'm sure you'll be okay," remembering he was supposed to feel bad for the rabbi's "injuries."

"Go talk to Sam right now and, if you can get him to do it, you can start the ceremony just about on time and you can explain to everyone afterwards what's happened to me but for right now, that doesn't matter. Go do what you have to do to get this thing moving, okay? And call me, call me as soon as you speak to him, and let me know everything's alright. I'll keep my phone on, even in the emergency room. Oh, Steve, I'm really sorry about this, really, really sorry."

"Yeah, okay, I know. I'll speak to Sam and I'll get back to you. And, ah, David, I hope you feel better."

Yeah, me too, I thought. I hope I feel better too.

Instead I said: "Give a special mazel tov to Elaine and the bride and groom and everyone there for me. Will you remember to do that, Steve? Thanks."

***

I waited at home through the evening for a call from Steve that never came.

That night I slept in spurts, dreaming on and off of taking a high school physics exam I hadn't studied for. I awoke for good at 5:30, aching to know what had happened at the Plaza the night before, knowing I couldn't call the Judge at that hour. Finally, at 7:45, when I could stand it no longer, I dialed Sam's number and waited six rings until Nancy answered, huskily: "Who is this?"

"Nancy, it's me, David. I'm really, really sorry to be calling so early but, please, I've been waiting all night to hear about the wedding. Did it go okay? Did everything turn out alright?"

"Yes, it was lovely," she said. "But here, I'll let you speak to Sam."

By now, Sam knew who it was on the other end. "Good morning, David. First, I want you to know that everything went beautifully, if I may say so myself. I'll tell you all about it, but before I go on, just tell me if you're okay. Everyone is worried sick about you. Did you go to the hospital? Are you at home? Are you alright?"

"Am I alright? Yes…yes, I'm fine," I said, remembering a fraction of a second too late not to be surprised at the question. "I went straight home after I came to and I, uh, I decided I didn't need the hospital after all. I just cleaned myself up all and bandaged myself and got myself to bed. But tell me about the wedding. That's much more important."

"Well, the wedding was great. Actually, it was wonderful. Maybe I'll have Nancy tell you about it, David, I don't know if I should be that immodest."

"No, Sam, you tell me. You've got my permission to be as immodest as you want."

"Alright," said Sam. "Well, you know I always have my robe and my manual with me, like I'm always telling you," he said conspiratorially. "So I ran down to the parking guys and had them let me in the car and I got out the robe and the service and I ran back upstairs and got the bride and the groom to sit with me for a few minutes and tell me about themselves. I guess people must have been getting pretty jumpy – and I won't even tell you about Steve and Elaine – but eventually we got started, at maybe about 8:30 or so. Anyway, I started off by telling everyone that you were hurt and that we'd all be praying for your recovery but then I just started. You know, David, I guess I have a sort of regular spiel that I do and, of course, I've known Jared ever since he was a kid so, even though I didn't really know the bride that well, I kind of faked it and everyone told me it was great. Got to tell you, David, it must be watching you through the years, but I just knew what to say and I think I did one of the biggest mitzvahs of my life."

"God bless you," I said and really meant it.

"Anyway," Sam continued in machine-gun fashion, "after Jared – and Jamie! -- broke the glass, it was like everyone just cut loose and, I don't know, maybe it was just such a relief after everything that had happened, but I'm not sure I ever saw a better party. I mean, everyone was up all night dancing and nobody sat out the horas and the speeches were cute and Steve and Elaine were obviously happy and all around, I gotta tell you, I felt really good about it."

"God bless you," I said again.

"But, David, tell me about you. Steve said you got mugged? Mugged? On Mt. Joy? How weird is that?"

"Well, yeah, I guess you could call it that, at least that's what I think it was. You know, I don't really remember it very clearly. I just remember being on the trail and these three big guys approaching me and then I came to and I was all beat up and bloody and kind of hurting everywhere all over."

"And you didn't go to the hospital?"

"No, I thought I would but eventually I just decided I'd go home and take care of myself."

"And what about calling the police? You did that, right?"

"Well, I haven't yet. And, to be honest, Sam, I'm really wondering if that's such a good idea. I mean, I don't seem to have any broken bones and I don't think I'll be out of work at all, so I'm thinking maybe it's better if I don't get the police involved in this. To be really honest, I'm afraid if I do, I'll have to deal with these three big animals and, believe me, I don't ever want to see them again! Anyway, there'll just be forms to fill out and questions I don't really know how to answer and, in the end, they probably won't even find these guys anyway, so what's the point?"

"But what about your wallet? You know you have to call the credit card companies and the DMV for your license and you're going to have to tell them what happened and they're going to want to know if you filed a police report."

"Yeah, I'm sure you're right," I said, thinking quickly. "But, maybe I'll figure out some other story for the card companies. Anyway, I don't think I want the police involved."

"Believe me, David -- and you should because this is something I really do know about – you should file a police report. It's your best protection. I think you're foolish if you don't. But, hell, it's your choice, I guess. The important thing is that you're okay. You are okay, aren't you, David?"

"Yeah, I'm alright, a lot better than I thought I'd be. Truth is I'd just like all this to go away and pretend it never happened. In the end, the only thing that matters is that the bride and groom got married and the Kurwitzes are happy and, thanks to you, Sam, it looks like this story has a happy ending. Thank you so much for pitching in like this. Do you know: the first thought I had when I was conscious again on Mt. Joy was, thank God Sam is there. He'll do a super job and everything will turn out okay. So, *kol ha-kavod*, congratulations, Sam. As for me, I'm just going to go back to bed and nurse my wounds for a while. I'm really hurting bad. Sorry to call you so early – but I just had to know. And you, you go back to sleep if you can."

"That's exactly what I plan on doing. I'll talk to you later. You get some sleep too."

We both hung up.

A flood of relief. Somehow, this had all turned out okay. Incredibly.

But, then, right after the relief came the nausea. How was I ever going to keep this story going? How was I going to explain to people that, after my "mugging," after having been pounded and kicked by three big men, I didn't have one cut or bruise, hadn't gone to the hospital, hadn't filed a police report? What was I supposed to do? Find a makeup artist? Throw myself over a small cliff? No matter what I might do to back up my story, I just knew it was a matter of time before I got found out. I wasn't that good a liar.

Then a sudden moment of truth: far better for me to take control of things, even if it's a little late now, because the longer I wait, the worse it's going to get. I knew that -- even though I could only imagine how terrible the fallout was going to be. This was worse than not showing up at the hospital when one of our congregants was sick, worse than canceling an appointment at the last minute, worse even than forgetting a wedding – unforgivable as that was. This was a major lie, a public lie, a lie on a monumental scale, and I was going to have to admit it and admit it to everyone I cared about.

I thought about it for a long time, then picked up the phone and called Mel Grafman.

I wasn't sure if Mel already knew about the wedding but it sounded like he did from the way he answered. When I suggested we should get together for lunch to talk about something important, Mel didn't hesitate and he didn't ask a lot of questions. He simply said: "Fine. Where and when?" When the arrangements were settled, Mel simply asked: "David, are you okay? Are you?" To which, I offered a quick "I'm fine, Mel. Just fine."

Usually we met at the deli; this time I knew we needed a more out-of-the-way place. So I suggested the Independence Tavern for a little privacy. "The Indie," as it was known locally, first opened its doors in the mid 1840's, when the country was young. Its current décor – and probably its last makeover -- was 1950's vinyl and formica. Somehow, no matter what the hour, the place was dark and smoky, like a set from a film noir. Between the smoke and the dim lighting, it was sometimes hard to know who was sitting across from you at the same table. Perfect.

Mel was there already sitting at a table in the corner, in jeans and a T-shirt, drinking coffee, when I came in at exactly twelve o'clock. I did my best to smile as I sat down across from him. He looked at me skeptically. We made a few stabs at small talk, glanced at the menu and then, after the waitress took our orders, I turned to him and said: "Mel, I have to talk to you about something important. I need your advice and your opinion and I need your promise – I mean a real promise, Mel, that you can't break for anyone or anything – your promise that you'll keep this between the two of us for now."

Mel, appropriately solemn, assured me that what we said would stay between the two of us.

"David," he said, "I get it. This is in confidence. So go ahead. Tell me what's on your mind."

As if you don't already know, I thought.

I had already played this conversation out about a hundred different ways on the drive over, like a child trying to negotiate a maze with a pencil, starting and stopping as I hit a dead-end, picking up the pencil to try again. Finally, I said: "Mel, in the spirit of the Holy Days, I want to admit to something that I don't feel good about."

Staring at Mel, looking for his genuine reaction hidden behind a world-class poker face. No way to know. Just got to jump in and pray for the best.

"Mel, look. I did something I'm not proud of. I told a lie. A big one. I told it so I wouldn't upset someone and also, frankly, because I had, well, painted myself into a corner and at that moment I couldn't see any other way out. But, anyway, now I know I have two choices: I can try to keep up the lie, although that will mean a lot more lying and I'm not very good at that. Or, I can get it off my chest and face the music which, I'm sure, is not going to be pleasant."

Looking more intrigued than upset, Mel said: "So, which way are you leaning?"

"Well, as you could probably figure out already, I think I just have to fess up, mainly because I don't want to have to keep lying. But, Mel, when this comes out...when it comes out..."

Completely unexpectedly, my voice caught in my throat. I waited to compose myself, hoping Mel hadn't noticed.

"When it comes out, it's going to upset a lot of people. I mean, let's face it, Mel, people expect their rabbi to tell the truth. They can forgive a lot, or at least they should, but they expect their rabbi to be honest and this time I haven't been, haven't been completely honest, haven't really been honest at all. Maybe they'll forgive me because of all I've been going through but, really, Mel, I'm not sure."

Mel looked at me intently, still not tipping his hand. He waited, then said: "So…I assume you're going to tell me what's weighing on your conscience. Go ahead, David, spill it. I think you'll feel better if you do."

At that moment, it was almost as if I had drifted out of my shoes and was floating somewhere in the air, as if this was all happening to someone else.

"Okay. So…I went hiking Saturday afternoon, up Mt. Joy. And when I got back down to the bottom, when I got back to my car, I realized that I had forgotten an obligation. You know how distracted I've been lately…"

Mel fought to suppress a smile.

"Well, I was supposed to be on my way into New York City to do the Kurwitz wedding at the Plaza. I'm sure you know that. And by that time, well, it was just too late for me to get into the city and be there to start things on time so I panicked. I panicked and I told Steve a lie."

Watching Mel's face. Just a twitch in one eye. Of course he knew!

"I told Steve that I had been attacked, 'mugged,' actually, was the word I used. I told him I was beat up and that I lost consciousness and that, when I came to, I called him immediately but that it was too late by then. And then the two of us came up with a plan to have Sam Silverberg, who I knew was there, do the wedding. Now, I understand everything worked out just fine with the wedding ceremony and I know the rest of the evening went off without a hitch. But when I spoke to Sam yesterday morning, and he was so concerned about me and I just started thinking about all the lies I'd have to tell to keep this story going, well, I just didn't have the stomach for it. Honestly, Mel, I don't want to be someone who could pull that off. I mean what kind of rabbi is good at lying to his own congregants…or anyone else for that matter? Not me. That's not who I am.

The truth is I panicked. And I made a bad decision, a decision to, uh, fabricate. And now I want to come clean and not be stuck covering this up for the rest of my life. And I'm hoping, Mel, hoping that people will understand how scared I was, how ashamed I was – I mean what kind of rabbi forgets he's got a wedding, for God's sake? I just hope people will give me the benefit of the doubt, and accept my apology. That's what I'm hoping, Mel. That's what I'm praying for. But I just don't know how people will be with this. And I'm scared."

Mel could see I had said all I was going to say. As he started to speak, his face and body language changed, from impassive to barely suppressed glee.

"Well," said Mel, "how do you think people ought to be with this? I mean, David, you're their spiritual leader. You're the one who gives the sermons about honesty and responsibility and now you, of all people, you're the one who's lying – and lying big time. You're the one who's trying to duck responsibility. I mean you can be a lot of things as a rabbi, David, but you can't be a liar. And, David, I'm sorry, I mean I'm really sorry, but how do you think people are going to respond? I can tell you right now. They're going to be outraged. They're going to be out for blood. And, I'll tell you what, I don't blame them."

"But what about the fact that I'm ready to make an apology? You said I'm trying to duck responsibility. That's not true. I'm ready to stand up and say I screwed up, say it in front of whoever I have to, to as many people as I have to. I'm willing to take responsibility for what I did and ask for people's forgiveness. Don't you think, after all these years, Mel, after all these years, that I've got enough of a track record, that they've known me long enough and, hell, haven't I earned their trust after all these years? Haven't I? Why wouldn't they cut me a break, Mel, after all this time?"

"You want to know why, David. I'll tell you why…No, let me put it this way. If you had done this, say, a year ago or five or ten years ago, if you had screwed up like this and you were proposing to go ahead and make a public apology for it, I would have said: 'Hey, Rabbi, these people love you and they believe in you.

You can be like that guy, you know, that minister who admitted cheating on his wife in front of everyone and cried and said he was getting help for it. You could be like him and you could do that and everyone would be mad for a while and, yes, of course, they'd be really disappointed in you. But they'd get over it. They'd get over it because, yes David, exactly as you put it, you'd have had a track record with them. And I think – I can't prove it – I think they'd have forgiven you before long."

"But…"

"But, it's different now. It's different David – and everyone knows it, everyone is talking about it, and you know it too. It's different…because you're different. You've changed. I don't know when it all started, I don't know, maybe a year ago – and I know it's gotten worse since Sharon ah…passed, and, David I am really sorry about that. But the truth is you seem to have turned into someone else, not the same David Chazen you've always been, the guy everyone loved.

"You've changed and you're different. And nobody really knows who you are anymore. You almost never show up to meetings and when you do, you don't seem to have any idea what's going on. You say, well, crazy things to people. I understand you aren't making hospital visits. And, David, your services, well, your services have become completely…let's say, unpredictable, for lack of a better word. No don't stop me, David. Let me finish.

"Your services are totally unpredictable. Nobody knows if you'll stay with the prayerbook or go off on some crazy tangent, if you'll start singing the same song over and over again and do it for an hour, if you'll stop to talk to somebody in the middle of services like there's nobody else in the room – yes, David, I've seen you do it! David, don't you get it? People see you acting, well…acting like you're acting and they think you've lost it. And they don't trust you anymore. It's like something has gotten control over you. And the old David we loved and trusted and respected – the one who made me want to be a synagogue leader -- well someone's made off with that guy and left us with someone who maybe looks like him and sounds like him but who clearly isn't him anymore.

"So, no, David, I don't think people will cut you any slack. I don't think they'll just let bygones be bygones. Actually, I think you're really in trouble here, in trouble if you try to keep up the lie…and don't think you'll be able to do that because too many people have already guessed you made the whole thing up. And you'll be in trouble if you admit it, because I think there's just a lot of folks in the congregation who have been looking for some way to get rid of you and now you've given it to them."

Like you? I thought. "So what can I do?"

"I don't know. I don't know that there's anything you can do that's going to make it all go away. Maybe if you announced that you were going through some kind of nervous breakdown because of Sharon and everything. Tell them you're going through an extreme grief reaction but that you're getting help. Tell them you understand you've got a problem but you're dealing with it, you're getting help with it and you'd like some time off to go work at what's eating at you and then, when you feel like you're ready, you'll let them know and maybe then they'll have you back.

"But, unless you're ready not just to say you lied, not just to say you panicked and did something stupid but that you understand that you're coming unglued and that you've got to get help and you know you're going to need some time to get your life back together – unless you're ready to do that, David, I think you're done here."

"Done? What does that mean, done?"

"Done. Period. You can build up all the good will in the world for decades, and you did David. Oh sure, there were some people who weren't crazy about you, people who went to other shuls because they didn't like something you said or did or a look on your face, but, let's face it David, that goes on in every synagogue with every rabbi. I talk to other synagogue presidents; I know. But even so, even so, after you've built up all the good will in the world, when you stop doing your job and people stop believing in you, it's very, very hard to get them to believe in you again. And I think, with this latest incident, you've crossed a line that you can't cross back over again."

I was up on my feet. "I'll be back in a moment," I said.

Running to the men's room, I knelt down and held my head above the toilet bowl, waiting to spew -- but it wouldn't come. Nothing there to come out, just bile. So I stood up, closed the toilet seat and sat down on it, wondering what to do next. I had expected discouraging words from Mel -- but this was way more than I'd bargained for. I composed myself and, cupping my hands together at the sink, drank a little to get the sour taste from my mouth and splashed some water on my face. As I returned to Mel, he asked, "Are you alright?"

"No, Mel, I'm not alright. Obviously, I'm not. How could I be? Look, I need to think about this and then I'll call you and tell you what I want to do next. But, don't forget, Mel. You promised me this would stay between the two of us and I need you to keep your word while I figure things out."

"I know I promised, David, but the cat, as they say, is already out of the bag and you can't stuff it back in. Steve Kurwitz has been busy telling everyone about what happened at the wedding and then the call he got from Sam Silverberg today telling him he spoke to you and what you were saying sounded fishy. He's been telling everyone and saying it's time for you to go. And maybe in a way, maybe it's a good thing because it forces you and us, all of us, to face this thing head-on and not duck it any more, like we've all been doing these last months. So…here's what I'm suggesting."

Ah, I thought, how typical! Mel just loved to make "suggestions."

"I'm suggesting we convene a special meeting of the executive board to talk

about this, about the missed wedding and about your…prevaricating and your
general conduct lately. And we're going to have to act quickly on this – like
tomorrow night. With the holidays starting on Friday evening, we have to deal
with this right now. We'll get together tomorrow night and we'll see what the
leadership has to say and what you have to say and then we'll know if we have to
go further with this."

"What exactly do you mean by 'further?'"

"I mean, quite simply, David, if we have to take this to the congregation. Believe
me, it isn't just the Kurwitzes or me or even the leadership that's been talking
about this, about you, these last few months. It's out there, David. It's everywhere, all through the congregation and even in the community. And, excuse
me, but it didn't start with Sharon's death. It's been going on for a long time.
I don't think you realize how much everyone has been watching you and how
concerned they are about you and your behavior. "

"'Concerned' are they? I love that."

"Yes, they are. They're concerned and worried and unhappy and sometimes
angry. And maybe the best thing we could do is let everyone have a chance to
weigh in on this. Maybe that isn't what either of us would have chosen but now
it's kind of chosen itself. And at least it might help us clear the air, so it might
really be a good thing for everyone after all."

I sat there silent, considering my options, unable to imagine how this might be
"a good thing after all." No, this was a bad thing, a colossally bad thing. And,
more and more, it seemed to me that I was the guy in the old Saturday afternoon
serials hanging on to the edge of the cliff by his fingernails with a yawning chasm
looming underneath.

When I got home that evening, there was a voice mail from Donna. "David, I'm
calling to tell you that this thing we're doing, this you-and-me thing, David, it

isn't right. It's just not. I mean: I'm not divorced yet and you're just widowed. And you're my rabbi, for God's sake. And well, I just…I just can't do it anymore."

I was stunned. After yet another all-night session with the uninhibited Donna earlier in the week, another morning-after waking up exhausted and guilty, wondering who would see Donna slinking out of my place before sunrise, I had been debating how much longer I could keep this up. But now suddenly she wants out!

I called her back, spoiling for a fight. After four rings, her voice on the answering machine asked the caller to leave a message. Waiting impatiently for her message to end, I blurted: "You are incredible, just incredible. Suddenly, you get a conscience? Suddenly, you're worried about morality. Unbelievable."

I stopped and took a breath. "Fine," I said. "Fine. We'll stop…because it's not right, just as you say, even if it took you a long time to figure it out. Just remember who started this. Remember it was you with the wine and sympathy. But okay, fine, we'll stop. Goodbye, Donna." Then I hung up. And quickly regretted leaving such a message on her machine and wished there was some way I could take it back.

Still shaking forty-five minutes later, I remembered there was mail in the mail box since Friday. I brought it back in and went through it, as I always did, letter opener in hand, two piles on the kitchen table – one for keeping, one for trash. In the midst of all the usual bills, advertising and requests for money from every liberal cause and charity in the country, I noticed the one "real letter" in the bunch, something from a "Ms. K. Barker" from Manhattan. It was addressed to Sharon.

In the weeks since Sharon's death, it felt macabre to receive a telephone call for her or a letter with her name on it. Rather than explain that my wife was dead, I'd just ask to have her name removed from the list; she wasn't interested in contributing. The form letters I'd throw into the trash.

But this was a personal letter from someone whose name I didn't recognize, someone who appeared – from the name on the return address on the top left front of the envelope -- to be from a literary agency, of all things! I could only guess that Sharon had submitted another poem, another short story and this was yet another in a long line of rejections.

I opened it.

The letter was warm and personal. "Kristy" was just checking in on her favorite aspiring novelist. She was pleased with the changes Sharon was making, how much better it was with the help of the editor she had recommended. It was quickly turning into one of the better things she had represented in a while. She loved the storyline, the truth-telling and especially the complex main character, the "rebbetzin" of the title. All things considered, she was convinced this book was going to get a lot of attention not just from Jewish readers but from all over.

I sat down, the letter dangling from my hand, and let it all sink it. Here was Sharon finally with a real chance to have something published – not just a poem or short story in some literary journal no one had ever heard of, but a novel, a full-length novel. Her agent had said she loved it, felt there would be interest in it. Poor Sharon, I thought, this was all she had ever wanted but now if her dream came finally true, she wouldn't be around to see it.

So, it seemed the book had the word *rebbetzin* in the title. How strange, it was a term she loathed. Then a thought. I went directly to the computer. Searching "Reb," I came up with the same file that had mystified me weeks earlier. I entered the password "Rebbitzin" and there it was – a large title "The Rebbetzin" followed by a story that ran some 212 pages with "The End" written on the last page in gigantic font as if to say: "Tada!"

I began to read, slowly and carefully at first, then, as it dawned on me what I was looking at, scanning pages, looking for familiar names, places, story lines. The "Rebbetzin" of the story was named Cheryl. Cheryl had a husband named Daniel. They had a son called Avi. The husband worked for a synagogue called Temple Sinai. He had been there for twenty years. He was a careerist. He was an egotist, who cared only for his congregants, not his wife or his son.

Here was "Daniel's" arrival at his new synagogue. Here he was chasing every woman in sight. Here he was playing out a charade as some kind of mystic. Here he was ignoring his son's loneliness and his wife's growing misery as he went out to play with his new girlfriend.

And here were the denizens of "Temple Sinai" – and a comically nasty lot they were. Here were the women, shamelessly draping themselves all over the suggestible young rabbi. And here was the president, a pompous windbag, superior, preening, self-serving.

I flipped anxiously to the last page. It read: "And what finally will be left of me?" Just as in the prayerbook, "Dust and ashes, dust and ashes."

The next day, Monday morning, I called the number in New York and asked for Kristy Barker. When she got on the line, it was clear she hadn't heard about Sharon's death, hadn't spoken with her since she had submitted what she hoped were her final edits some weeks before. She was audibly shocked and needed to stop to catch her breath.

"Oh, I'm so, so sorry. I've come to really, really like her. Oh David, I'm so sorry." Then as an afterthought, "May I call you David?"

"'Of course."

"Oh, I'm really so sorry. Tell me what happened."

In quick strokes, I told her about Sharon's death, the funeral, the whole thing. I did not call it "a suicide" or tell her about Sharon's prior attempt. I referred to it as "an accident." She listened quietly, commiserating. At the end, she said: "David, I can't tell you how sorry I am for her and for you and for your son. I wish there was something I could do." Somehow, that's where most of my conversations ended up these days.

Then she said: "Actually, there probably is something I can do. You read the letter so you know how I feel about Sharon's book. I think it's really good – especially for a first-timer. I think it is going to do very well. I'm so sorry she won't be there to see it, but I think we have to publish it as a kind of tribute to her. This is a really strong book, David. Have you read it?"

"Well, actually, I didn't know anything about it until your letter. But the last few hours I've been racing through it so I've got a pretty good idea what it's about."

"So, what do you think?"

"What do I think? Are you kidding me? I think Sharon probably violated everything sacred between us…and between me and my congregation…and between us and Ari. I mean really, everyone – and I do mean everyone – who reads this book here is going to know exactly who the "rebbetzin" is and the "rabbi" and everyone else in it. I don't think anyone's ever going to look at me the same way again. And I wouldn't be surprised if it ends up costing me my job. Outside of that, I think it's great."

"But David…it's a novel. People have to be able to make the distinction between fact and fiction. And besides, you didn't write it. She did. And it's good, very good – don't you think? I'm sure you don't want me to pull the plug on it now, do you?"

A long silence. "I don't know. I guess I need to think about it. It's all so new to me." My mind was racing. "Let me think about it and I'll get back to you."

"OK. But unless you tell me not to, I'm going to keep this process going so we have the option to go ahead if there's interest. And David, don't forget, there's potentially some money in this here as well. I don't think you want to walk away from that, do you?"

I said nothing.

Kristy said: "I'll let you know if anything happens."

***

The executive meeting was called for Monday night at 7:30. When I walked into the board room from my office at seven twenty-five, everyone was already there. Most were casually dressed, a few still in business attire, obviously having come straight from work. With the exception of Donna, they all averted their eyes like a jury set to convict the defendant on all counts.

Mel glared up at me as he found his place around the long, rectangular table, then announced: "Alright, I know we all want to have a discussion tonight about the Rabbi. And I know we all came ready to say whatever's on our minds. But before we start, I want to turn it over to the Rabbi. I think we owe it to him to hear whatever he would like to say first. I think that's fair, don't you?" They all nodded like a collection of "bobbleheads."

Nothing to do now but start. I did my best to make my case. My wife had died, by her own hand. I was in shock. I acted in the passion of the moment, exercised colossally bad judgment. The Holy Days were coming up in a couple of days – a time for forgiveness. Couldn't they forgive me and together we could start the New Year fresh and clear?

But it wasn't to be. The die was already cast; minds were made up. It wasn't just one event, they explained, but rather a continuing series of incidents in which I was seen as distracted, irresponsible, uncaring. People were leaving the syna-

gogue, going elsewhere. For the good of the congregation, it was time for me
to step down. So I was offered the chance to resign, was promised a settlement.
Otherwise, they said, it would go to a congregational meeting and that could get
pretty ugly.

I sat in silence for a time, then said: "Let it go to the congregation."

I could tell by their stunned faces that they hadn't expected this.

"Don't you think there are enough people who still appreciate what I've done
for them over the years," I said, "people who will come out to a public meeting
and cry bloody murder when they find out what you're planning on doing to
me? And don't you think, even if you're successful at getting rid of me, if you
see people leaving now, don't you think there will be a lot more if you forcibly
remove the one rabbi they've ever known, the one who's been here for over two
decades?"

Now Mel, not waiting for anyone else to chime in, spoke up. "Maybe you're
right, Rabbi. Maybe you are. But, Rabbi, I've got to warn you. If you think
there's unhappiness in this room tonight, I think you're in for much worse when
we get the whole congregation together. But, hey, that's just my guess. Besides,
this isn't a dictatorship, it's a democracy. So we'll let the people decide. That's
the way we'll do it."

With that, Mel gaveled the meeting to a close. Just that quickly, just that easily,
it was done.

***

The next day, an emergency congregational meeting was called for two nights
after Yom Kippur. Suddenly everything kicked into gear. The phones began
ringing, the email ricocheted through cyberspace. Seeking allies, seeking supporters, seeking like-minded congregants in anticipation of the big meeting – as

it quickly became known – everyone was busy choosing up sides.

Although my friends had quickly sprung into action, I told them clearly that I wanted no part of it – either people would come to the meeting, remember what I had done, appreciate it and want to keep me or they wouldn't. They shouldn't have to be cajoled into doing the right thing. I wouldn't demean myself by making personal pleas for their support; I simply would not do it. And they shouldn't either.

But, of course, they did.

Every once in a while I would get a report from one of my zealots (yes, there were some of those) letting me know the good or disappointing news from the last phone call, the last email, the last conversation in the check-out aisle at the Foodmart.

I began to wonder what my life might look like if I were no longer rabbi of Temple Emmanuel. First off, I would never have to attend another late-night meeting again. That would be okay. But what would I do for money? How would I keep myself – and Ari -- going? Then I remembered Sharon's book. Maybe we'd actually make a deal and it would get published. Maybe I'd go on Oprah, I joked to myself (at least I think it was a joke.) At first, I had to admit, I'd been shocked by the book and what was in it, afraid of the fallout. But now I was beginning to see it as a kind of lifeline, a sort of insurance policy for Ari if I lost my job.

In the days before the meeting, I spent a lot of time alone, reading, taking long walks in the crisp early autumn air, mediating and, of course, writing sermons -- sermons that would be thoughtful and serious but which would avoid address-ing the elephant in the room, the congregational meeting looming just after the Days of Awe.

The only person I was happy to talk to was Ari. Incredibly, it was to him I now turned not so much for advice as for support. After our talk right after Sharon's funeral, Ari was clearly on my side, thought I deserved better from the congregation. I took comfort that he was indignant on my behalf and that he, of all people, was so passionate in my defense.

He said: "What do you want me to do, Dad? Can I make calls, can I…"

I interrupted: "No. No. Thanks, Ari, really…thank you, but no thank you. I really don't want you to do anything, although it means the world to me that you're offering. Actually I really don't want anyone to do anything for me right now, so don't take it personally."

"Why not? After everything you've done here? Don't they know this place wouldn't amount to squat without you?"

Looking into my son's eyes, moved by his righteous indignation, all I could say was: "Thank you, Ari."

***

The Holy Days came and went. I'm still not sure how. The sermons were delivered. The choir and cantor sang. The people came and listened and prayed. But there was an air of unreality to it, as if we were all in a state of suspended animation, all collectively holding our breath.

Then, forty-eight hours after Yom Kippur, it was like a reprise of that sacred day all over again. The same crowds, the same hum of anticipation. As more people arrived, the custodians set up rows of chairs in the social hall all the way to the back, with overflow in the lobby and hallways. For them and for me, it was truly a Day of Judgment.

Tonight, of course, I wasn't presiding, so I had to choose a place for Ari and me. We sat in a section of friends and supporters, all squeezed in close together, not an empty space in the pews anywhere.

At the front of the sanctuary, on the raised *bimah*, Mel, dressed in a business suit, was scurrying around, busily engaged in whispered conversations, pointing out something or other on a pad he was carrying around with him, making sure the lectern was set in the right place and the sound system ready.

At ten minutes past the appointed starting hour of 7:30, Mel gaveled the meeting to order. He made a great show of looking out over the room from side to side, front to back, as he had undoubtedly seen me do so many times over the years.

He said: "Good evening, everyone. It's time for us to begin. Quiet. Quiet, please."

With that, the din in the room slowly subsided.

"We all know what we're here for this evening. But before we begin, I want to remind everyone in this room of the importance of what we're doing here tonight. There is so much riding on our discussions – not just for Rabbi Chazen…"

He glanced over to me and Ari and our supporters around us.

"…but for all of us. There is so much at stake in the decisions we'll reach tonight. So I want us all to stop and think for a moment, think about we're doing here and maybe even pray a little prayer that we do the right thing tonight."

He paused for about fifteen seconds, then continued on.

"Alright." He cleared his throat with some drama then said again, "Alright. As we all know, we are here tonight because there have been some complaints against Rabbi Chazen, some fairly serious ones and, because they are serious complaints, some of our congregants have asked that we have a meeting to air them and then see what, if anything, we want to do about it. Now, let me be clear right from the start. We do not know what people might say here tonight so we cannot possibly know what will come of all this. But we know that one of the possible outcomes is that we may not want to continue our contractual relationship with the rabbi. So let me say a word about the rabbi's contract…"

"It is what's called a 'continuing contract,' which means, in theory that the rabbi is here until retirement. But there is a stipulation that details the procedure we are to follow if there are allegations of, and let me quote here directly…"

Here, Mel took his reading glasses from one pocket and a copy of the contract from another and read:

"'In the event of gross misconduct or willful neglect of his responsibilities, the congregation will have the right to call an open meeting where these charges will be publicly aired and discussed. Events that may cause the congregation to terminate its contract with the rabbi include but are not limited to: moral turpitude, felony offenses or those of similar severity, inability of rabbi to perform his duties, loss of ordination or professional license or violation of standards of rabbinical behavior as set forth by the rabbi's professional association.

For this meeting, there must be a quorum of the congregation and all who attend must be afforded a chance to speak. After such discussion, a vote may be taken to determine whether it is the will of those present to terminate the rabbi's contract. If a vote is taken and there is a majority of three-quarters of those present – who must be members of the congregation in good standing -- who wish to terminate the rabbi's employment by the congregation, this contract shall then be determined to be terminated and no longer valid or binding.'"

Mel looked up. With probably fifteen hundred people present, there wasn't a sound in the room.

"So this is what we're dealing with here. I hope that's clear. Are there any questions so far?"

A man had his hand up at the back of the sanctuary. Mel asked him to stand and speak loudly. It was Mike Greenwald, one of my first presidents at Emmanuel.

"I want to make sure I understand what you're proposing. We have a room full of people and every one of us has the right to speak with no limit on how long we can speak? Right?"

Mel shook his head in agreement. Mike didn't move. Mel asked: "Is that all?"

"No, Mel, I'm just getting started." Some laughter.

"Okay, everyone here in this room – and I would guess there are more than a thousand people here – everyone has the right to speak. They can say anything they want, for as long as they want. And then, we'll have a vote. Now, I've got some questions about this vote."

Mel was shifting his weight from one foot to the other.

"First off, how do we know everyone in this room is allowed to vote? How do we know everyone here is a member in good standing?"

Mel said: "Well, Mike, actually, as everyone came into the building tonight, they signed in on one of our sign-in sheets. You must have done it too. And right now we have members of the executive board in the office, going through our rolls making sure that they are members in good standing and that they have the right to vote. So, I think we've got that one covered." He smiled but Mike wasn't having any of it. He had clearly come "loaded for bear."

"Actually, Mel, I'm not sure it's 'covered' at all. So, okay, we'll figure out who here is a member in good standing and we'll, what, put a purple mark on their thumbs?"

"No, of course not, Mike. We'll just hand out ballots only to those we've determined are members in good standing."

"Oh, so this vote will not be a show of hands. This will be a vote with actual ballots we'll have to fill out? I see....Okay, next question: If we hand out a ballot to someone, who's to say they won't then pass that ballot on to someone who is not qualified to vote?"

"Oh, Mike, I think that's extremely unlikely. Why are you worried so much about all the little details here?"

"I'm worried about the 'little details' as you call them, Mel, because, if you want the truth, I'm not sure this is entirely on the up-and-up and I want to make sure that we do things properly here and that the rabbi gets a fair shake."

Applause from some parts of the room; hard to tell how many joined in. Mel was visibly agitated now.

"I assure you, Mike, I assure you this will be nothing but scrupulously fair." Then he paused and looked up, a hurt child unable to hold his tongue: "Mike, why would you doubt me? Why would you doubt that I want what's best for the congregation? I assure you that everything tonight will be absolutely fair. Nobody wants a fair procedure here more than I do. Okay, can we move on now? Can we?"

"No, I have some more questions." Groaning now from some parts of the room.

Mike turned from facing Mel, toward what he perceived to be the source of the groaning and said: "Listen, folks, I'm sorry but this is too important to rush through. We've got the fate of this congregation and this man in our hands and I, for one, am not content just to take somebody's word that things will be done right. I want to guarantee it – or else we're going to have a real mess on our hands and maybe a lawsuit to boot. And besides, I think we owe it to Rabbi Chazen, don't you? So let's take our time here and go slowly and do things right. Okay?

"Okay, next question: What happens if there's a couple here tonight. Do both partners get a vote?"

"Yes, they both get a vote."

"Okay, next question: Who's going to count the ballots?"

Mel turned to say something to someone nearby then responded: "They will be counted by the executive board as a group," which was greeted by cries of "no way" from the sections of my supporters.

Mike quickly chimed in: "No, Mel, that's not going to cut it. We all know it was the executive that engineered this meeting here tonight. We all know it was the executive who double-checked the contract to make sure you could do it. We all know it was the executive that wants to give the rabbi the boot. So why should we…"

Now Mel was banging his gavel and the room was in a loud uproar that continued on as Mel tried to respond.

"Alright, Mike, that's enough. I mean really that's enough. I'm not going to let you continue with this…This is just so unfair of you. You do not have the right to impugn the integrity of this executive board. No, we're going to do it exactly as I said. We're going to have the executive board count the ballots. There is no reason to doubt their integrity. That's settled."

There was so much noise and tumult in the room that not everyone heard him so they turned to one another asking what they had missed. Through the din, Mel plowed on.

"Okay, alright, are there any other questions? Does everyone understand the procedure we're going to follow here tonight?"

He waited a moment, then said: "Good, let's go on. Okay, the floor is open. Those who want to speak should come forward now and form a line here in front of me to the right and everyone who wants to can speak for no more than…five minutes."

Already he'd changed his mind. There would be a time limit.

At first, everyone looked around at each other, uncertain what to do but then, slowly, people began to rise from their places and walk forward. Soon the line was joined by about twenty-five or thirty would-be speakers. It was clear we were in for a long night.

At the front of the line stood Steve Kurwitz, looking pleased with himself. Mel called on him, saying: "Well, I think everyone here knows Steve Kurwitz, a longtime leader and a great friend of our congregation. Steve and his wife, Elaine, just married off their son, Jared, in New York City and I know we all join in wishing them mazel tov. Let's listen to what he has to say."

Someone shouted: "Why does he get an introduction? You didn't introduce Mike Greenwald and he's a past president." But then the room got very quiet as Steve, in tan slacks, a striped casual shirt and a blue blazer, stepped forward to the microphone.

"As many of you know, what brings us together here tonight really came to a head at our son's recent wedding. As you may have heard, I got a call from Rabbi Chazen just a few minutes before the ceremony was supposed to start, saying he'd been beaten up, mugged by three strangers, and couldn't get to New

York on time. So we all felt bad, very bad, and then we turned to Judge Silverberg who was an invited guest and who could perform the ceremony, to pitch in. And, I might add, he did an absolutely beautiful job…

"Anyway, not long after this I learned that the rabbi admitted that he was never beaten up, that he had just forgotten about the wedding – forgotten! -- and that he had made up all that other stuff to cover his…to cover himself. Well, I can tell you: when I thought he might have been hurt, I was worried sick, but when I heard the truth – and I thought about how worried we were about him all night long at the party – I felt, well, I felt betrayed. And I thought…what kind of a rabbi does this? What kind of rabbi forgets to do a wedding? And, more important, what kind of rabbi tells a lie to cover himself and thinks that's okay? So I talked to some people and I guess they talked to other people and here we are tonight."

Mel, looking at his watch, said: "Time's almost up, Steve."

"Okay. I want to finish by saying this, and this is very important to me. I have nothing personal against the rabbi. In fact, for the longest time I've held him in the greatest esteem. But it's clear to me, not only from this episode but from a lot of other things I've seen lately, that there's something wrong with him, with his life lately…"

There was loud grumbling now from the crowd.

"Well, there is, and even if it's not nice to say, it's true. We can all see it. And it means we can't rely on him when we need him and isn't that exactly what we pay him for – to do what we need him to do for us? Isn't it? Well, it isn't happening, and I'm not sure it's ever going to happen again. So I think, sadly, we need to terminate the rabbi's contract and move on and find someone who's willing to do the job we all need him to do."

Someone -- it wasn't clear who, although it looked like Donna -- called something up to Steve as he was leaving the microphone, at which point he quickly ran back and added "Or her, of course. Or her." And then he sat down to the vocal appreciation of friends and family nearby.

The next speaker was a lovely woman in the congregation who spoke passionately about how I was there for her when her mother died and she knew that was true for so many other people and how could there even be a question of "David" continuing on as Emmanuel's rabbi? It was inconceivable to her that anyone else could do the kind of job "David" had done and she, for one, didn't want to be at Emmanuel any more if he wasn't going to be there.

This was greeted, in turn, by applause.

The next two speakers in a row told bitter personal tales, each a variation on the theme of how I had let them down when they had come to me in their hour of need, all within the last few months. I couldn't be reached. I didn't return their calls and never checked in on them. They were disappointed. They were angry and they couldn't see how I could continue to go on like this without destroying the congregation. One man also alluded to some "questionable moral choices" I had made since my wife's death, as a few eyes shifted in Donna's direction. But, thankfully no one was indelicate enough to spell it out so this evidently well-known "secret" never found its way into the open.

For me, these speeches were an agony -- to hear the bitterness, anger and disappointment and to know that they were all watching me. I tried to keep my own eyes down and my feelings to myself but it wasn't easy. More often, I fixed my gaze on the snaking line at the front of the room, examining each upcoming speaker and wondering which way they would go. For or against?

Through it all, Ari sat stock still, unmoving, unwilling to let anyone see his reactions to what was being said. But he never left my side, not even for a moment.

As chairman, Mel made every pretense at being even-handed, and was just enough so that he could escape censure from my more vocal supporters in the room.

At first it appeared that the lineup of speakers would never end. As soon as the line began to shrink a little, others – who had been, at first, reluctant, now spurred perhaps by those who had already spoken -- arose from their seats to join in. As the evening wore on, I kept an informal tally of speakers pro and con; it seemed to be roughly even.

After about two hours and with people increasingly repeating almost verbatim what previous speakers had said, Mel stepped forward to the microphone and said: "Friends, it's over two hours since we began here this evening and, while I know this is very, very important and I know there are a great many of us who have something to say – and, in theory, everyone should have the right to speak if they want to – I want to make a suggestion."

Ah, a suggestion, I thought.

"I want to suggest that we have perhaps three, or maybe four more speakers and then close things off. Does that seem reasonable? Can we agree to do that? Is that fair?"

There was a lot of noise from the assembly, a lot of shouted yeses and nos, with no clear consensus so that finally Mel said: "Okay, let's see a show of hands. How many agree with my suggestion that we finish with three more speakers?" Hands were raised, a majority of the room.

"Okay then. We're agreed. Three more speakers and then we'll go to a vote."

Then someone shouted: "And what about the rabbi? Doesn't he get to speak? How can we say this is a fair discussion without hearing what he has to say?"

This was greeted with the loudest and most sustained applause of the evening.

Then Mel, looking to his cronies in the front row, said: "Okay, the suggestion is to let the rabbi have the final say. Is that what we want to do? Let's see a show of hands."

It wasn't unanimous but it was close. Almost every hand in the room was raised, even those who had spoken most angrily against me. Everyone wanted to hear, expected to hear from the Rabbi and, of course, I had counted on it all along – and had come prepared.

After the last three speakers, an interminable wait, I stood up from my seat and walked toward the dais and the microphone. I looked around the room from front to back, from side to side. As I did, I looked out at the faces in the room, attaching a name and a backstory to each one. Then I launched into what would be, I knew, the most important sermon of my life.

I began by reminding them of how I had come to them as a young man so many years before, the hopes I'd had for this place and the hopes I knew they had in me. I talked of my years in the pulpit, the weddings, funerals and bar mitzvahs I had officiated at, the classes I had taught, the services I had led, finally talking about the personal relationships that I had formed over the years and how much they meant to me. It was, so far, not so very different from the speech I had made at the executive meeting a few days earlier.

But then I stopped, looked dead ahead and said:

"I am well aware of what is at stake here tonight. No one understands that better than I do. So I want to be totally candid with you. You know that I've been going through a terrible time this last year. In a lot of ways, my life has really gone off the rails. I went searching for God in a more serious way – and that was something that was real and that really meant something to me -- but I let that search distract me from facing up to a life that had gotten confusing and unhappy. I focused exclusively on myself and forgot about everyone else who matters to me. I wasn't there for you. I wasn't there for my family. And I caused a lot of damage. A lot of damage…

"I alienated a lot of you here in this synagogue, you who always trusted me and believed in me. You reached out to me and I wasn't there for you. I was too preoccupied. Tonight I want to apologize to you from the bottom of my heart.

"I also know I wasn't there for my family." I looked straight at Ari, whose eyes met mine, unblinking.

"I got all wrapped up in my work, in my own search for meaning and, along the way, stopped seeing you and caring for you. I thought I was embarked on some kind of holy endeavor but I see now that I used that to avoid taking responsibility for the ones I loved – and I see what's happened."

I paused to control myself but it didn't work. My eyes began to sting and the tears began to flow.

"Sharon is gone. She's gone and I can't bring her back. And that is something I'll have to live with for the rest of my life.

"But my son…my Ari…he is still here, thank God. He's still here and, God willing, I have the chance now to show him I love him and take care of him when he needs me and be the kind of father I always wanted to be and…and still hope to be.

"My friends, you've heard me say it a thousand times up here from this lectern. God gives us second chances. That's what our tradition teaches. We get a chance to start over again if we are ready to do *teshuva* -- if we admit what we've done, feel real remorse for it and try to make amends and promise ourselves and the people we hurt that we'll devote ourselves to doing things better in the future.

"That doesn't take away the past. It doesn't undo the harm we've done. But it does allow us to stop doing harm and start being better people. And that is what I commit to doing – from this day forward. I understand now, that is where I have to find God.

"I know I have to start doing things differently. I have to be a better listener, a better friend, a better rabbi – and a better father. Tonight, I stand before you and I promise that is exactly what I intend to do if you give me that chance. I ask for *rachmanes*, a little compassion. Let me know that you want this flawed, imperfect human being to be your rabbi. Let me know that you can forgive me when I'm wrong and admit it. I am part of this community too and now I need your help. Let me know that the relationship we built over two decades is real. Let me know that you still remember and believe in that person you welcomed into your hearts so many years ago and that you are not going to walk away from me now even after I've made such a terrible mess of things.

"I know this is an awful lot to ask. But I ask it of you humbly and in all sincerity. Please, give me another chance."

Then I sat back down at my seat, where Ari greeted me with a hug and a kiss. And, as applause rolled over me, I hoped for the best.

Mel stood from his seat on the dais, walking distractedly over to the microphone. He looked up at the congregation from under furrowed brows, saying, as if by way of afterthought,

"Uh, thank you, Rabbi. Thank you very much."

Then, looking down to his friends in the front row and realizing they expected him to seize control of the moment, he took hold of the microphone with both hands and said forcefully:

"Alright then, it's time for us to vote. Ushers, please distribute the ballots." Pandemonium. Finally, after perhaps twenty excruciating minutes, it was time to vote.

So…I'm going to ask all of you to take out a pen and mark your ballot. Remember that the vote is whether to terminate the rabbi's contract or not. That means if you want to do so, you vote 'yes.' If you don't, you vote 'no.' Is that clear? Does everyone have that? Good. Then let's fill out the ballots and then pass them towards the center aisle to one of the ushers there. They will immediately place them in a box they are holding. When everyone's had the chance to fill out their ballots and pass them in, we'll take all the boxes into the office and count the votes and we'll be out with the totals as quickly as we can. Okay…I'll ask again…are there any more questions? Okay…go ahead and do your duty."

The noise in the room, at first minimal, began to rise as ballots were completed and passed in. People stood and talked, some waving wildly, others more subdued, each in an effort to explain their vote, each trying to figure out the sentiment in the room, which way the tally would go.

Through all of this, I sat quietly beside Ari, whose support was the greatest surprise of all. A number of friends and supporters gathered close around us, talking louder and louder to each other as the volume in the room continued to rise.

"Are you nervous, Dad?" Ari asked me.

"Nervous? No, not really. I've been listening and watching everybody here tonight and, honestly, it's hard for me to believe they're going to get three-quarters of this room to terminate me. Anyway, like I said, I'm content to just let things take their course. I'm ready for whatever comes. I just wish they would get the count done already and get this thing over with."

It was now going on forty-five minutes since the voting had started and the noise in the room was tremendous. It was hard to believe they were still counting but, with what looked clearly to be over a thousand votes, and, I assumed, double- and triple- recounting just to be sure…the crowd was getting restless.

Finally, at a little over fifty minutes, Mel came out with a piece of paper in his hands. Aware that every eye in the place was on him, he strode, like the leader he wished to be, up the steps to the microphone. He began to ask for quiet until he realized there wasn't a sound in the place.

"The ballots have been counted and the result is clear," he began. "There were not sufficient votes…"

A cheer went up from many parts of the room – but not from the front row where so much of the executive board was sitting -- as Mel went on: " …there were not sufficient votes to terminate the rabbi's contract."

Now the cheering was more widespread but again not universal.

"Therefore, Rabbi Chazen continues to be Emmanuel's rabbi under the terms and provisions of his existing contract. So I thank you all for coming and for being part of this historic evening. And I would ask one more thing…"

He waited for quiet as many in the group, having heard the only thing they cared about, began to head toward the exits.

"Please, he said, please, before you go, please one more word."

To little effect. The noise and tumult continued. Then again, "Please, please sit down and stay with us for one more moment. Only a moment. I really need to say one thing more. Please, it's important."

Reluctantly, most of those who were standing found their way back to their seats, although they perched lightly in anticipation of a speedy get-away.

"Thank you. Thank you very much. Listen. There's one thing that I have to say, one thing that really needs to be said before we go. On a personal note, I want to say that I have always been a huge fan of our rabbi…"

Some laughter and even some hissing.

"I have honestly always been a big fan and, as much as I always felt this way, I knew it was my responsibility to hold this meeting when the executive board voted as they did. But I know this: neither I nor the executive board nor any of the people we heard speaking tonight about problems with the rabbi, none of them, I am certain, hold any kind of ill-will toward him. And we do know that this has been an exceptionally difficult time for him. So now I'm confident that we will all of us be able to put this all behind us and really come together as one."

Ari, sitting pressed up against me, whispered: "Blah, blah, blah."

I didn't really hear him. Instead, as though charged by a spasm of electricity, I rose from my seat and said: "Mel, there's something I need to say."

Mel, thankful that I seemed ready to take control of a moment he couldn't quite manage, turned to me and said, with a forced smile: "Of course, Rabbi. After all, it's your congregation."

I walked forward to the microphone and said: "Well, Mel, it's nice of you to say so but, really, that's exactly what's not clear to me. I'm really not at all sure this is still my congregation. I want to know what the vote was, I mean the actual numbers. I need to know that before I can move on."

"No, no" – from the front row filled with executive board members. "No, no" – from the auditorium front and back. "No, no" – from Ari, who looked imploringly at me.

And from Mel? "No, David, I really don't think that's a very good idea. The vote failed. That's all you, all any of us need to know. Anything else can only be negative. Let's leave it, okay? The vote failed. You're still our rabbi and will be, God willing, for many years to come."

"Hear, hear"…from places in the sanctuary.

I stopped to consider, looked behind me momentarily at the ark doors, then around the room, then turned back to Mel and said: "I'm sorry. I need to know the actual numbers. I can't continue on until I do. Do you understand? I need to know the numbers."

Mel looked up, helpless. The room was silent. He looked to the front row for advice. By now, they were impassive. This was his problem. He looked up at the faces in the hall, hoping that someone somehow would bail him out.

Finally, he said: "David, I really think this is a terrible idea. And you can hear from everyone here, David, everyone on all sides of the issue, everyone here thinks it's a bad idea, a really bad idea. Do you really want to insist on this?"

I shook my head, "I do. I have to."

"Alright," he said, taking that piece of paper he had been carrying before out of his jacket pocket. "The vote was 548 in favor and 621 against." Noise from the room.

I stopped for a moment to consider, then said:

"So, in this gathering here tonight, this gathering that represents the members of this congregation, I have the support of slightly more than half the people and almost half the people would prefer that I leave? It reminds me of that old joke about how the rabbi is away sick from a board meeting and the president calls to tell him they voted 7 to 5 with 3 abstentions to wish him a speedy recovery."

Then I stopped smiling.

"But this is no joke. This is real. No, it's pretty clear what I've got to do here. Ultimately, this job is all about relationships and I see I've done them irreparable harm. I can't stay here anymore. I've got to resign."

Loud reaction from the congregation as I continued:

"Don't you see? I've got to resign because I've lost your confidence. I mean, after all, I'm supposed to be spiritual leader here. Well, how can I possibly lead a congregation where almost half the people don't want me? That's never going to work. I've got to go. It's as simple as that."

I waited just a moment, then said: "So…yes, I resign, effective immediately. And I wish you all good luck."

Then, turning again in the direction of my seat, I proceeded down the steps, grabbed Ari by the hand as I passed by him and together we went out of the door and into the night. I drove him straight over to the Pontarelli's place, gave him a hug and kiss, and proceeded home.

When I got home, the phone was already ringing madly. I decided to let it ring. When it didn't stop by midnight, I took the receiver off the hook.

The next morning when I awoke at 5:45, I said my prayers, then walked down the stairs to the kitchen to make myself a cup of coffee. The disabled telephone was emitting beeps, imploring me to hang it up. I set the receiver back on the hook. Almost immediately, it began to ring; I removed it once again.

After coffee, it seemed like a good time for a run. Why not? I felt healthy, clean, relieved, like a man relieved of an heavy burden. I felt it as I savored my coffee and moved about the house. I felt it in my prayers that morning – intense and focused.

Walking outside, the sunlight poured over me, not overpowering but warm enough. I set out to…well, I didn't know precisely where. Later on in the day, I'd probably have to start answering some of those phone calls and talk to Ari and my father and Kristy Barker and whoever else. But not now. For now I just wanted to run.

And I did. I ran easily -- shoes comfortably broken in, gym shorts and T-shirt so light I felt almost naked – step after step, block after block, mile after mile, without conscious thought. I was just completely happy to be running and thinking of nothing else.

Where I'd go next, what I'd do, I really didn't know. Perhaps another congregation in another town. Perhaps I'd become a teacher in a Hebrew day school or a Hillel or go to work for some organization or foundation somewhere. Perhaps a year in an ashram in India or a yeshiva in Jerusalem. Who knows?

For now, I was content to run, feeling alive and happy and free, taking longer and longer strides, running confident and strong, lungs filled with clean, fresh air, at one with the world around me, running.

Running and completely alive.

* *

ACKNOWLEDGMENTS

I want to express my sincerest appreciation to three special individuals who helped give birth to this work:

-- Bonny Fetterman, whose wisdom, understanding and expertise helped give shape and form to my writing.

-- David Sandman, who lovingly, thoughtfully, brilliantly created the cover design and laid out the pages of this volume.

-- My wife, Susan, who was hugely responsible for giving voice to the character of Sharon and, more important, for having the patience, understanding and creativity to help me realize my vision for this story.

NORTH MERRICK PUBLIC LIBRARY

1691 MEADOWBROOK ROAD

NORTH MERRICK, NEW YORK 11566

(516) 378-7474

48260334R00152

Made in the USA
Charleston, SC
30 October 2015